The City of
Broken Angels

Alan Janney

The City of Broken Angels
Copyright © 2017 by Alan Janney

@alanjanney
alan@ChaseTheOutlaw.com

First Edition

Cover by Damonza
Artwork by Anne Pierson
Formatting by Polgarus Studio

Ebook ISBN: 978-0-9983165-5-0
Print ESPN: 978-0-9983165-4-3

Sparkle Press

This book is dedicated to...

Anne

Becky

Bob

Danny

Debbie

Larry

Liz

Matt

Megan

Mike

Teresa

and William

Cast of Characters

Infected - Pure-born Variants

Blue-Eyes - Secretary of State / President's mistress

Nuts - mechanical genius

The Outlaw - masked vigilante

PuckDaddy - internet hacker

Samantha - sniper working with the Resistance

Tank - dangerous drifter

Walter - terrorist living in the northwest

Carter - powerful mercenary

China

Pacific

Russia - warlord in San Diego

The Zealot - vagabond, missionary

Kingdom Variants

Becky - scavenger

Carmine - Queen of New Los Angeles

Kayla - Mistress of Communication

Mason - leader of the Falcons

Travis - leader of the Giants

Others of Note

The Cheerleader - mysterious recluse, girl on fire

Dalton - queen's bodyguard

General Brown - military commander

The Governess - supervisor of New Los Angeles

The Inheritors - children infected with Hyper Virus

Isaac Anderson - leader of the Resistance

Miss Pauline - Orphan Overseer

The Priest - Law Keeper Overseer

Andy Babington - high school colleague

Prologue

From the blog of Teresa Triplett
The Ides of March, 2020

Queen Carmine, the Red Butcher, the girl once known as Katie Lopez, is an early riser. To put it mildly. She granted permission for this "Day in the Life" piece but, despite sleeping in the same tower, I've missed her three mornings in a row. So today I'm up before the songbirds and the roosters, shivering in the Olympic's parking garage. She can't leave me behind if I'm sitting on her Land Cruiser's bumper.

The two questions I'm most often asked by outsiders are:

1) How do you still have a webpage?

2) What is Queen Carmine doing right now?

To answer the first question, I have no idea, other than to note modern technology is impressive and I've heard it's easier to maintain the internet's infrastructure than, for example, the car manufacturing supply lines.

As to the second question, you'd know the answer if you lived here. Queen Carmine is *everywhere*, and doing all things.

She arrives five minutes after I do, walking side by side with Dalton, her ever-present bodyguard and New Los Angeles's most eligible bachelor, though don't mention this to him. His handsome scowl still hints of burn wounds, partially healed reminders of his proud devotion to our queen.

Before I can slip into the backseat, Carmine pinches me on the butt without a word and gets behind the wheel. Perhaps she's in a playful mood today; not many world leaders goose their biographers.

She drives. Always. Which aggravates Dalton to no end. He grips the handle over the window and growls for the duration, and I don't fault him; she is not a subtle driver. I'm thrown all over the backseat, sliding across polished leather and crashing into doors before I can buckle in. The streets are clear of debris and most gaping holes have been filled, but the journey is still a harrowing rollercoaster.

We slam to a stop near the 8th Street cafeteria. I barely get out of the truck before she and Dalton have loaded two large crates of steaming biscuits and hot sausage through the Land Cruiser's hatchback.

In the four months since the Castaic Massacre, Carmine's been a woman possessed. A whirlwind of production. She shoulders the weight of the world (and nearly lost it all last November) so it's hard to blame the queen for outworking her inner demons. Especially considering the constant CNN reminders that the east coast is militarizing. Blue-Eyes hungers for revenge, and Carmine is determined we won't be caught unprepared.

She and Dalton bring breakfast to Ascot Hills Park in the northeast. The park is a wide oasis of grass and rolling hills in the middle of suburbia, and currently home to hundreds of chickens and goats. What do we eat in the Kingdom, you ask? Eggs. Lots of eggs and chicken. The Shepherds, sleepily munching on apples for breakfast, are flabbergasted. Queens do not deliver breakfast to the proletarian.

Usually.

She stays to chat as the sun comes up. The Shepherds are too starstruck to contribute much conversation, so she asks questions, listens politely to the fumbled answers, and praises them for their hard work. She smiles for selfies and then she's back in the Land Cruiser. I'm nearly left behind.

Next stop, the 110 Marketplace, erected below the raised cloverleaf junction. Rumors are she intermittently visits this place incognito to test our systems. Today she and Dalton browse the merchandise in plain sight. Well, she browses, and he glares at the staring patrons and Vendors, as is his wont.

She's here to test our new digital currency, which is still in infancy but quite easy to understand: you work all day and you're given ten credits by your Overseer and the credits can be used to purchase goods from the markets.

It's apparent the queen's joints cause her pain. She massages and stretches them, especially her elbows and wrists, and has twice tightened the compress on her right knee to palliate the discomfort. The famous red silk is now a fashion statement around the world, a fact which befuddles and amuses her.

She purchases a pair of Lululemon athletic pants and deposits three credits with her phone. She closely monitors the process and then talks with the sleepy Vendor about the possibility of patrons returning things in the future, and how that would affect credits. The poor woman is mortified she doesn't know how that'd work, but Carmine is unaware of her distress. She rarely notices how she affects the rest of us.

Carmine thanks her and quietly confides to Dalton, "The currency still works. Not perfect yet, but…" She trails off, working on her phone.

The local Black Market took advantage of the credits immediately after the launch, charging high prices for liquor and toilet paper and other luxuries. So many credits were hoarded and stashed with fake IDs that the mighty internet genius PuckDaddy himself stepped in to help correct the problem. After the reboot, currency is flowing with fewer hiccups. (In case you're wondering, physical dollar bills still hold value in the Kingdom but are primarily used for trading with the outside world.)

Carmine now heads east. She listens to dance and pop music saved on her iPod and played over the truck's speakers, far too loud for Dalton's taste. When it's his turn to pick, he chooses smooth R&B and cranks it down. My opinion is not solicited. She thinks out loud while she drives, and I shamelessly eavesdrop as we pass the Magnolia power plant. She worries we're not generating enough electricity, and that we aren't manufacturing solar panels yet, and that Nuts works too hard, and that burning natural gas for electricity is dangerous, and that we aren't training enough qualified electricians, and so forth. She worries obsessively. Dalton speaks rarely, and only then to remind her to "Put down the damn phone." Fortunately we're one of the few vehicles on the road for much of the day.

Fun Queen Carmine trivia — until recently, she was taking classes at Stanford University. It's true; the irrepressible warrior at the wheel is also erudite. She took online classes to keep her mind sharp, and to retain her humanity, she tells me, until January when the university closed for temporary relocation to Kentucky. Now she churns through books on leadership and history and the occasional fiction.

We arrive as ten eighteen-wheel tankers laden with oil and gasoline are being subjected to rigorous inspection outside our border, and so are the three armored escorts. Carmine waits in a Texaco truck stop's expansive parking lot and greets the drivers after they're granted entrance. This oil comes straight from Texas, a stronghold for the Resistance.

"We don't need the oil," she explains later. "Our reservoirs are holding strong. But we have a surplus of fruit that will expire soon, so the Governess wanted to trade. She's shrewd."

"Why do you greet them personally?"

"We need as many loyal people as we can get," she says. "And I want those truckers returning home freighted with positive stories about us."

Carmine is, as you know, quite pretty. A welcome sight for the trucker's weary eyes, and they can't help but stare. She's no Kayla, our self-proclaimed Minister of Communication (or Mistress as she prefers) who is overwhelmingly beautiful. But she's Girl Down The Street attractive, if that girl was a light-skinned Latina made from triathlete material. She moves with natural poise and strength, and she radiates authority. Her hair has grown long enough that she tucks it behind her ears now. She wears black activewear to suit her busy lifestyle and not because it shows off her eye-catching physique. But it does.

The truckers report a smooth passage. They avoided the highway robberies we read about plaguing the middle of our former country, a vast expanse of land dotted with embattled cities, reminiscent of wild west stories from the 1800s. The new lawless 'frontier' stretches east to west from Colorado to Kentucky, and north to south from Oklahoma to Minnesota. No Man's Land, unless you're safety ensconced inside a city or armed farm country. The bands of roving pillagers haven't grown that bold yet, nor have they approached our borders. To play it safe, the tankers will steer clear of the lawless country and drive over twenty-four hours straight until reaching mid Texas.

Carmine listens, a grim twist to her lips. It's well known she pines to head east and draw the leaderless Variants home. The Variants aren't evil, she repeats to anyone who listens. Just lost. And if she doesn't collect them, Walter might. Or the Herders will find them. Or worse.

She puts the truckers and security escorts up in a nearby hotel for the night, and we're off. Next stop, the Orange County and Anaheim Medical Center, the Kingdom's second fully functioning hospital.

On the way, Carmine asks me over her shoulder, "How many people in America died from flu this winter? Do you know?"

"I'm not positive. A lot." Actually, I do know. But I don't want to interrupt her, now that she's talking to me.

"Over two million so far. Forty times the average," she says. "Do you know how many we lost? In the Kingdom?"

"I heard five?"

"Four. And it's not just because our demographic is younger, though that's part of it. But we're stronger. Harder working. We have purpose, and something to live for: each other. We're too busy to die."

New Los Angeles has a population over 300,000 now. Still only a fraction of the former eighteen million. More would come but they're afraid of the Red Butcher; the gruesome Castaic Massacre videos still reverberate through the land. Those who immigrate into New Los Angeles are stouthearted to begin with, not easily overcome by influenza.

Carmine doesn't stay long at the hospital. She hits the halls like morphine, powerful but brief. She walks the wards, waves to the sick, and encourages the doctors. Forty minutes total. She thinks (and she's correct) that even a quick visit will make a difference. And she covets that difference. Any edge helps.

Are you exhausted yet? I am, and it's only lunch time.

I'll fast forward a few hours to 5 PM. She never actually stops for lunch, but rather she eats continually. Mostly granola bars and carrot slices. At 5, she visits a barracks in the north to watch training. If you live here, you know barracks is slang for mutant housing. They don't live as the rest of us; they don't iron their clothes, or make their beds, or dust their bookshelves. Most mutants aren't blessed with the clarity of mind that Carmine has, and those who are are given positions of leadership like Kayla and Mason, the infamous leader of the Falcons. But the rest? They operate on instinct and impulse. Even when they aren't engorged with adrenaline, the Variants don't always think lucidly. Their barracks could more accurately be labeled as caves or hives. Or pigpens.

Perhaps you get confused by the mutant terminology? It took me a while to master the jargon. Here's the easiest way to remember:

- Anyone 'enhanced' is a mutant
    (Some of them swore fealty to Carmine)
    (Some swore fealty to Walter)
    (And some rampage across the mid-west)
- A more polite term is Variant, but you probably know this.
    (Carmine herself is a Variant - a powerful one)
- Carmine refers to her Variants as Guardians

Following me so far? Here are two sub-categories:

-Within the Guardians, there is a small team called Falcons
    (Falcons are elite fighting Guardians - Extremely cool)
- Lastly, the mysterious group who call themselves Infected
    (born with the disease, instead of injected later in life)
    (vastly fewer in number, vastly stronger in strength)
    (The Outlaw himself is Infected)
    (So is Blue-Eyes, though she denies this)

Now you know what I know. It goes without saying, we live in a much different world than we did four years ago.

Carmine sits crisscross on the roof of her Land Cruiser and watches Guardians train. She's obsessed with self-control, and today's exercises are about fighting with restraint. Queen's orders. "Control yourself!" she calls every few minutes. "Discipline your body!" It's like watching professional kick boxers battle at hyper speed. If those kick boxers were also partially insane with the temper of tigers.

If you observe Carmine long enough, you'll see her flipping a knife. It's an exercise she does when deep in thought. She balances the point of her blade on the inside tip of her fingernail, palm up, and then flips it. The blade rotates one time and she catches it on the inside of the adjacent fingernail. Her nails are not long, and it's mesmerizing to watch her flip the knife from pointer finger down to pinky, and back. Mutants are weird.

"Dalton," she says, mid flip. "We still have an hour before sundown. Let's visit the Wall."

Her bodyguard grunts something unintelligible.

The Wall, a massive work in progress. Some of it's a physical wall, but most of the miles are monitored simply by infrared surveillance and cameras. Anyone is welcome in the Kingdom, but she wants to know who's here. Especially after her best friend was kidnapped and almost drowned last year.

It's easy to forget that our queen is only nineteen. And that she's not really a queen, but rather one third of the Kingdom's governing council. If nothing else, she's our Kingdom's founder, our identity, and our hardest worker. Royalty or not, we'd follow her anywhere.

She's tired. Anyone can see that. She's yoked to her many concerns, which weigh like a millstone around her neck. Her shoulders sag and she rubs her vivid green eyes often. But she won't stop. Maybe she can't stop.

I can stop, though. I'm exhausted. And starving. Instead of visiting the Wall, I'll hitch a ride home. This reporter has an early bedtime tonight.

As I turn to leave, I notice she's staring east into the purpling horizon. Into the wild country. Towards the lawless No Man's Land, and towards Blue-Eyes herself on the far coast. Carmine carries responsibility I can't imagine, but her jaw is set. Her eyes sharp. She won't rest.

She knows. She knows what we all know.

This peace won't last.

Trouble is coming.

The City of Broken Angels

Queen versus the Machine

Los Angeles, when will you save me?
Los Angeles, when will you save me?
…
Wake me when this war is over
Meet me where the skyline ends
- Blink 182

Part One

March. 2020.

"The wicked draw the sword and bend the bow
to bring down the poor and needy,
to slay those whose ways are upright."
- Psalm 37

- 1 -

Carmine

I'm hidden behind a thicket of coyote brush, impatiently watching the second hand on my watch. Tick tick tick. My silhouette in the small glass surface blots out a portion of the brilliant stars above. I've been waiting forever, at least six minutes. I hate watches; this one's borrowed.

The problem with New Los Angeles is that it's expansive. Too many hiding spots for interlopers, and not enough manpower to pinpoint and evict them. Or womanpower. I must not truly believe that, though, because I'm planning our next expansion and we're behind schedule.

Finally the watch reads 10:10 PM, and I move up a scrubby ridge on the western side of Kagel Canyon, a valley in Angeles Forest, tucked out of sight on the edge of our borders. Formerly a quiet, pleasant habitat for several hundred naturalists, now the valley is dark and forbidding. I reach the crest of the ridge and peer into the hollow on the far side.

This hidden declivity is home to three cabins and an overgrown campground clearing. And base to a group of thieves styling themselves the Asaltantes Norte, or the Northside Raiders. This particular gang of irritants has been using Dexter Park Road as their ingress, stealing gas, goods, and valuables, and traveling at night with their headlights darkened. Approximately fifty thieves camp here, men and women living off spoils. I don't begrudge their survival instincts, but if they want to survive in *my* territory then they'll need to work like the rest of us.

13

The canyon's occupants are dispersed among three cabins, five popup campers, four tents, and a handful of trucks. A small fire crackles in the approximate center of their camp, and on the outskirts they burn citronella torches and lanterns for light. The sky is big and clear and balmy like most nights in southern California, but without the previous century's electric glow. A perfect evening for an ambush. I could have sent the Law Keepers to roust them but this is more fun. To keep the madness at bay I need to stretch my muscles every so often.

Precisely five minutes after leaving my coyote brush hideout, I release an ear-splitting war cry. So loud it even hurts my own ears; I want to win this battle before it begins. The trenchant sound caroms off the far side of the valley and returns. All eyes turn towards the source but I'm gone. I circumnavigate the camp's periphery at warp speed, extinguishing torches and breaking lanterns, and the pillagers are plunged into darkness. Shouting. Screaming. Mayhem. Ghost Carmine, operation shock and awe.

A few of the more resilient thieves open fire with semi-automatic pistols. Evanescent blasts but they can't hit me. They aren't aiming in the right zip code. Their flashlights click on just in time to illuminate the angry colossus thundering into their midst from the west. His voice shakes the earth. He's close to seven feet tall, as thick as an oak tree, and wielding a great double-bladed ax. He roars and swings at their popup campers, hewing off chunks like some prehistoric demigod. If my scream frightened them, the colossus, glowing red from firelight, renders them delirious. A lone gunman, wearing jeans and nothing else, is brave enough to aim a shaky weapon but I disarm him with a brisk overhand chop. The rest scatter north and south through Kagel Canyon or hide in the cabins. Those heading north will soon be out of the Kingdom, and those running south will be taken into custody by a regiment of waiting Law Keepers.

Sixty seconds after the giant's dramatic entrance, the campground is deserted. Dalton, my bodyguard, steps out of the brush and holsters his pistol. "You two are damn fools."

Tank, the colossus, laughs, a deep aural vibration from the chest, and says, "I enjoyed that. Been more fun, though, if you let me hack a few in half."

"Load up. I want to be gone soon." I get behind the wheel of a U-Haul truck and find keys in the ignition. As I hoped. Dalton climbs into a second truck. Tank barely fits into a third. We observed this crew long enough to confirm each truck is laden with stolen supplies, and all three engines turn over on the first crank. Gas tank is over half full. For once, everything goes as planned.

A terrifying augury - that can't be good.

We pass through the Law Keeper checkpoint, give them a thumbs-up, and head west. Tank leads us up Ventura Freeway into the once bustling San Fernando Valley. Formerly home to millions, now San Fernando has a population of forty thousand and comprises the northwestern wedge of our rebel Kingdom. The silent land is dark this late at night and nothing exists outside our headlight cones. Tank turns into Tarzana, a once posh town and neighborhood surrounded on three sides by national parks. The wildlife here grows brazen without the threat of traffic and scary millennials, and we honk repeatedly to move a small herd of California mule deer.

Citizens of New Los Angeles never venture into Tarzana on account of rumors that the extravagant homes are haunted. Those rumors aren't exactly wrong. We slowly motor south on Redesa Boulevard and park on a private street near Braemar Country Club. These houses used to be worth north of twenty million each, but now they're essentially cabins with campfires burning on the front lawn. Tank parks first, spills out, and opens my door.

He's a large man, about my age. Big bones, big muscles, big ax. Hispanic, like me. His blue t-shirt looks ready to pop its seams. Eighteen months ago he suffered third degree burns over much of his body, and the right side of handsome face is twisted with scars. "Welcome to my home," he rumbles.

I climb down and reply, "Dalton and I need to go. I appreciate the help tonight. Distribute the supplies among your crew, and extend them my best—"

"Come on." His hand envelops mine, and he pulls me after. "Can't leave yet, babe. Come meet the kiddos."

A giant is approaching. A huge man. My bodyguard Dalton balks from climbing out of his truck when he sees the giant. "Oh hell no," he growls, eyeing the giant from inside the truck's cab.

The approaching behemoth is named Travis and he is an astonishing sight. Travis sways closer, covering six feet with each stride. He is over eleven feet tall and weighs six hundred pounds, I'd guess. If Tank is an NBA player, Travis is the backboard.

"**Queeeen**," Travis thunders. "**Th'Queeeeen is heeere!**"

"Hello Travis." I cannot help the smile. He's an irrepressible toddler the size of a telephone pole.

Travis wears Big'n'Tall sweatpants, which fit like capris, but no shirt or shoes. He has trouble stopping, so we brace our hands against his abdomen. His arms spread wide, a herculean wingspan, and Tank says, "No, Travis! No hugs!"

"**Awww.**"

"Come on, kid. Let's show Katie around."

"My name is Carmine," I growl. Dalton begrudgingly exits the truck, muttering something about 'freaky ass giant stuff.'

These giants are victims of a macabre enhancement surgery gone wrong. Our creator was a transhumanist envisioning a utopia, but the virus he used as his mutation agent ran out of control. The giants keep growing and growing until age twenty, when they stall at eleven feet. A handful reach twelve. The virus, which burns in my veins too (though differently), breaks their mind. The giants have the mental powers of elementary school children, and so they use Gateway and Canyonback Parks as playgrounds. Their collisions can be heard for miles, creating the haunted Tarzana rumors. Tank fell backwards into the roll of their caretaker.

"**My hooooome**," Travis announces as we approach a two-story golden palace. A small campfire on the front lawn reflects off a thousand windows. Another giant is sitting at the fire, staring deeply into it. He doesn't glance up at our arrival. He and I are the same height when he's seated.

"Where are the others?" I ask.

"**Sleeeeep.**"

"Its two hours past their bedtime," Tank explains. He leads us on a tour and points out various attractions, such as the bathing pool, the drinking pool, the forbidden goats which keep the grass short, and the cooking pits. Through the windows I see giants sleeping on mattress pangaeas, using couch cushions as pillows.

Tank talks for the tour's duration, but I'm lost in wonderment. It's like a neighborhood playhouse for huge children. One of my hopes is that many of Los Angeles's former occupants will return to their homes and share the workload of survival, but this part of Tarzana will never again house the former owners; it's being trampled beyond recognition by clumsy, playful giants. I snap back to the present and hear Tank say, "We keep clean water running into the drinking pool because I don't want chemicals. I make the kids squeeze a couple hundred lemons and limes into the water every few days so they get some vitamins. The big idiots won't eat vegetables."

Travis waves a paddle-like hand for us to visit one final spot, and we follow. "The armory," Tank explains, in a backyard near the golf course. Looks like a salvage yard. Car doors and iron grates and heavy wooden tables are being repurposed and beaten into shields and body armor. Dozens of metal husks are propped against the house. Dalton, a former Navy SEAL, looks impressed.

I ask, "The giants prepare for war?"

"Yep. They hate Walter."

"They're too innocent, Tank. I can't let them fight."

"You don't have a choice, babe. If Walter doesn't show his ugly face soon, they'll go find him. I talk them out of heading north every week."

Travis retrieves the largest broadsword I've ever seen. Hilt to tip it appears five feet long. For Travis it's a long knife. He presents it to me, and if I use two hands on the leather hilt I can lift it. Barely. **"My toy. Hurt."**

Tank says, "Travis found that in a comic book shop, bolted above the door. It's real. He named it Hurt. He sharpens it every day. You can't lift it?"

"It'd be easier if I was angry." I chuckle to hide my displeasure. Tank and Travis can heft it easily but I can't, not unless my adrenaline is pumping. I'm irritated and envious of their strength. Dalton refuses to try.

17

Travis takes Hurt back, and slips his hand through the large leather wrist loop at the bottom. He walks into darkness and begins slashing the air, as a six-year-old would, great sweeps of the blade like a windmill. He forgets us immediately.

I yawn, "I'm going home, Tank."

Dalton sniffs his approval and leads the way.

Somehow, during our return stroll to the trucks, Tank and I get very close. His arm is slung around my shoulders.

I remember nothing from 2015 until May of 2019. My memory was wiped clean by the same surgery which created the giants. I remember nothing, that is, except Tank. Tank I remember clearly. He dated Katie Lopez, my alter ego, and in his mind I'm still her. Having amnesia and remembering only one human being creates a powerful affinity for that individual. I don't want to be with Tank. He's a rascal. I wish I wasn't drawn to him, but I am. Very much so. He's the only home I know.

"You doing a good job here," I say.

"You know it."

My arm slips around his waist, a familiar and comfortable motion. A little voice in the back of my head says, *Stop that this instant*. I say, "Don't let the giants go north, Tank. We can find creative outlets for their energy here."

His grip tightens on my waist and he halts our forward progress. Dalton walks ahead in the dark to the Land Cruiser we parked here earlier. I want to look up at Tank but I don't dare. No eye contact.

"Stay," he says.

"Tank…"

"Stay. With me. I got a whole house for us. Me and you, kid. You barely get a bedroom to yourself in that tower downtown." He draws me into an embrace, his arms around my neck, mine around his midsection. "They don't deserve you."

I don't answer.

No, the voice in my mind says. *No no no. Absolutely not.*

"Already got breakfast ready for us tomorrow," he says. "Eggs, fruit, and coffee. Then a walk up Corbin Canyon."

"This was a trap," I say, my voice muffled into his shirt.

"Some prizes are worth trapping. Besides, it's your own fault, wearing them skintight spandex."

"They're leggings, you big oaf."

"Whatever, they're hot as hell."

Let go. Let go let go let go let go let go.

"Tank—"

"Don't answer yet. Listen. No one deserves you, 'sept me. We don't have to be with all these people. They can help themselves. Together we'd be the most powerful couple on the whole damn planet. Let's go live in the White House. Who could stop us?"

"The current occupants. The President and Blue-Eyes?"

He chuckles, a sound I feel through the meat of his chest. "No chance. Think she can stop me? About time someone cut her down."

"I can't stay, Tank."

"But do you want to?"

"That doesn't matter."

"Does to me."

"I don't always get what I want," I say.

"You want me. You get me."

With a supreme effort of willpower, I pull away from him. Or at least I try. He doesn't budge an inch. "Hey. Let go."

"No way, mama. If I let go, you leave."

"I'm stuck."

"Yep."

It's as if I'm being hugged by a statue. I'm hopelessly pinned. "You get two more minutes. Then I'll resort to violence."

"I like it when you talk dirty."

"Gross."

"Do you like me, Katie?"

No.

I say, "My name is Carmine, and yes I do. But so what?"

"Then come inside with me."

19

No.

"No."

"Why not?"

"Because I don't trust myself, and I don't trust you."

He squeezes a bit tighter. "We'd have a good time. I'll make sure of it."

"Life is not about having a good time. At least mine isn't. I don't want to get mixed up in you."

"Why not?"

"Because, Tank."

"Because of Pajamas, the Boy Wonder?"

I don't answer, but we both know that's part of it. There's someone else. Kinda. I haven't seen him in months, but technically he exists. My life is too busy for romance, but if I had a love life I'd want it to be with him. If I ever saw him. Maybe.

Maybe not. At least with Tank I get tactile interaction. Maybe Tank—

No. Not with Tank.

You're right. No. Not with Tank. Probably not.

He asks, "Have you even seen that runt recently?"

"No. But that doesn't matter. I can't get mixed up in you because I don't have time. I have to stay focused. And you're a big distraction."

"Baby, you need a big distraction."

Two minutes turn into ten, and still we stand. He hasn't released, but to be fair neither have I. I'm not sure why. Maybe everyone needs to feel nostalgic now and then, and he's all I've got.

Finally, after ten minutes of teeth gnashing, my bodyguard lays on the horn. Not a pleasant beep beep, but a solid strident blare. He's going to cause a giant stampede if I don't go. I release. Tank releases, and we turn away with no words. All has been said.

Tank's lonely.

So am I.

- 2 -

Carmine

The following night is Becky's birthday party. She's the big Two-Oh. Every Guardian is twenty, or soon will be. Our creator only injected adolescents about to turn eighteen, something to do with the frontal cortex development. Our particular year has been labeled Generation Broken, which seems unfair to most kids born around 1999.

Becky is my friend. I really only have two girlfriends; she's half my social life. My attendance is mandatory therefore, even if I'd prefer being run over by a train. It's always weird when I go to social events because I'm one third of our Kingdom's triumvirate and I dampen the fun. As though everyone needs my permission to relax, and even then they can't. Dalton agrees to take the night off because I'll be surrounded by Guardians, and I think he might be having a fling with Teresa Triplett, the reporter.

At 7:30 I decide on a whim to go early. Get in, get out, and the attendees can enjoy the remainder of Becky's party in my absence. I'm wearing my standard outfit: black activewear and red silken compresses on my aching joints, even my shoulders. Kinda blah. Maybe if I dress differently I won't be so noticeable. I rifle through my disaster of a closet to retrieve jeans and a green strapless top. Selecting shoes is an art form I cannot even begin to fathom so I go barefoot. Time Magazine, one of the publications still circulating in the east, often has Queen Carmine caricatures depicting me shoeless. Whatever. Heels are stupid.

21

I jump down the stairwell (which takes four minutes) and hurry to Little Tokyo. The sun has set and the pavement is cool on my feet. Coal fires are lit in braziers on the corners and I get waves and stares the whole way to Becky's tower. She lives in the Miyako Hotel, a twelve-story slate blocky building. The Miyako is one of the barracks on the east side of Downtown. Housing for Guardians.

The party is on the top floor lounge, a large room with red walls lit with rechargeable lanterns. It's decorated in classy Asian decor. Becky and the handful of early party-goers are staring at the door when I walk through; they *Felt* me coming.

"You're here!" Becky grins. She's short and cute. Thick dark hair and big smile. "I'm glad you came. But…you aren't staying. I can tell."

"What? I can—"

"You want to go home and read."

"Becky—"

"You're miserable."

"Stop it!" I put my hand over her mouth. She's so good at reading people it's creepy. Sometimes she has whole conversations with herself, playing her part and mine. And she usually gets it exactly right. "It's your birthday. No way I'd miss it. So shut up."

"Thanks for coming." She hugs me.

"Of course."

"Love you."

"That's…okay—well, good, and me…me too."

"You don't have to say it back. Your whole body clenched. You're allergic to affection. Do you see that boy over there? No, not that one. The boy with the good hair. The one who's worried his shirt isn't tight enough. I can tell. Anyway, you can have any boy tonight except him. I want that one."

"You can have them all."

"I wish."

At 8 PM, Becky starts the party by plugging her 'Party in a Box' into a battery. It's a powerful speaker and light system, and the lounge transforms into a kaleidoscope of colors and music. The room is instantly full of life and people acting silly.

I enjoy dancing, but this is not ideal. I've drawn a crowd, and they all want to talk. One girl in particular, I'm almost positive her name is Liz, gets me in a conversational headlock while the others listen and nod.

"Queen Carmine, I hear the fruit harvest is going well."

"Yes," I nod. "It is."

"Oranges?"

"That's right. And asparagus."

"So not just fruit?" she prompts. We're having to shout over the music. "Vegetables too?"

"Correct."

"Pears too?"

"Yes. Pears too," I say.

"I like pears!"

"Too bad all our cottage cheese is gone."

Yes, they all commiserate. This is terrible, our cottage cheese shortage. Liz says, "Maybe we could make some!"

"Maybe so," I agree. This is *such* a good idea, the crowd thinks. We should *totally* make cottage cheese. A long pause ensues and everyone bobs and stares at their feet. I offer, "And artichokes."

The crowd murmurs in a general appreciation of artichokes. The is the most boring conversation ever, and it won't stop. We talk about California's different seasons, and how so many abandoned fields are ripe with fruit. They ask about my plans for tending the fields in the coming months. I admit I have no idea how we'll do it.

Liz asks, "Do we have too much fruit?"

"We do," I sigh. "We don't have the power to run big freezers, so we're canning a lot of it."

"All of it?"

"No. Not all."

"Oh. How much of it?"

"I'm not sure. Much of it will spoil soon, so we send big containers to the Navy strike group off our coast in the Pacific. They're short of supplies."

Ooooooh, the Navy, they say. How interesting.

Ohmygosh I'm slowly dying. They're trying to be polite because they think I want them to but, really, go away. I'm so bad at small talk and parties.

Yes. Yes you are. You are a disaster.

Shut up Katie.

Becky eventually comes to my rescue and shoos them off. Before I can argue she grabs my hand, and with sincere alacrity she pulls me into the pulsating mass. Her joy is infectious and I dance far longer than I intend. This party is exclusively for Variants, and the atmosphere quickly goes to my head. Mutants like Becky and her friends 'broadcast' their virus and it creates a connection with me, especially when we touch. It's a heady sensation, almost like an out of body experience. The more excited we are, the stronger our bond. I *Feel* what they feel and vice versa, and tonight our hearts beat as one.

After an hour of dancing, Becky calls for a break to cool off. The building has no power for air conditioning, and open windows can accomplish only so much. We are unsavory. About fifteen of us take the stairwell to the roof and to cooler air. Sweet delicious oxygen. I pace between a row of rooftop tomato planters and wipe the sweat from my eyes, while Becky and the guy with great hair and the other couples move to the darker far end. Young kids in dark corners. I smile. Variant teenagers are still teenagers at heart. And twenty-year-olds, I guess.

On my third trip between the planters, as my heart is resuming normal rhythm, a long arm snakes out of the darkness and encircles my waist. I'm yanked into the shadows by the penthouse. Before I can yelp in surprise, a hand clamps over my mouth.

"Hah." A familiar voice in my ear. "That was smooth. Just like Batman."

"Mmmmpff."

"You're right. I'm way handsomer than Batman."

I growl into his hand.

The arm and voice belong to Chase Jackson, a boy better known as the Outlaw. A mysterious vigilante romantically involved with Katie Lopez, a part of my history I can't remember. He's a globally recognized war hero and, despite my best efforts, I'm irresistibly drawn to him. At the moment, quite literally; he's behind me with iron hands on my mouth and and hips. He removes the hand from my lips and we stand motionless, content to simply rest against one another, an intrinsic fit. I've missed him more than I realized.

He's wearing the cologne I bought him.

"Batman has a cape, though," I whisper. Two days and two hugs from handsome boys. I could get used to this.

"Yeah, well, his budget is bigger. Some of us don't need capes to look cool."

"And he has a sexier voice."

"Perhaps you'd like to get Bat-pinched."

I snicker. The Outlaw has the Hyper Virus, same as me, but his power dwarfs mine, tremendous and terrible potential he keeps bottled up so it doesn't draw the attention of other Variants. His strength used to anger and frighten me but I experienced a biological shift in perspective after I surrendered to the truth: he's scary but he's good. He can suppress his strength and I can suppress my fear.

He says, "Your hair is getting longer. I like it."

I ask, "How long are you staying?"

"I'm not positive. Maybe a long time."

"Uh oh. That doesn't sound good."

"Why not? We can kiss for days."

I elbow him in the ribs. "You wish."

"Yes, yes I do."

"What I *mean* is that you coming here to stay is an indication you believe trouble is brewing."

"Not necessarily."

I ask, "But does it?"

"Why don't you want to kiss? I can find some Chapstick first."

"Focus, Chase."

"Some girls would consider it an honor."

"Which girls? I'll assign them to Sanitation. Or toss them into the Pacific."

He draws me further into the shadows and we press against the wall, out of sight. Becky and her crew are returning to the party. They file through the door and never see us. For the moment, we're alone.

"What's the occasion?" he asks. His lips brush my ear.

"Becky's birthday. She's twenty."

"You turned nineteen a few months ago."

"I did? When?" I ask. I haven't thought about my own birthday since…never.

"You don't remember your birthday?"

"Mmmmmmm no. I can't remember."

"I'll throw you a surprise party."

"Where have you been recently?"

He takes a deep breath as if he's assembling his thoughts, and rests his chin on the top of my head. I raise my hands to the arm around my shoulders and chest. He's human but he doesn't feel like it; more like he's rock wrapped in soft leather. "Everywhere. The Federal Government is closing in on the Resistance in a thousand different towns."

"And if you show up the hostilities stop?"

"Sometimes."

"Where is the world's deadliest sniper, Samantha Gear?"

"Samantha is in DC, hoping she gets a chance to knock Blue-Eyes's head off. But she knows Samantha is there, so she's hiding."

"I'm glad you're here," I say.

"Me too."

"But you're worried."

"Nah."

"Tell me what you're worried about. Why'd you come back?"

He says, "It's not pressing. We can talk about it tomorrow."

"But—"

"Tonight, we should dance."

Oooooo, he's right.

Downstairs the party is pumping. The Variants will turn on Chase if they sense him (he's a powerful intruder they don't trust), so we sneak in the back and stay out of the crowd. Katie must have been a dancer because it comes naturally. Music provokes me, imperative movements, and the beat is almost pre-choreographed in my mind. Much less so for Chase, but he does the White Man's dance moves as well as the next guy.

He loves me. Or he loves Katie, the girl I can't remember. One of us. Either way, it's a rush. He's obvious in a thousand ways, and I find the sensation of being loved overwhelmingly sexy. When I catch his eye, see that special smile he reserves for me, notice how he responds to affection, it's all I can do to maintain composure. I refuse to let a boy control me, but my boundaries grow harder to enforce.

After twenty minutes of dancing my curiosity is too strong to ignore. I shout at him over the music, "Tell me!"

"Tell you what?"

"Why are you here?"

"Tomorrow. We'll meet with Mason and General Brown and talk about it."

"No! Tell me now! I'm worried. Is it about the Infected? The pure-born Variants?"

"Yes."

"More are coming?"

"I don't want to shout about it."

"Let's go to my place. Keep your head down!" I grab his hand and pull him towards the door. I won't wait until tomorrow; I need to know now or I won't sleep. We'll talk at my apartment.

The stairwell door opens before we arrive and a pizza delivery guy enters carrying four pizzas. I bet this gathering wasn't hard to locate. Poor guy walked up a lot of stairs. Maybe we should stay for pizza? I'm kinda hungry...

The party's atmosphere is shattered by a scream. Becky takes one look at the pizza delivery guy and identifies the danger, realizes what I don't; we don't have pizza delivery guys. It should've been obvious. His disguise is simple but effective. He's an imposter.

Those pizza boxes aren't full of food...

The delivery guy's backpack is too heavy...

He's wearing a thick vest under his jacket...

He's a walking bomb. A young guy, covered in sweat.

A suicide bomber.

We're all going to die.

Becky's moving at the speed of fear but she can't reach him in time. He sees her coming and he triggers the bomb. Mission accomplished. Everything happens in slow motion.

The Outlaw saves my life by three tenths of a second. He embraces me and launches us towards the windows. So slow.

The suicide bomber's pizza boxes and backpack and vest are heavy with explosives, probably triacetate triperoxide plates, maybe a hundred and fifty pounds total. They ignite like one bright star, a savage chemical eruption. The top of the Miyako Hotel detonates upward and most of the southern wall is shattered and flung into the Japanese Village Plaza. An avalanche of noise. The blast reaches me and Chase, swallows us, and flings us through the glass.

Becky and all the closer Variants are instantly vaporized by the intense heat and pressure. I'm in midair when I feel them die. Nineteen total, including Becky. Their bodies weren't ready for combat. Adrenaline had no time to solidify their structures or harden their skin. Their flesh was destroyed as anyone else's would be. My mind and spirit are connected with theirs as they die, and the loss hits me as though my soul is being crushed. Like the bomb erupted inside my chest. Like I'm dying too.

Chase and I land and skid across the adjacent Citibank building. Debris and fire rain down in chunks. Katie is crying between my temples, but other than that I'm deaf. The world moves in delayed hazy jerks. Chase should be dead but he's not. His back is a mess. Muscles and skin flayed from the bone. Ribs exposed. His body smokes. But he breathes. My arms are black and my shirt is on fire. I notice all this coldly, detached as though the cords connecting my brain to my soul have been severed.

Above us the Miyako burns.

I blink and see Becky scorched in the constellations.

I blink and Chase is trying to move.

Chase.

I blink and alarms are wailing.

The bomb was meant for me.

I blink and heavy streams of water are launching in rainbows towards the fire.

I blink and see firemen swarming.

Eyelids heavy.

I blink…

I blink and they don't open.

For as long as it takes to draw a deep breath, I'm somewhere else. Los Angeles is gone, and I'm in a dark chamber. Like a temple. The sound of muffled voices throbs in my ear.

I cough in pain and it's a masculine sound. Not my own.

A woman watches me. She is beautiful.

Where? Where is she? the woman says. What can you see?

I…

As quickly as the vision comes, it fades.

I blink and suddenly I'm in a bed. In Los Angeles again. The scalding silence of fire is replaced by the sharp quiet of a hospital.

Dalton is at the window, fists on hips, staring at the angry sunrise. My bodyguard…

I blink and daylight has infiltrated the room. Dalton sleeps in the red chair. Kayla sits crisscross at the foot of my bed, resplendent in designer jeans and an ivory top. The room smells like a thunderstorm so she must be worried.

Can you hear me, she asks. Carmine? Sweetie?

I watch her from a distance of eternity.

He's alive, Kayla says. Chase is alive. Are you there?

I can't respond. I have nothing to say.

I don't move.

I wish I'd died with Becky.

Becky.

Another blink.

- 3 -

A Queen Broken

Carmine dreams.

Carmine's body detaches from her spirit.

Carmine wakes up at six. A dinner tray rests on the table beside her hospital bed. Chicken, asparagus, and applesauce, but she doesn't touch her food. Instead she stares at the wall-mounted television which displays a satellite broadcast of CNN. News prognosticators are silently arguing over the headline 'DEADLY EXPLOSION IN LOS ANGELES: Queen Carmine Feared Dead.'

A man clutches her hand and squeezes. Dalton. "Hey kid. Gonna stay awake this time?"

Carmine does not respond.

Kayla and a physician scurry in. The doctor pokes and prods and asks too many questions, and Carmine nods to make him go away. He explains things she doesn't care about, and then he leaves after one final lingering glance at Kayla. It's hard for men (and most women) not to ogle Kayla, the world's second most downloaded woman.

At the moment, Carmine thinks Kayla smells like apple pie. She's exhausted but alert, and she strokes Carmine's hand. "You're going to be okay, sweetheart. You're going to be okay." Carmine isn't positive what she's talking about, and her eyes return to the television while Kayla prattles, "You're in one piece. No broken bones, which are *ew*, but you have a severe concussion. General Brown won't let me release a statement. He thinks reports of your death might reveal the culprit, or whatever. The Outlaw is injured, but he'll survive. His body sustained major damage but he heals so *fast*, Carmine, it's like pow. He burns through nutrients faster than the nurses can pump them into his stomach. Your arms and shins have first-degree burns, sweetie, but they'll heal. The doctor pulled out the shrapnel. I have some great long-sleeved options which will hide the burns and highlight your pretty eyes."

It's not her arms that Carmine is focused on. It's her soul. It's gone.

She blinks. She sleeps.

Becky is seared into Carmine's eyelids. Each time she closes them, Becky is there. Screaming and reaching for the pizza boxes. So she opens her eyes for good around nine that evening.

Nineteen dead. She experiences each death like a scar across her chest. So profound are the wounds that all other emotions are meaningless. She feels no fear, no hope, no relief, no pain. Just a sense of loss.

And anger. Entire mountain ranges of anger. Her body anneals with adrenaline. Skin thickens. Nails lengthen.

There was a bomb, she thinks.

Dalton sits on a chair barricading the door. No one getting through there without his approval. He glances at her when she begins nibbling on asparagus but he knows better than to intervene or offer help. Carmine's scowl is enough to keep him in his seat. The television is on mute so she thumbs up the volume; CNN is still diagnosing the explosion. The connection is patched through satellite feed so the television flickers occasionally. The asparagus agrees with her stomach so she eats the chicken and applesauce, and drains a large plastic container of water too.

"The President and his inner council have yet to respond to the tragic news coming out of New Los Angeles, which cannot be much of a surprise given that he's declared the annexation of Los Angeles an act of war. It's well documented that he and the Secretary of State have

repeatedly demanded Carmine release the harbored Variants, issuing any number of injunctions against the self-proclaimed queen, and this suicide bomber will only serve to strengthen his claim—"

She listens with interest. I'm Carmine, she thinks. They're talking about me. She has trouble codifying information through the fog of insensibility. Someone bombed us.

Becky…

"If you're just joining us, our story of the day took a dramatic turn twenty minutes ago when the criminal warlord in San Diego released a statement claiming responsibility for the suicide bomber. Experts had predicted Walter would take the credit, but so far his camp has been quiet. The military doesn't know much about the warlord other than he calls himself Russia and he seized the abandoned city with a small army of gunmen last December. Kingdom insiders assert that Carmine planned to attack San Diego and oust Russia and his regime in the coming weeks, so if Russia's claim is accurate then perhaps this was his preemptive strike. We still don't know if Russia is working with Walter and his terrorist network in the northwest corner of America, but certainly it appears as though their purposes intersect."

Russia. So that's his name.

He killed Becky. He killed the other eighteen.

They died instead of me.

Carmine climbs out of bed and pulls her heart monitor off. An IV needle is stuck inside her rock-like flesh so she breaks off the protrusion.

"Oh damn, you need to use the bathroom?" Dalton stands and moves his chair. "Where the hell's Kayla? This is stuff girls should do together. Don't move, I'll find her." He steps into the hall; Kayla isn't there. He snags a doctor by her white sleeve and forcefully pulls her from the nurses' station towards Carmine's room.

But the warrior queen is gone.

General Brown is standing at his window on the twenty-fifth floor of the Olympic apartment tower and completing his nightly ritual; he watches the dark skyline and lets his mind wander over the day's events until he's too tired to think. This happens like clockwork at 2050 hours each night. This evening he's musing over Carmine and what it will mean for New Los Angeles and the Resistance if she's out of commission for several weeks. So much depends on her, including the future of his grandchildren. How can he and his soldiers help pick up the slack? Probably can't. Carmine is one of a kind, a stabling force on the deteriorating planet. Brown's already undressed down to his boxers and t-shirt, ready for sleep. His uniform is laid out for tomorrow, agenda set, lamp extinguished, but before he can reach hypnagogia his cellphone lights up. Incoming calls at bedtime are rarely positive.

General Brown checks the caller ID and answers, "Kayla, what can I do for you?" He listens a moment and his eyebrows rise slightly. He clears his throat and asks a clarifying question, "She hasn't spoken? Do you know where she might be going?"

Carmine dreams.

She dreams she's young and beautiful. Her hair is long, thick, and brown. No scars on her arms or legs. She laughs and doesn't worry about protecting an entire city. She rides on her boyfriend's back as he jumps between towers, as he *Leaps* into the stars like earth is a place they can visit or leave at will. He loves her and she adores him and they are suspended in the golden air of youth and irresponsibility, and all that matters is not getting caught by her mamá.

Her mamá.

Two hours after the escape, Carmine finds herself in a commandeered Honda Accord idling in Tarzana. The vehicle is dusty and smells of mold. She doesn't remember how she got here. But she knows why she came. Her stolen jeans fit well. The white shirt is too small and the jean jacket is too big. She kills the engine and sits in silence for five minutes with the windows down, listening to insects chirp.

There is no youth. No leaping in the stars. No irresponsibility.

Russia killed them.

Russia the warlord from San Diego.

She leaves the car door open and moves noiselessly to the nearby row of mansions. The fires on the front lawns have been doused and everyone is asleep. Great thundering snores emit from inside. Behind the fourth house Carmine finds the giants' makeshift armory, a junkyard of repurposed metal. A tall broadsword is shoved into the earth almost up to its hilt. Hurt. That's why she came. She cannot aim a firearm accurately but she can swing a sword. Carmine easily withdraws Hurt from the soil, the weapon issuing a soft metallic rasp. The sword is no longer heavy because her body is swollen with simmering rage and epinephrine. She hefts it and gives an exploratory slash, as though she has the strength of ten strong men.

She's crying. She doesn't know why; her insides feel dead. Zero emotion other than anger. But tears stream freely down her cheeks.

The sword is not as tall as her, but it's close, and it's awkward to carry. The large leather wrist loop slips easily over her head but if she wears the weapon like this then the sharp tip will drag the ground behind her. She experiments by wrapping the leather strap under the cross-guard first, and then over her head. It's a snug fit, but now the sword sits higher on her shoulders almost like a backpack. This arrangement will suffice, she decides.

She returns to the car but finds Tank waiting there. He has ducked his head into the Honda and is inspecting it suspiciously. Not wishing to be discovered, Carmine hides behind overgrown boxwoods and waits. In her current state of mind, she wants no distractions. She'd rather hurt Tank than talk to him at the moment. She doesn't even know if she *can* talk. Nothing inside her appears to function correctly except anger and instinct.

Tank knows it's her. He recognizes the fragrance of her disease and her sweat, and he circles the car looking for footprints in the dirt but she was careful. He won't be able to track her. He's heard the speculation she died and now he's both relieved and confused. Could she have gone to his house? He hopes so. His thick fingers play with the buttons of his shirt a moment before he turns and strides up the far hill towards his home.

She watches him leave, waits another moment, and then sneaks down the street. She'll find another vehicle after she exits his neighborhood. No need to fire a car engine in close proximity. A half mile down the road she discovers the three U-Haul trucks parked on Rosita, but she doesn't stop for them. Too big, too noisy. She moves on.

At the intersection of Hermano Drive, Carmine stops dead in her tracks. *Tigers.* Two of them. They move off the Caballero Golf Course, onto the sidewalk, and into the street. The night is pitch black but Carmine and the tigers see each other perfectly. Massive animals, nearly her height and weighing over a thousand pounds each. She is without fear. She *should* be afraid but she cannot experience the emotion. Instead, she approaches the tigers boldly.

She steps between them and extends her hands. The big cats nuzzle their furry faces into her palms like they want to be scratched, and she obliges. She scratches behind their heads, their necks, and under their chins. The male opens his mouth to bite her hand, but the motion is playful. He's restless. The female is slightly smaller and content for the moment. A powerful musk invades Carmine's nostrils, and she thinks one of the tigers recently marked the golf course with pungent urine. They press heavy heads against her chest, seeking further affection, almost enough to knock her over. The longer they play, the more emotion they subsume from her. They soak and magnify her anger. They share the disease. They are one.

Inspiration strikes. Carmine turns and walks back the way she came. The tigers will follow; she knows they will, and they do. The big U-Haul's latch isn't locked. She releases the door and it rolls upwards into the cargo storage's ceiling. The truck is empty. With no prompting, both big cats leap effortlessly into the capacious cargo area, circle the thick moving blankets, and lay down.

The warrior queen smiles, but with no humor. Her eyes are cold.

Todd Hodges is lounging with his feet up at the last checkpoint on Interstate 15 and trying to stay awake. He sits on the very edge of the Kingdom's boundary; to his left is New Los Angeles and to his right is wild country. A pointless post, in his opinion, because nobody in the Kingdom ever ventures this far east, and there certainly aren't any vehicles trying to get in. His checkpoint is in Corona, an abandoned city in Riverside, twenty miles from Anaheim.

'Abandoned' isn't exactly correct. Eighteen months ago a hundred thousand people lived in Corona so it *feels* abandoned now. In reality, however, several hundred still live here, surviving off scavenged goods and the local wildlife. Todd hears them most nights, making noise in the once trendy neighborhoods. The Kingdom doesn't have enough Law Keepers yet to fully monitor the many communities within its border, so who knows, maybe the scavengers might live here another couple years. What the Corona creeps do isn't that dissimilar from the rest of us, Todd thinks. Simple survival.

At 11:15 PM, he gets a text. A group message sent to all sentries on duty.

>> Alert. Alert. Please report any sighting of Queen Carmine. Whereabouts unknown. Condition unknown. Contact the Priest directly.

Queen Carmine's alive! Todd figured as much. It'd take a lot to kill the queen. He met her twice, once right here a month ago when she surprised him with breakfast. She shook his hand, gave him a chicken biscuit, and inquired about his job. He'd been so nervous he couldn't speak. Often he wishes he could relive that morning and make a better showing. He would like the queen to know how reliable and competent he is, instead of a mumbling jackass.

She's lost now? Why would the Priest be looking for her?

His lip curls in distaste at the thought of that man. Only the Priest's original zealous followers respect him, and the rest despise him. He maintains control through his large organization of informants and through fear. Most Law Keepers are hopeful the queen will remove him from power soon.

Sure, Priest. You got it. I see the queen, I'll let you know.

Todd returns to his phone, playing a stupid tower defense game. He's already beaten it twice, but it passes the time. And keeps his mind off how spooky his outpost is.

At 11:35, Todd hears a distant engine. Traffic is a rare occurrence and never this late. He walks into the middle of the freeway and looks both ways. A pair of headlights pierces the darkness in the valley below, traveling south towards him. He curses and wishes he'd been looking in that direction so he'd know if the headlights came from the north and drove through Corona or if this is a local scavenger out for a joyride. Either way, he returns to the guard shed for his flashlight and firearm. Better safe than sorry.

The vehicle begins to churn up the long gradual incline towards his post, and Todd develops the impression this isn't a local scavenger. This is someone from Downtown. A supply truck perhaps? If so, it's a week ahead of schedule. Reinforcements?

He doesn't grow alarmed until the headlights are a quarter mile distant. They aren't decelerating. He waves his arms and flickers the flashlight. "Slow down, idiot," he grumbles.

This close he sees the vehicle is a U-Haul truck traveling at ninety miles per hour. He shouts and jumps up and down, but the truck barrels closer and blows through the security gate. The metal barrier is dragged fifty yards before wrenching free. Todd watches the red taillights recede for several minutes.

What the hell was that??

He follows the cone of his flashlight to retrieve the heavy gate and drag it back. Better call my supervisor, I guess. Not like he can do anything now, but I should cover my ass.

Todd doesn't remember the alert about Queen Carmine until he turns his phone back on. He stares at the message and wonders. Could that have been her? Couldn't be. Nothing is down that direction for a hundred miles until San Diego, and the queen wouldn't be going there. That's where the warlord named Russia is.

Carmine dreams.

She dreams she's at a football game but not in the stands. She's on the field. In one of her hands is a bouquet of flowers, and in the other is the boy she loves. They're alone in the universe, only the two of them, but the lights are on and applause thunders down from heaven. The boy wears a football uniform, and he's sweaty and handsome.

She dreams they go to a dance and she wears a dress and he wears a vest. Her hair is tied up with ribbon. Kids without faces come to the party but only to watch the two of them. He drives her home afterwards and she's so happy she can't catch her breath, so excited her teeth chatter. A car ride that never ends.

Kayla lays on one of her couches. She stares at the ceiling and fingers the cashmere blanket pulled up to her stomach. Her dog Princess sits silently on her feet. Her apartment is dark except for scented candles; a somber but appropriate mood for their war council.

Despite the two sets of furniture, General Brown can't find anywhere to sit. Ranks of sparkly throw pillows rest on the couches and chairs and he's too dignified to dump the pillows onto the floor. So he paces and tries to avoid kicking artwork stacked near the walls. This room is like a monument for everything Girl. Mason sits on the floor next to Kayla, knees drawn to his chest. He's dressed in his customary vest. "She's gone," Mason says for the tenth time. "She's just…gone."

The Priest is outside in the hall, talking to someone on the phone.

The Governess is tired and grouchy. While she waits, she inspects the panoply of designer creams and lotions on Kayla's kitchen counter. She's a woman not given to appearances; she wears a black skirt and button-up blouse every day, and no makeup. Her hair is fixed in a bun and Kayla's never seen it otherwise. But the lotions are interesting, especially if they can help with crow's feet. She dabs several on her wrist before nodding in satisfaction. She picks up a glass container and says, "This one, I like."

Kayla glances her way and sighs, "Good choice. I use La Mer every day. That bottle costs over two thousand dollars."

The Governess knows the dollar amount is meaningless. Merchants abandoned the bottle when they fled LA, and Kayla simply found it in a boutique. However, the Governess is startled that the meaningless number is so large. She fumbles and drops the glass container. It shatters on the kitchen tile.

For a long uncomfortable moment, Kayla appears as though she's been both electrocuted and petrified. She's weary and heartbroken as it is, but she manages to achieve an additional level of anguish as she surveys the La Mer smeared across her tiles.

"Ah Kayla. I am sorry! I dropped your bottle."

"Oh…I mean…that's…" Kayla manages. "…that's okay?"

General Brown ignores the disaster. Anyone foolish enough to spend thousands on a face cream deserves what they get. He's got bigger problems. He nudges Mason with his boot and says, "Shake it off, Mason. We're soldiers. We're leaders, and we lead. We'll get the queen back."

Mason does not look up.

The Priest opens the door and proclaims, "Got her! A U-Haul broke through our border ten minutes ago. Has to be the queen."

Mason looks up and asks, "Where?"

"Heading south on the fifteen."

"Huh? Where's that?" Kayla asks.

"She's going to San Diego."

"Yuck. Why?"

"Russia," the Governess answers. "She will go to kill Russia."

General Brown's fists go to his hips. This is trouble. The Kingdom can't afford a war with San Diego. Not without the queen. His mind already churns with possible solutions.

The Priest continues, "Dalton is downstairs waiting with a car. We're going to get her back. She's got an hour head start on us, though, so we're leaving now."

No one speaks. The Priest wants to risk his life for the queen? This is new. Those two are well-known rivals.

"Should not Mason and his Falcons go?" the Governess asks.

"He can't," the Priest replies, not without a certain degree of disdain. "Their Alpha has been removed."

"So?"

"The Variants are beginning to crash. Just like when the Chemist died. Mason has gone into a depression. So has Kayla. And it'll get worse before it gets better."

"Wait a damn minute," Brown growls. "The mutants will start rampaging?"

"Maybe."

"Musth," Kayla says in a quiet voice.

"Repeat that? Musk?"

"Musth. Carmine researched it, and she says it's like musth."

Mason's eyes are bloodshot and he's inspecting Kayla curiously. "I don't get it. What's musth?"

"It's a state of frenzy triggered by increased hormones," she responds from memory. "A condition common in the animal kingdom. The dominant animal in a herd constrains the frenzy of the young. Keeps them in line. But if the dominant animal is removed…"

"The animals rampage?"

"Yes. So gross, right? We're like elephants, which is *ew*. Young adolescent elephants need the influence of older bulls, otherwise they get violent. Carmine is the dominant animal. Biologically, we need her influence."

"Without her, you go crazy."

"Kinda. Yes. Maybe."

The Governess throws her hands up in the air and says something in another language. General Brown says, "The Outlaw is in the hospital down the street. He's an Alpha. Won't he do until she gets back? Can't he make you elephants shut up?"

"No," Mason replies immediately. "The Guardians hate him."

"He's not the same species," Kayla explains. "He's pure born, not genetically engineered like the rest of us. Plus, he hasn't woken up yet."

General Brown shoots the Governess a worried look. They can handle the day-to-day operation of the Kingdom, but not the mutants. They are a whole different animal. Once their greatest asset, the Variant army just turned into a time bomb. This nightmare won't end. "Okay Priest. Go get her. We need Carmine."

The criminal warlord known as Russia is reclusive. He lives somewhere downtown, his men know, near the ocean, and he doesn't like to be disturbed. San Diego is without order, without structure, without law. Do what you want, Russia has told them. Only be ready to fight. He maintains control through pack mentality, thrives in the chaos. He is a quiet man but a cruel and powerful one.

The walls separating America from Tijuana have been broken and the brave and the violent come and go as they please. This is no place for the meek. No place for families. This is a captured province and Russia's gunmen live off the fat of the land. Which is mostly liquor and fish. At night they burn couches in the streets, and the occasional house in Logan Heights.

Qualcomm Stadium sits near the edge of downtown San Diego. The stadium is the former home of the NFL's Chargers, and is without power. A vast arena now serving primarily as a campground for homeless drifters. All is quiet except inside the lavish suites high above the field. There, criminals reside and they often don't sleep until dawn. Like their warlord, the criminals are violent, lazy, and free of responsibility. In fact, the Qualcomm group of mercenaries has only one job; watch the interstates and shoot unwanted intruders. Qualcomm is conveniently located at the junction of Interstates 15 and 8, and many days are spent on the roof of the stadium suites staring through sniper scopes, taking potshots at anything stupid enough to move.

This particular band of pillagers traveled all the way from Minnesota. The world's ending, they decided. Let's ride it out in Coronado. They looted and stole their way to San Diego to find it freshly occupied by a powerful insurgent army, twenty thousand strong. Can't beat'em, may as well join'em. They moved into Qualcomm Stadium and began racking up a list of atrocities. Mercenaries paid in promise, booze, action, and firearms.

Tonight they play poker. Every night they play poker. Three tables are erected in the owner's box; other suites are used for sleeping, but not the owner's. Battery-powered lights burn and cards fly in the smokey atmosphere. Phil is one of the dealers, a former security guard turned bar tender turned murderer and mercenary. The men trust him to handle the cards, so he shuffles and deals every other hour.

Phil is the first to notice a tiger walk into the owner's box. Not simply a big cat, but a cat the size of a Camry, head larger than a car engine. Claws like Ginsu knives. Phil is thunderstruck; he's stricken mute and nearly insensate, powerless to warn the others. Tigers do not simply prowl in Qualcomm. Unthinkable. Unimaginable.

A striking woman strides purposefully into the room, carrying the biggest damn sword Phil's ever seen. She's pretty and thin, with short hair, but she's tall enough to attract the attention of Phil's comrades, and subsequently they notice the tiger. The poker suite goes deathly still.

"I need answers. If you don't touch your weapon, you get to live," she says with an eery calm. Like a robot. Phil believes her, but his friends are high. His group shoots first and doesn't bother asking questions later. A man in the back is the first to fire; he unloads his pistol, loud cracks in the enclosed space, bullets digging into the tiger's flank. The animal is not wounded, only angered.

Half the men in the room are stupid enough to go for their guns. That half dies, either by tiger or blade. The woman moves like a ninja warrior from hell, efficient and merciless. It's not a fight, it's an execution. Phil closes his eyes and groans, unable to watch his friends fall. After the longest minute of his life, the noises stop. The woman grabs Phil by his collar, lifts him from the floor, and pins him to the wall with her forearm.

"No! No, stop, please, no," Phil cries. The tiger snuffles at his hand. "Please, stop, please."

"I can't," she says. "I don't know how."

The girl holding him is crying. Why is she crying?

"What do you want?" Phil asks.

"Where's Russia?"

"Downtown."

43

"Where?"

"I *swear* I don't know! I'm not lying." Phil jerks away from the tiger and loses control of his bladder. "We don't know. I've only met him once."

"What's he like?"

"He's...I don't know. He's big."

"Get your phone. You need to send a text message. To everyone in San Diego."

The Outlaw wakes up at three in the morning. Confused. Tired. His brain fights through a fog made of medicine.

Where am I?

He smells laundry detergent and ointment and rubbing alcohol. He's lying face down on a bed in the dark. He tries to move but his back screams in protest, a far off agony. What's going on...

"Don't move, Mr. Jackson." A nurse lowers herself to eye level and glares at him. "I am your nurse and I expect cooperation. Do you understand?"

He nods. But not really.

"Your back needs to heal, so you will lie still and you will not complain."

He mumbles, "My back?"

"You should be dead. Do you know why I'm your nurse? Because I'm the best. And all the younger nurses were fawning over you. I'm fifty-six and you'll get no pity from me. You need to get better. Fast. I treat Guardians and they heal, and you will heal, and I will get you out of here. Soon. Nod if you understand."

"There was a bomb."

"Yes."

"Where's Katie?"

"I do not know a Katie."

He wants to ask more questions but can't. He's gone again.

Carmine emerges from the Trader Joe's on Vermont Street at five in the morning. Almost everyone inside the derelict market is alive. Her enemies are beginning to take the text message warnings seriously.

Put down your weapons and live.

Downtown, they all say. Russia is downtown! Don't kill me!

It's been a long miserable night. Carmine can't remember killing anyone, but she knows she has. Far too many. She hates it. Wants this nightmare to be over. Wants Becky back. The sun will be up soon. She needs to be deep in the heart of San Diego's tower cluster by then, and she's close. Over her shoulder, in the distance, fires still burn from the night's many fights.

She walks up University Avenue and merges onto Cabrillo Freeway, tigers in tow, and she's greeted by a haunting sight: Balboa Park. The park is over a mile long and leads directly past the Palisades into the heart of San Diego's downtown. At night with no street lamps, the overgrown park might as well be the amazon. But this is the quickest route. She experiences no fear, but even in her broken state she recognizes danger.

Gunmen are materializing out of the park. Dozens of them. Unlike Walter's army in the northwest, most insurgents Carmine has encountered here in San Diego are Hispanic. Like her. By now they've received the text messages. Probably multiple warnings about the crazy woman with the sword and tigers. The woman too fast to be shot, and the animals too powerful to kill.

Much to her surprise, one by one the gunman begin laying down their weapons. Pistols, shotguns, assault rifles are all placed on the pavement.

Carmine doesn't like this. She recognizes a trap when she sees it. Russia has heard of her, and he beckons. Come to me, he says.

I'm coming, Russia. Coming for you.

She knows death awaits. She's ready to die.

Russia's army lines the street and witnesses her plunge into brooding Balboa Park.

She dreams. Dreams and walks.

She's with Tank in his gargantuan Hummer, marveling at the opulent vehicle. He wants her to be impressed and she is. Their evening is spent traveling to investment properties he's purchased with money from his trust fund. He holds her hand, this handsome boy already coronated by the high school football gods, and she begins to hope. To hope he's lost his bitterness, to hope their sputtering romance might blossom, to hope he'll ask her to his prom.

Suddenly she's with Chase in a crowded high school cafeteria. She squeezes his hand and his headaches fade and he smiles gratefully at her. He's in so much pain…

At the far end of Balboa, there is a man waiting for her. He stands in her path.

Beyond him, at the peak of a tower in San Diego's skyline, a massive black flag is flying. Looks like an entire acre of fabric flapping in the breeze; Russia's flag. A banner of terror. Carmine wants to rip that flag down, but she can't get there. Because of the man.

He waits, in her way, near the San Diego Air and Space Museum. He blocks her path into the looming towers beyond. The sun is rising but can't yet pierce the park's shadows, and so the mysterious stranger remains hidden inside his cloak and cowl. His scent is rich and wild, like a herd of horses. She doesn't know why but her heart quickens with uncertainty, the first true emotion she's experienced. He holds up his hand, palm out. Rings decorate his thumb, index, and pinky fingers. He lowers his hand towards the ground, and her two tigers obediently sit on their haunches. They watch him with interest.

How did he do that?

She wants to ask, Are you Russia? But she cannot. She has no voice.

"Your long night is over, Carmine," he says. His accent is thick, like English isn't his first language. She shivers. "The man who waits in the city, Russia, he is beyond you. Your mind has been destroyed already but he will smash your body."

Tears fall from her cheeks. She's surprised she has any left.

"The man in the city is strong. And violent," he says. He walks towards Carmine, and her tigers surge with excitement like kittens. Suddenly she's tired. So tired. "I know him. And you must live a while yet."

Upon closer inspection she sees he's ancient. A black man with a wispy beard and penetrating brown eyes. His clothing is dirty and his necklaces and rings are tarnished. The tigers rise and go to him. He scratches deep into their pelt with dirty fingernails, and speaks kindly to them. "You have had a hard night, my friends."

Who is this, Carmine wonders. Exhausted. Barely coherent.

"Go home, beautiful animals. And kill no more." He commands them with a strong sincere tone, and they obey. The animals turn and pad into the shadows, and Carmine is too spent to object. She doesn't even watch. The stained sword drops from her hand and clatters loudly onto the road.

Carmine collapses but the man is ready. She collapses into his arms and he cradles her close, like a father would his daughter. She is asleep instantly. "Sweet beautiful girl, that sword does not suit you," he says. He hefts her a little higher so he's able to press the button on his earpiece. The cellphone dials and rings, and he steps carefully over the freeway's barrier and into the trees, towards the car he parked at Marston Point. The line is picked up on the other end and he says, "PuckDaddy, my dear friend. I have her. She is safe."

Part Two

You can have Los Angeles
Just give me back my girl
- Fiction Family

- 1 -

The Outlaw

The girl named Kayla enters the hospital as I walk out. She's wearing heels, and jeans so tight they could be painted. Her eyes widen when she sees me and I swear they change color from blue to green, like mood rings. "Outlaw!" she gasps. "Err...I mean, Mister Chase...sir."

I'm painfully pulling on a zip-up hoodie, and she reaches behind me to help. She smells like fresh cookies. "Chase. Just Chase," I grunt.

"I was coming to see you. Are you...you're leaving?"

"I think my nurse was trained in Agoge. I need to rest somewhere else."

She says, "Agoge? What's that?"

"It means I hate her."

"It means he's a wimp." My old pal Dalton climbs out of his red SUV near the sliding doors where he'd been waiting for Kayla. He grins. "Agoge was rigorous Spartan education. His nurse was too rough on him."

I try to shrug but it hurts. "Well. She was. So shut up."

"Get in, Outlaw," he says, and he opens the rear door.

Kayla claps, honest to goodness claps, and says, "Oooh, good idea! We'll take you anywhere."

It's a beautiful day for a walk but I accept the offer. I wasn't going far anyway; everything hurts and I'm already exhausted. I limp into the back and Kayla sits next to me. Its like sitting near a bakery oven. Dalton closes the door and gets behind the wheel.

"Your jacket looks too small," she observes.

"I have no clothes of my own. This one belonged to my nurse from hell."

"You stole it?" she gasps. "Oh my. I'll pick you out a new jacket. You're built like a mannequin, so this will be fun."

Kayla sounds worse than the nurse. She produces her phone and begins typing faster than I thought possible.

Dalton asks, "Where to?"

"I'm hungry."

He nods and guns the engine. "The 8th Street cafeteria."

I haven't been outside in days. The city is hurting. Variants are everywhere, sitting on the sidewalk with their knees pulled up, staring out windows, laying despondent in the streets like dead insects after a gas bomb. Fear and gloom are palpable. Even the southern California sunlight seems watery. A kingdom without a queen.

The makeshift cafeteria on 8th is a large tiled room with tables, like a cafeteria should be. I wonder if the cafeterias were Katie's idea originally; her subconscious projecting high school lunch rooms onto her new Kingdom. We get a LOT of weird looks when we walk in. A guy I kinda recognize comes to eat with us. I've seen him around. Dark, brooding guy, thick eyebrows. His vest reminds me of the style I wear. Kayla refers to him as Mason, and the two of them watch me eat like it's fascinating. Dalton rolls his eyes and eats his soup without comment.

Mason looks mildly depressed, but after a minute he asks, "Do you remember fighting in the Gas Tower? Before the Chemist died?"

"Sure. I remember that night."

"I was there."

"Oh yeah? Small world."

"You hit me with your stick and broke my arm."

"Oh." I wince. "My apologies. Coulda been worse, though. I cut some other guy's head off, if I remember correctly."

"Yeah, Carlos. Good riddance."

Dalton mumbles into his spoon, "I was there too but nobody cares."

"Where's Katie? The nurse wouldn't tell me."

Mason frowns. "Who's Katie?"

"We don't know where Queen Carmine is," Kayla answers. "PuckDaddy says she's safe. That's all."

"Call him."

"Call him?" Kayla asks. "Call who?"

"Puck."

"Are you kidding?"

"No?"

"I can't simply *call* PuckDaddy," she sputters. She's gone very red in the face. "He's…he's…like a god."

Mason says, "I don't see what's so great about that computer nerd."

"I'm confused. I thought you two talked on the phone all the time."

"We message in chat rooms." She blushing so furiously it's like an alarm. "Text now and then, but it's no big deal. Why? Did he say something? Because you have to tell me. What did he say?"

"Let me borrow your phone."

"Why? No."

"i want to call him."

"I'll die first."

Dalton growls, grabs my empty tray, and says, "I'll get you some more food so I don't have to listen to this crap."

"Mason, can I borrow your phone?"

"Not to call the nerd."

Dalton slams his phone on the table and stalks towards the food. I pick it up and dial a number from memory and put it on speaker.

Kayla's about to hyperventilate.

The phone rings once and PuckDaddy's voice issues from the speaker. "Dalton, my man, what's up homie."

"Puck, it's Chase. Where's Katie?"

"Chase! OUTLAW! Hell yeah!" The phone rattles on the table with the force of his volume. Kayla's eyes are massive and she's covering her mouth. "It's so freaking good to hear from you. Puck's been deeply lonely."

"Where's Katie?"

"How's your back?"

"Hurts. A lot. Where's Katie?"

"She says I'm not allowed to call her that. Her name is Carmine."

Kayla smothers a giggle, like a little girl would. Mason scoffs.

I rub my eyes in irritation. "Puck. Where is she?"

"She's safe. Zealot got her."

"Zealot? *The* Zealot? I thought he was in Africa."

Mason and Kayla share a glance and shrug - Who?

"Not anymore, homie. He's here."

"Do we trust him?"

"Yes. I trust Zealot more than I trust Samantha. Cause she cray," Puck says.

"I've been stuck in a dark room for days. I know nothing. Do we know who sent the bomber? Was it Walter?"

"Nah bro. It was Russia."

"*Russia?!*" I shout so loudly the entire cafeteria hops. "Why? I thought that jerk kept his nose out of our business."

"Not anymore. He's cashing in."

My brain is swimming. I lower my head to rest in my hands. "This is a lot to process."

"Yeah," the speaker says. "Hey, Puck just looked up your phone location. You're near Kayla. Looks like she's right outside the cafeteria."

Kayla gasps and shakes her head. She waves her hands back and forth. I'm not here, she mouths. I'm not here! I can't!

I say, "Yeah, she's…probably nearby. I guess. Doing weird stuff."

"Why are you on Dalton's phone?"

"Mine got blown up. I'll find a backup. Puck, do you—"

Suddenly Kayla smacks the phone with her palm and the call cuts off. Mason and I are so startled we jump in our seats.

"Why'd you do that?!"

"I don't know!"

"What is wrong with you?"

"I can't deal! I can't deal with this." She's fanning herself with both hands. "Call him back."

"Then why did you—"

"Call him back! He probably thinks you're being rude."

"But—"

"Tell him that I'm here. No, don't. Yes. Just do it."

I dial Puck again. I say, "Sorry Puck. Got cut off."

"S'okay. Cell signals ain't what they used to be."

"Yeah? Guess who's here. Your friend—"

Kayla smacks the phone again, and she squeals. The call cancels. I throw up my hands. "What. On. *Earth*. Kayla!"

"Sorry! I didn't mean to!"

"This is muy loco," Mason observes.

"Kayla—"

"Call him back!"

"Sit on your hands."

"I'm okay. I'll do better. I promise."

"No, you'll sit on your hands this instant."

"Okay. Now call him."

I call him back and move the cell phone far away from Kayla. She sits on her hands and closes her eyes. I say, "Sorry, Puck. Me again."

"What's going on over there, bro?"

"Mason just walked in. You know Mason? Kayla's here too. I got you on speaker."

Puck sharply inhales and the line clicks. Call canceled. I stare stonily at the device. Kayla opens one eye and peeks at us. "What happened?"

"He hung up."

"Why?"

"Because you two have issues."

"What? I don't...what?"

"He's just as scared of you as you are of him. And I'm the most frustrated person on earth."

Her face brightens like the dawn. "He's scared of me? Why would PuckDaddy be scared of me?"

"Because you're crazy hot and he's a wimp."

"He's a wimp?" Now she's no longer the dawn, she shines like a noonday sun. "He's shy? Really?"

"I don't know. Apparently." I pinch the bridge of my nose and take deep breaths.

"That's the most adorable thing I've *ever* heard! Yay!" She claps and bounces.

"How is that adorable?" Mason argues. "Everyone in the city is nervous around you."

"He's sooooooo sweet."

The cellphone rings. Puck's calling back. It's like I'm the parent of middle school idiots. I answer and he says, "…sorry Chase. We, uh…got cut off…again."

"Uh huh."

"Hi Kayla." His voice is weak.

"Hi PuckDaddy," she replies in a high squeaky voice.

"Great," I say. "Now we're all adults. So, Puck, what do you know—"

"Where are you right now, PuckDaddy?" she asks.

"In California. Near Utah. I think. I read your post last night on Reddit. Loved it."

She stares down and begins picking at her manicured pink nails. "Oh. Thanks! I worked on it a long time."

"I can tell. It has over a million replies so far, the majority in approbation. I think you're the most popular person on the boards."

"Puck," I shout. "When is Katie coming back?"

"Do you mean Carmine?"

"Yes," I groan. "When is she coming back?"

"Dunno bro. Zealot says she's really sick. Might be a while."

"Sick? What do you mean sick?"

"Her mind. Something happened in the explosion, homie."

"She didn't speak all day," Kayla says.

"But she's safe?"

"Yes."

"Is that why the Variants are mopey?" I ask. "Because she's gone? They look sick too."

Mason nods. His eyes are red and he needs a shave. "We need her back."

"What happens if she's gone for a long time? A month or more?"

"I think we'll be depressed," Kayla answers. "And then get agitated. Really angry. We're connected to her. She's our leader. Our queen. Our purpose."

"That is super strange. And alarming."

"It gets worse," Puck says. "Multiple videos of her are going viral on the internet. Videos of her in San Diego. The whole world knows she's not in her right mind, and that she left her Kingdom."

"Walter will see the videos."

"Exactly. Walter's already on his way, bro. He left Medford, Oregon this morning. He's bringing *everyone*. I've already alerted General Brown."

The hairs on my arm prickle and stand up straight and my chest turns icy. Walter's coming. Judging by Kayla's face, she already knew. That's why she was coming to see me in the hospital. "When will he arrive?"

"He and his Variant soldiers should arrive tomorrow. His army of mercenaries will take a few days longer to move."

"Tomorrow."

"Yup."

"And Katie's Variants can hardly function," I note.

"*Carmine's* Variants."

"She calls them Guardians," Kayla says. "Not Variants."

"Whatever! They need a new Alpha. Right?"

Mason says, "We need Queen Carmine."

"Can't you be the Alpha?" I ask. "Until she returns?"

"I'm not strong enough." He shakes his head. "Not to be what we need. If I tried it would cause jealousy and piss off hundreds of others. I'd have to fight my way to the top. It'd never work."

I say, "It can't be me."

"Right. You make them nervous," Kayla agrees. "You smell funny."

"Thanks."

"No...I mean..."

"Puck, where's Samantha?"

"She's on her way. Be there in forty-eight hours. Navigating across America isn't easy these days."

"So when Walter arrives tomorrow he can waltz in and immediately assume command of Carmine's Variants?" I ask. "Because he's strong?"

"Maybe." The once proud and mighty Mason looks brought low and miserable by the idea.

"That's our worst case scenario. If that happens, we're all dead."

"General Brown thinks they can hold him off for a little while, but not long. Walter has two thousand mutants trained for war," Puck says from the speaker. "An unstoppable force."

Dalton brings me another tray of food and I begin popping apples and potatoes into my mouth. An idea is forming in the back of my mind, but I hate it and desperately search for another. No one speaks. I bet Puck has the same idea but won't admit it.

Finally Kayla asks, "What are we going to do?" I don't answer. Neither does Puck. She looks at me and then the phone and back. "Well?"

"I have an idea. A terrible one."

- 2 -
Carmine

Salt water.

The rich scent wakes me up with a start.

Dreams. I was dreaming about fire. So real. But now…

Water.

Waves are lapping against my headboard.

I need to get up. Need to open my eyes. Need to move, to talk.

But I can't. I'm unable to muster the resolve for locomotion. My body is a rag without frame, without energy, without life. Breathing takes every ounce of determination I possess. But when I do, I inhale pure bliss. Delicious ocean air.

I'm inside a small cabin on a boat. In the Pacific Ocean.

My mattress begins to rise. The entire dimly lit cabin rolls softly upward, crests, and pitches down again, an easy pleasant motion. A broad wave has passed beneath the keel, I realize. I find the sensation to be impossibly pleasant. Soothing, like the ocean is massaging my spirit.

I'm not getting up. Not ever again.

Somewhere above, a man sings. A vibrant tune released with a deep voice. Optimistic, as though the singer likes to laugh. The boat's frame creaks, and I hear the sound of ropes tightening and fabric snapping taut. We're on a sailboat.

Another wave lifts the bow and I smile into the pillow. My headache doesn't pound. My joints don't ache. A powerful emotion wells inside, a sentiment turning the world a shade brighter, a feeling I'd forgotten.

Joy. Contentment.

- 3 -
The Outlaw

I sleep twelve hours on my stomach in Katie's bed on the 22nd floor of Olympic. The apartment is devoid of any decoration, another sign that Katie is buried deeply under the hard Carmine exterior. Her Devotee, a big good-looking dude in a robe, isn't happy about me but he doesn't have a choice. I'm not happy with him either; the buffoon's robe is short and he tries to bunk on the floor in my bedroom. No sir, not while I'm here.

I find items from Katie's childhood. There are photos and clothes and lotions I recognize from our past life. Her pillow smells so good I cry. But not when the Devotee is watching.

I get up at six the following morning. I'm still weak and my back screams in pain, but we're out of time. I grab an apple and granola bar, and open the apartment door. Kayla's waiting in the doorway and she says, "Are you sure this is a good idea, Mr. Chase?"

"How long have you been here?"

"I don't sleep. And I'm worried about your plan."

"Yeah, me too."

Kayla calls for the elevator and we ride down to the dusty garage where Dalton waits with a car. He drives us north following my direction, swerving to miss Variants wandering aimlessly on Olive Street. He parks at a dilapidated storage unit warehouse. Kayla wrinkles her nose with distaste and says, "Yuck."

The warehouse stands like a dirty gravestone marking the past. Dalton and I spend an hour unclogging hallways leading deeper into the complex. These are personal storage units long since abandoned and many of them have been looted. Cleaners stuffed rubble into the entrances to clear the streets, and they must now be unstuffed. I move gingerly to avoid ripping newly knitted muscles, and Kayla explores the units for valuables, "like jewelry and clothes and anything fabulous."

Finally we reach my old compartment. The padlock is still attached. I tug until bolts in the floor crack free from the concrete, releasing the latch. Kayla clasps her hands under her chin and says, "This is such an honor. I'm so excited."

"An honor?"

"You were the *Outlaw*. Time's Person of the Year. I used to wear a black tank top with your face on it," she gushes. "Before the surgery. And now here we are. At your Batcave. Everyone guessed you had a hideout downtown."

"Prepare for disappointment," I remark and roll the metal security door upwards into the ceiling. The air is dank and dense with particles. I find the bin of flashlights and click one on, primarily for Dalton's benefit. Kayla and I see well in the dark.

Memories come flooding back. This place saved my life a couple times. Before the great evacuation. Before the collapse of the west coast. The unit is a large space complete with a twin bed, computer desk, television, big car batteries, and boxes full of supplies. Dalton is unimpressed. Kayla says, "Wooooooow."

Dalton helps me open the boxes while Kayla goes through desk drawers. I discover what I'm looking for in the fourth bin; a backup Outlaw vest, gloves, and wing-suit pants. "Why do you need this stuff again?" Dalton asks.

"Showmanship. I'm merely Chase Jackson. No one is scared of me. But hopefully a lot of Walter's army will be afraid of the Outlaw. The outfit is important, I've learned."

Kayla calls, "These drawers are *stuffed* with cash. Thousands of dollars. And credit cards! Where'd you get all this?"

"It's a long story."

"This is so romantic," she sighs. She places her hands on the mattress and tests the bounce. "Did you ever bring Queen Carmine here?"

"No. I wish."

"Too bad. Because this place is sexy."

"How the heck is this dark storage unit sexy?"

"Because it is. Boys are so unromantic." She shakes her head and smiles wistfully in the dark. "Did you ever light candles in here? Because ooooh."

It's clear from his scowl that Dalton thinks Kayla might as well be an alien. I tend to agree. He helps me out of my shirt, which sticks to the wounds. Kayla takes one look at my back and pronounces it, "Seriously disgusting."

Dalton tosses me the pants and says, "You're on your own for that."

"Hey! I found you a backup phone!" Kayla chirps. "In this drawer. There's also a love note in here. May I read it? I'm going to read it." The room smells like a field of flowers.

I glance at my watch. We need to hurry.

A little after nine in the morning, I stand at the intersection of Grand and 4th with General Brown, the Governess, Mason, Kayla, and Teresa Triplett. We are the motliest crew ever assembled. Teresa is a reporter, and she's sitting on the berm typing into her laptop and furiously snapping pictures with her camera. The intersection is surrounded with Variants too depressed to stand. In other parts of the city, the depression has worn off and they're angry; Kayla informs me the Arts District is being smashed to pieces. In the towers above, hundreds of New Los Angeles citizens stare from the windows.

It's a typically beautiful day in southern California, with a blue sky that stretches to forever. This part of the city is well tended and still carries the City of Angels atmosphere. Too beautiful a day for death, but that's a very real possibility.

General Brown is at my elbow and he mutters, "This is a good plan, kid. As far as desperate, last minute, hair-brain, half-baked plans go, this isn't terrible."

"Thanks General."

Some of the Variants glare at me and release a primal growl. My scent is bottled up as tightly as I know how, but they still detect me. I smell like an intruder. An outsider. A threat.

I say, "I'm less confident than you are."

"Why's that?"

"He hates me. He's tried to kill me…I don't know, a bunch."

"Can you beat him?"

"Not right now. I can barely stand."

Brown curses and gives the windows another inspection. He has snipers and soldiers with electroshock weapons at the ready. I check the General's watch; Tank is late.

My cellphone rests on the hood of Dalton's SUV, adjacent to a bluetooth speaker. I call, "Puck, is he close?"

PuckDaddy's voice comes rattling out from the speaker, "Yes. Sixty seconds out. Puck hasn't monitored Tank for a long time. Lost track of him. I have to admit: I'm freaked out."

"Freaked out? Why?"

"You'll see."

Soon Tank Ware strides into view. He turns the corner at 3rd Street, coming around the Wells Fargo Bank Tower, and approaches our intersection. That big dumb idiot has a double-bladed ax resting across one of his shoulders. His face hasn't healed. He's dressed in a white button-up shirt and gloves, as usual.

How I hate that guy.

I'm about to shout at him, something deeply offensive and brilliant for old time's sake, when someone else turns the corner behind him. A lot of someones. A lot of *big* someones.

General Brown whistles. Dalton says a very bad word.

Tank is being followed by giants. Huge massive enormous bulky men, so big they appear to move in slow motion. Their fists are full of rebar spears. They carry heavy iron plumbing pipes, like clubs. Their chests are protected by manhole covers and car hoods. Forearm bucklers made from trashcans.

"Of course Tank has an army of giants," I groan. "Of *course* he does." Our intersection, full of Variants, is struck silent. The depressed mutants stand and gape. So do the rest of us.

Tank reaches the intersection and halts. His overgrown infantry does too. He glares balefully at me but he doesn't speak and neither do I. The rest of the intersection waits.

Finally Puck's speaker bursts, "Those dudes are HUGE! I can tell even from the satellite feed."

"This better be good, Pajamas," Tank rumbles. "You said Katie needs help."

Behind him, from within the ranks of walking mountains, a giant roars, **"The Outlaaaw!"**

"Oh crap," I mutter.

The giants begin to roar in anger and for an instant I worry about a stampede. A Crush-the-Outlaw stampede. It'd be nice if these guys didn't remember me.

Tank holds up his hand and orders, "Wait." The giants grumble but they don't charge. I'm safe for the moment.

All the Variants are staring at Tank; not at me and not at the giants, only at Tank. He asks, "Where is she?"

"Katie's safe."

"Where?"

"I don't know. Zealot has her, and I trust Zealot."

"The hell is Zealot?"

"An Infected. A lot older than us. He says he can help heal her."

Tank stops watching me and turns his glare onto General Brown, Kayla, the Variants, and the towers. He's not satisfied with my answers. "All you people couldn't keep her safe?"

"At least we're trying. Instead of hiding."

He says, "You're still an ugly little boy, you know that."

"Nice ax. You use that for shaving? Looks like you accidentally cut half your face off."

"If you don't have a good reason for asking for my help, I'm going to be displeased, tiny man."

"Walter's coming. With his mutant army."

Like I flipped a switch, his giants howl. An earsplitting blast which rattles the tower windows. Teresa Triplett is so startled she drops her SLR.

"They ain't big fans of Walter," Tank explains.

The closest giant, a man wearing huge jeans like capris, drops his iron pipe and calls, "**Kaylaa!**" Kayla, startled to a cartoonish degree, screams and turns to run. The giant takes two steps and catches her. He picks her up like she's a six-year-old and holds her at arms length. "**Kayla. So preeetty.**"

An instant before she succumbs to fear and faints, she recognizes the man. "…Travis? Is that you?"

PuckDaddy shouts from the speaker, "What's going on?? Who just called Kayla pretty? Puck hates him."

"Travis, can you put me down?"

"Tank," I call, "the Variants need you. Until Katie returns."

Mason mumbles, "Her name is Queen Carmine."

Tank asks, "Why me?"

"It's complicated."

"Don't care. Tell me."

"Katie underwent a round of gene therapy. He didn't simply inject her with the virus, he also planted stem cells. The Chemist used his own genes, and he used yours too."

Tank sets the axe down and leans on the handle. His eyes are far off, mulling over the facts and implications. Travis thuds back and forth across the intersection, smiling at Kayla who politely asks to be released.

I continue, "Katie is their Alpha, Tank. I think your leadership can pacify the mutants who bonded with her. Because you two share their DNA."

"Why do they need to be pacified?"

"I don't really know. Think of the Variants as a pride of lions with no dominant male. The Variants need an Alpha. That's why they flocked to Katie and to Walter, and those who didn't are rampaging across the mid-West. She calls those loyal to her Guardians."

A Guardian I don't recognize has approached Tank. She's approximately our age and she's watching him curiously. Tentatively. He scowls at her but she keeps coming. She reaches to touch his arm. He smacks her hand and growls, "Stop it."

Kayla has surrendered to being carried like a baby. She's still held in Travis's fists, and she calls, "Let her touch you. It helps, Mister Tank. I don't know why."

"Don't care," he says. "Katie's the only one who gets to touch me."

"Aw. That's sweet."

I say, "That's sweet? No. No it's not. That's gross. Katie doesn't want to touch you."

"Beg to differ, Pajamas. She's done a lot of touching."

General Brown looks like a man watching Gilmore Girls and he wants to throw his remote through the television. He still hasn't spoken.

Even big Travis recognizes the rising antagonism and he stops pacing. The simmering hatred between Tank and me is almost visible. The last thing we need is to tear this city apart with a personal grudge match.

Actually I'd lose that fight quick. I'm so tired, and my back is killing me. Blood is leaking from my vest and seeping into the pants.

Puck asks from the speaker, "Is it awkward there? It sounds awkward."

"We don't have time for arguments, young men. Walter's at the edge of the city," General Brown barks.

"**Walter**," Travis snarls and he drops Kayla. The giants rumble like a thunderstorm.

"Let him come," Tank announces to the intersection. "We'll grind him into powder."

"We can't. The Variants aren't bonded to you," I reply. "That takes a while. They might latch onto Walter instead."

"Can't the General just drop a bomb on them?" He waves his hand in General Brown's direction.

"Easier said than done," Brown answers. "They're a small mobile force. They'd scatter, and his militia isn't easily killed."

"We need to make a show of strength, Tank. Stall him. Force him to wait. And then we'll pray Katie comes back."

"We outnumber him," Tank says. "Right? What's so hard about this?"

The giants roar in response, a truly astonishing sound. I wait for the tumult to die down.

"His soldiers are trained warriors, and they're bonded to him. They'll fight like a single entity, but we'll be disorganized, unfocused. It'd be a slaughter. We have to trick Walter."

"We launch rockets only as a last resort," Brown says. "But they'll be ineffective."

As we speak, dozens more Variants appear. They crawl across the towers. The intersection is clogged with humanity forming a circle around Tank. He glances at them, irritated, and continues leaning on the long ax handle. There's no denying his effect on the mutants; they respond to him. Even Mason. This plan might work. Even though I'm worn out. Need food. Need a nap. Shaky on my feet.

Tank gives me a long, penetrating inspection, "You're standing funny, Pajamas. And sweating."

"Because you smell so awful. Shower now and then, would ya?"

"You injured?"

"You wish."

"Okay," he relents. "Let's meet Walter and tell that son of a bitch he can't come in. For Katie."

- 4 -
Carmine

I remember Chase.

No. That's not right. I remember…dreaming about him. I experience him inside Katie's memories. Of a dance. Something about a car ride. Something that keeps slipping away. I'm hit with a swirl of emotion so strong my breath catches. Tank was there too.

I used to rub Chase's shoulders after football practice! We were kids then. I remember that. We were only friends but…ugh, it's gone already.

The sailboat's cabin pitches enough to remind me I'm on a boat. The mattress and pillow contain a faint damp musk but it's a pleasant, lived-in scent. My jeans and shirt are unfamiliar and they don't fit well. No shoes.

I emerge from the cabin into blinding light. I'm on a field of diamonds so brilliant it hurts. The air thrums with rays of warmth and the breeze is brisk and heavy with salt. The deck sways and I grip a railing until I'm able to open my eyes. A man laughs and says, "Here you go. Put these on." Sunglasses are pressed into my hand, and they help. We're on a smallish sailboat, maybe thirty feet. The fiberglass hull is faded ivory. The big sail is down but our boat is being pulled along by a smaller orange sail at the bow.

A man sits at the wheel, reading a yellowed paperback. He wears old green khakis and a tattered blue henley shirt. Dirty boots. Four rings, a bracelet and a thin necklace, all gold. Attractive bright smile. "She lives."

My voice cracks. I can't remember when last I spoke. I clear my throat and try again. "Forgive my abruptness, but I need a few questions answered. Immediately. Who are you?"

"A friend. Your companion PuckDaddy refers to me as Zealot. But I prefer Saul."

"Zealot," I repeat, searching memory banks. "Zealot. I know the name. You're Infected."

"That is a recent term, but yes. I am. We used to call ourselves Cursed. But that was a long time ago. A long time."

"Where are we?"

"Can you see the coast?" He points off the right side of the boat, the starboard side, to a large island in the distance. "That is Santa Catalina Island. We are not far from your home. Santa Catalina has been mine for the past six months."

"I didn't know people still lived on Santa Catalina."

"Yes. Many. Over ten thousand, I think. The number grew during your great evacuation, or so the story goes. We live on fish, and we trade with your black market. It is a peaceful place."

At the word fish, I'm suddenly ravenous. Wonder when my last meal was? Saul seems to sense my discomfort and he nods to a small galley behind me. There is a pan with, what else, fried fish, and an unopened bottle of orange juice. "Caught it this morning. Eat and drink."

I do. He goes back to his book. The juice is past expiration and it's warm, but delicious. I drain the bottle and refill it from a big jug of water and drain that too. Wipe my mouth with the back of my hand. "What happened last night?" I ask. "I don't remember much. Only…tigers. And anger. And violence."

"That is an adequate summary. Your mind came very close to breaking. Too close. Too close to insanity."

"I was going to kill Russia."

"No, sweet girl." He shakes his head sadly and closes the book. He looks maybe seventy, which is well over a hundred in Infected years, I've learned. "You were going to *be* killed by Russia."

"How do you know?"

"I know. I am ancient. I know."

I let that marinate a moment, stung by the gentle rebuff. "You have an accent."

"I was born and raised in Rwanda. Lifetimes ago. When I was little, Rwanda was governed by Germany. Isn't that strange? I left Rwanda for good in 1965. Long before the genocide."

"How long have you known Russia? Or known *of* Russia?"

"Good question. Maybe, since the 70s."

"So he's old?"

He shrugs and smiles. "Depends on who you ask. Still young to me."

"Russia needs to die, Saul."

"What an awful conviction to have."

"You should have let me try."

"Your journey is not yet over, I think. Russia has the illness. Same as me. You cannot win that fight."

I'm stunned. Amazed. Russia? *Another* Infected in California? There's only like fifteen total, and they're all coming here. That's how I know the name Russia; Chase must have mentioned it. What do I know about the man? Nothing that I recall. "What happened to my tigers?"

"They are *your* tigers? I sent them home."

"Sent them? How?"

"Can you communicate with them? You think you're the only one? Better you should learn to control yourself, instead of controlling them."

He pulls on a rope, reties a knot, and adjusts our heading. The sea is calm and we slowly cut through it on nice easy swells. I ask, "Why did you help me?"

"You needed it. And I wanted to meet you."

"I appreciate it. Very much. But I need to get back."

"In time. In time. What you really need, Carmine? You need to heal."

"Am I injured?"

He nods, and his kind eyes are sad. "Severely. In your mind."

"How do you know?"

He pulls a phone from his back pocket. Presses the screen a few times and hands it to me. "Hit play," he says. I follow directions. The video is of me. It's a dark grainy picture, captured by a camera phone, and the sound is garbled, but the truth is obvious. I'm screaming and butchering a room full of people. There are bursts of gunfire and tiger snarls. I'm swinging something. A sword? Eventually the fight stops. The survivors have surrendered and I stand in the middle.

I glance down at myself. I find dried blood on the cuffs of my jeans. More on my shirt. Under my nails. My tears fall freely onto the cellphone. On screen I'm wearing a jacket. I bet he simply threw the sodden garment away.

Saul says, "Those were not innocent men, Carmine. But death comes at a price, and not all of it is borne by those who die. God did not intend for his children to kill one another."

I hand the phone back and wipe my tears. So much of myself I don't remember or understand, but I'm glad that awful night is erased from my mind. Like it happened to a stranger. "When was that?"

"Two nights ago. The trauma was too great, and so you slept. Your body does not like what you did."

"I'm not happy about what I am. But I accept it."

He tilts his head back, as if pondering a great question. "And what are you?"

"I am what I have to be."

"Which is?"

"Ruthless. A leader."

"And?" he presses.

"And violent. And mean. But I do it to protect others."

"Go on. What else are you?"

"A monster."

"Ah. But are you truly?"

"I am. Didn't you watch the video?"

"Or are you sick?"

We both grow quiet. I am sick. That's glaringly obvious. I scrape dried blood off my hands. When that's not enough, I lean over the upper edge of the boat's hull and rinse them in the ocean.

"You are no monster, Carmine. You are overly burdened. And sick. But you are God's beautiful creature."

"I used to think that, Saul. But I don't see how that could still be possible."

"Never doubt the great hound of heaven, precious girl."

"I feel better. On the boat, I mean. Better than any time I can remember."

"The disease inside your body is a storm of agitation. It demands attention. Demands action." He makes fists and shakes them, and that's exactly how my insides often feel. "But the motion of the sea calms it. You will never be as calm as you are when at sea. There is a woman, you would call her Infected, who has been at sea for over a hundred years. That is how she stays alive. How she stays sane. It is medicine."

"Is she your friend?"

"No. She is not my friend. I avoid her."

"So you think I should stay out here? I can't do that."

"Not forever, no."

"How long?"

"Until we finish talking."

"Saul, I don't want to sound ungrateful, but a long pleasure cruise is untenable. A lot of people depend on me. They have to be wondering where I am."

"Your friends know you are safe. I contacted them."

"May I borrow your phone to make a call?"

"There is no need for phone calls."

"But—"

"No, Miss Carmine. You may not borrow my cellphone."

"What if I take it from you?"

He cackles. A pure sound. Innocent mirth. "You are so young! So proud. So foolish. If you try to take it from me, you will learn a valuable lesson."

"Which is?"

"That you should respect your elders."

I believe him. I don't try. "What do we do now?"

"See that boat to the north? He's a trader. We're going to buy a pineapple."

Hours later I sit on the bow of Saul's boat, enjoying peace. My feet dip into cool water every time we pitch forward. The rise and fall feels like a baby's bouncer, like I'm held within a compression blanket. For the first time in a year I feel no all consuming drive. No compulsions.

Saul is below me. Somewhere in the chroma of blue. I spot him every few minutes, a dark shape flashing ten feet under. When he surfaces for air it's with powerful kicks which jet him from the ocean like a dolphin. He swims like one too. Take all the time you need, Saul. Our sails are down and we aren't moving, and I'm happy.

I try turning on his phone but it's password protected. Darn it.

After an hour he erupts from the sea and lands feet first on the stern deck. A large fish squirms in his hands. He streams water and blows air and says, "We are blessed. God gives us bluefin tuna for dinner!"

He uses a knife to quickly sever the fish's head, because, he says, "I do not like it when animals suffer." We prepare tuna steaks with olive oil and seasoning and put them on his grill. I'm irritated because he thinks mundane tasks like preparing my own food will allow my spirit to relax. I'm also irritated because it's working.

I ask, "Where did you live before Santa Catalina?"

"I sailed from Mombasa in November, and stopped for a short time in China. I lived in Africa for many years. The people there are sometimes very poor. They are ignorant, and I told them how much God loves them. This is part of the human condition, you understand. The need to be loved."

"Is Africa affected by our societal collapse?"

"A little. Yes. But it will get worse. Much of Africa grew too dependent on your aid. It is sad." He takes his steak off the fire before I do, and he uses his fingers to pop hot chunks into his mouth.

"How is the rest of the world? Do you know? I've been too busy with my city to care."

"The world withdraws. Shuts down. Fear is powerful, yes? There are mutants in other countries. Mutants like you. They'll be hunted down and killed. Eventually."

"Did you know the Chemist?" I ask.

"I knew Martin Patterson, yes.."

"And?"

"And? And I miss my friend."

"You can't be serious."

"There are very few like me. He was a good man for many years."

The steak is glorious. Fresh. Tender, but crispy at the edges. Maybe I should start preparing my own food. I finish a piece and say, "The Chemist was insane."

"Martin was sad, at the end. I think. He did not know his creator and placed too much value within himself."

"His actions were evil. He abducted and hurt me."

He places his hand on my shoulder and squeezes. I won't look him in the eye. "I am sorry he did that. Please accept my apology. I would prevent your pain, if I could. It was perhaps past time for Martin to go."

"He should have been killed long ago, Saul."

"Maybe so. So it seems now, but I find it hard to judge the people who operate from mental instability. He was sick. Same as you." He retrieves his phone and waggles it. The same phone on which I watched videos of a madwoman hacking her way towards San Diego. "I do not enjoy judgement."

I don't respond. Fissions radiate in my brain, tiny pinpricks of lightning.

He says, "Hate is a powerful thing. Our world has been broken by it. Hatred is a poison in your mind. So is violence. It can destroy you."

"Like the other night."

"Like the other night. In San Diego. Can you still feel them?"

"Feel who?"

"I bring you into the Pacific to get separation from the others like yourself. You call them Variants, yes? And you were connected. You felt them, like they were inside."

"I did. How did you know?"

He smiles and pats his chest. "You and I have that in common. I can do it too."

"The bomb in the tower killed my friends, and the link nearly destroyed my mind."

He nods, and grunts in agreement.

I say, "I don't feel them now. We have to be close. And excited."

"It is the same in me. Emotion is contagious, and with you and me it is enhanced. In time you will most likely begin to link with others. Humans without the disease."

"Is that how you were able to communicate with the tigers?"

"Yes. The interaction of minds."

"What freaks we are."

"It is a powerful and dangerous thing. An ability you must learn to control. You cannot absorb their deaths without paying a heavy price. The last time, as you say, it nearly destroyed you. If it happens again..."

"What do I do?"

"You manage the link. Manage is the right word. Build a barrier that you control, little one. Don't let them in, unless for a specific reason."

"How?"

"Practice. Above all else, do not link to great numbers. It will overwhelm you. You can lose yourself," he says, and then all of a sudden I *Feel* him. I am me, and he is Saul, and we are one. We are separate but we are also something else. A connection. Like being dunked in warm water. A pleasurable experience. He is a vast source of peace and knowledge and I sink into the comfort of intimacy. "You experience me."

"Yes."

"You do?"

"I do. It's like you instantly became my twin," I say, and I cannot help but laugh at the absurdity. "You feel like home."

"And you feel like pain," he says. "Such anger and hurt you carry."

"It's been a rough year."

"Push me out. Out of your mind."

"I don't want to."

"Now you see the danger. This ability you and I have. It is not safe. If I died at this moment, you would too. Close yourself off. From me."

I try. It's like fighting myself, like trying to intentionally forget something. I close my eyes and concentrate, searching the halls of my skull. Time passes as we battle. Soon I'm able to differentiate that which is Carmine from that which is Saul. His spirit is clean and content, while my spirit throbs with anxiety and anger. I pull from him. It works, and he allows me to rest a moment before pressing in again. I push at him and pull at myself, an uncomfortable process because I like the way he feels. It's a time-consuming wrestling match, and when I finally open my eyes again I'm shocked to see how far the sun has travelled.

"Good," he says. "We will practice again. You have a powerful spirit, Carmine. I understand why your people cling to you."

He withdraws from me completely and I nearly fall over. My strength has dimmed, and I'm exhausted. He reaches out to catch me and I fall asleep on the deck.

- 5 -
The Outlaw

Walter traveled the entire night, pushing six hundred miles in twenty-four hours to take us by surprise. That distance is jaw-dropping given the country's clotted arteries and fuel blight. Despite his haste, we manage to cobble together a defensive facade.

We drive the Variants and giants in trucks to our border, and there we assemble on Interstate 5 inside East and Rice Canyon. The hills are desiccated and dotted with dusty brush. An old west showdown at high noon. He can't get past us, not without a fight.

If he attacks, we lose. We're an army of unconnected variables. I can barely move. The mutants aren't sure of Tank, not yet bonded with him. They follow him, but how far? Our only hope is in a unified show of force. Four thousand of us are arrayed in ranks across the interstate and adjacent hills. If he inspects us closely he'll notice the Variants are depressed and nervous. He'll notice I'm bleeding.

I'm wearing my red mask, which contains a bluetooth earpiece. Puck speaks directly into my ear canal, "Walter's just over the rise, homie. Puck is SO frickin' nervous. He has an advanced sentry you should see any second."

Tank stands beside me and the giants move restlessly at his back. He holds up his hand and says, "Travis, you and the boys need to remember. Today is not the day we fight Walter. You stay."

A motorcycle appears at the crest of the rise, a mile distant. Even this far removed we hear his brakes lock and tires lay down thick rubber. I have enhanced eyesight and I zero on the rider; it's a woman. She retrieves binoculars from her backpack and spends a minute scrutinizing our unexpected army. Her torso is covered with Kevlar body armor. Satisfied, she stuffs the glasses into the pack and retreats the way she came.

"So it begins," Tank rumbles.

"I'm going to meet him," I announce. "Mason, you stay here with the army."

"Let Walter come to us," Tank objects.

"I don't want him close to the Variants. They aren't bound to you yet. They're biologically susceptible to hijacking. You coming?"

I walk north on the interstate, up the gentle rise. Tank growls and follows. Our army watches its makeshift generals leave for parlay, hoping we return. Walking's hard. I want to meet Walter at least half a mile from Mason and the rest, but I'm out of breath after a hundred yards. "You should leave the ax," I comment.

"You should lose the clown costume."

"You don't need that thing. This should be a peaceful shouting match."

"Whatever. I'm bringing it. Might decide to cleave his head in."

"Really?" I ask. "You need an ax? That's disappointing. You're seven feet tall. Are you compensating for something? And my clown costume rocks."

"You look pathetic. Always have."

"Over there is the Oak Tree Gun Club," I pant. "Used to go there with my dad."

"Maybe you should save your breath. Sound like you're about to die."

"Maybe you should...okay...good idea..."

Puck talks into my ear, "Real witty banter there. It's like you guys got dumber." Another two hundred yards, getting closer to the top of the rise, and he reports, "Get ready. He's coming."

Walter himself crests the horizon, being driven in a silver Nissan truck. The driver yanks the wheel, and Walter hops out before the vehicle skids to a stop.

"Hah!" he calls. He throws his head back and howls. It's a laughter tinted with rage. His voice caroms off the hills. "Hah! If it ain't a pair of little girls dressed up for halloween." He's wearing boots and camouflage cargo pants. And Ray-Bans. And gold necklaces. His hair is cornrowed. Iron claws are bolted onto his fingertips.

"The stench emerging from your truck is truly unfortunate, Walter," I say.

He makes a show of peering over our shoulders, south down the interstate. "Well. Gangs all here. Ain't this a pretty picture. A damn pleasant surprise."

I've never seen him this riled. Usually reserved, now he's so mad he's stomping. I say, "Turn home, Walter. Get in your truck and go."

"Naw. Came all this way to speak to the queen. Where is her royal highness? Didn't get her sexy little ass killed in San Diego, did she?"

Tank raises the ax and points it at Walter. "Watch your mouth, freak. That sexy little ass belongs to me."

"Well…" I waffle my hand. "…no. No, not really. But that's beside the point."

"Where's the bitch with the gun?" Walter asks, referring to Samantha Gear. He glances at the hills and chuckles. "You cowards hiding a sniper?"

She's not here. Not even close, but let him think whatever he wants. "You may not enter Los Angeles, Walter."

"The hell I can't."

"Not with your head still attached," Tank grunts, and I nod grimly. Our threats are pure bravado. We can't back it up. If we attack him, his mutant army will surge and we've lost.

"Appears you bred giants," Walter comments, glaring down the road towards our impressive army. "Imma build collars for them boys. Make them pull my damn chariot around."

"Leave your Variants here," I suggest. "Let Carmine heal them. You go elsewhere."

He hisses, "Tell you what. Make you two little boys a deal. You run away. Run far away, and Walter won't cut yo' ass in half."

"You'll lose this fight, Walter," I lie. "I beat you before by myself, and I don't hate you half as much as Tank does. No reason for your Variants to die. Go home."

"Los Angeles *is* my home. And I'm taking it back."

"Not today."

"You ain't leaving?"

Tank responds, "We ain't leaving."

Walter storms to his truck and stops at the open door. "Give ya a day to think it over. If you won't leave, I'll rip the place apart." He slams the door, tires squeal, and he's gone.

We watch quietly for a moment, and I breathe a sigh of relief. "Can't believe that worked."

Tank whacks me on the back, hard. The burst of pain is so intense I nearly black out. "Ain't no surprise. You always been good at lying."

- 6 -

Queen Carmine

I'm up at dawn. The sun torches the sky and turns the Pacific into rippling magma. So beautiful my soul aches. Longings nothing in this universe can fulfill. I pull on a bathing suit and vault into the water and swim laps for hours while Saul rests in a hammock slung forward of the mast. Minute fish sparkle like flecks of silver around me, and a curious shark circles the boat after the sun rises. The shark is small, only four feet, and of some sharp-nose variety. He swims close enough to touch several times. I experience no fear. We are comrades.

I'm able to hold my breath for several minutes. Over and over I swim downwards into the bruised darkness of the ocean until I can no longer see. The water is quite cold but I don't mind. If Saul moves like a dolphin then I move like a hippo. Slow and unimpressive, unable to fully launch into the air. Some of our Swimmers move like Saul. But not me.

Finally my hunger wins out. I need caloric intake. Saul hands me a sandwich after I climb aboard. I eat three, and the remainder of the pineapple. He's cooking a fish he caught with bait dangled over the side.

I indicate his paperback. "What are you reading?"

"Octavia Butler. You know her?"

"I don't."

"I've read her in Somali. Yes, but in English she is even better." He nods at the water and below the surface I see the dark shape of my shark. "You made a friend."

"I was hoping he'd attack. Thought it'd be fun to wrestle."

He laughs, flashing brilliant white teeth. "You sound like the lady in the boat I told you about. She likes to fight sharks."

"Is that part of the violence you think I need to forget?"

"No," he shakes his head and tries a small bite of the fish. "No. You crave adventure. That will always be with you."

I dip into the cabin to change and I call, "Tell me about the disease. I know nothing."

"I do not understand much either," he says. "Martin knew much more than I. The Chemist. He was a physician, but he kept his secrets. Before arriving to your coast, I visited a girl in China. She researches the disease."

I emerge from the cabin wearing dry clothes. "And?"

"She does not believe there is a cure. And she is a genius, I think is the word. That our illness is a combination of others, including something like rabies."

"Rabies," I repeat. "That would explain the aggression. The rage."

"The rage, yes. But not the hate. Anger will always be with us. Even God grows angry. Hate is a choice."

"Does Russia hate?"

"Oh yes. Russia hates. Russia has always hated. I do not know Walter or the other one. The girl you call Blue-Eyes. But I assume their hearts are poisoned. The disease prevents them from self-regulation."

I lower myself into his hammock. It creaks and smells like an old boat, but I stretch out and close my eyes. "They hate me," I sigh. "Though I don't know why."

"Hate often has no purpose other than itself. They hate to hate. They hate you for what you stand for. You stand for hope. And taking care of those less fortunate. And equality. This they cannot abide. Do you see? The same way the sea satisfies you, violence and cruelty do so for them. Which is why you must heal. Before you turn to other medications. Before you turn to dark addictions."

Soon his spirit begins probing at mine. Seeking to establish a link. I want to connect with him, to experience his peace and joy, but it's a test. I'm supposed to block him, and I try. I retract from him as if from an unpleasant memory. Still he grows on my consciousness. I force my mind against his, and it's effective. It's obvious he isn't trying hard, but for the moment I'm successful. He retreats.

We grow quiet. He tends his fish and reads his book, and I doze. I'm like an infant on this boat; my only responsibilities are to eat and play and sleep. I dream, and I wake up periodically to note the sun's progression across the sky.

I miss Kayla. And Mason.

And Chase. And Tank.

And Becky.

Towards evening Saul the Zealot sits at the stern, tossing bits of fish to gulls crossing our wake. He laughs and says things I don't understand.

I stretch and sit up. "So you connect with all animals?"

"I cannot. Not really," he says. He shoos the birds away and wipes his hands on his pants. "Only mammals. That is all."

"Like the queen of a hive?"

"Perhaps."

"Can all the Infected do it?"

"No. Only you and me, that I know. We are cursed differently. Like fingerprints."

"Idiosyncratic freaks, more like it," I mutter, and on a whim I ask, "Do you know Nuts?"

"I do! I do know Nuts. But I haven't visited him in years. What a funny nickname he has. I plan to see him soon. We are approximately the same age, give or take a decade."

"Nuts keeps our kingdom afloat. He fixes everything. What about Samantha Gear? Nicknamed the Shooter? Do you know her?"

"Yes, I know her. We message. And I worry about her soul. All that violence. I worry. She is walking down a dangerous path."

"But aren't we all violent by nature? All of us with the disease?"

"That is a good question. A very good question. I would say we are not violent, but rather addicted to adrenaline. Do I pronounce that correct?

Adrenaline. I don't know about your Variants. But the Infected tend towards solitude, not violence. We are suspicious by nature, and have each fled to our own continent."

"Why?"

"We do not enjoy each other. As I said, suspicious. We don't tolerate others well and we need to control our surroundings."

"That sounds a lot like me."

"It is the nature of our curse. As we age, it worsens. It affects us all. Well. I should say, it affects us all except for the Outlaw. He is an exception, it would seem."

"The Outlaw? How so?"

He and I both sit on the bow, under the railing. The sails are down and the ocean is calm, almost like a mirror. He kicks his feet in the water and says, "We are drawn to him. To the Outlaw. I spoke to Martin. To Carter. To Croc and Pacific and PuckDaddy. It's his gift. He is not solitary. He pulls us."

"Yes! He pulls me too! Exactly, that's exactly how I feel. That's not fair, right? How do I make him stop?"

"You want nothing to do with him?"

"No. No, I don't mean that. It's just that…he has an unfair advantage. I can't resist him."

"You love him."

"Yes," I say. "Wait, no. No no. Jeez, wow. No. I…*enjoy* Chase. Too much."

"I look forward to meeting him. Even the boy called Tank feels the pull. The destiny of those two are intertwined."

"You know Tank?"

"I've watched Tank. I've learned. Much of it from PuckDaddy, my good friend. Tank, he battles against the disease. He experiences the hate but he resists. Tank reminds me of myself. A hundred years ago. Before I followed God."

"Tank's a handful. You know, Saul, I'm not afraid of you. Is that strange? You don't smell like Chase. Chase is so powerful that his scent repelled me in the past."

"The boy is stronger than I, it's true. Much stronger. But from what I understand, the revulsion is something Martin built into you. Did I pronounce that right? He implanted his own genes into all his creations, and even into Walter and Caleb. We should never play God, but Martin tried. Anyone with the disease, the Hyper Virus as it is called, is an enemy to you, unless they have Martin's genes. The genetic code. PuckDaddy has told me all of this, and I believe him."

"Do you know Caleb?" I ask. Caleb is the boy who fled Los Angeles as I arrived.

"No. I know of Caleb. I know he is fragile." He shakes his head as if he's disappointed in Caleb, and he scratches at his beard.

"That's my impression too."

We sit for a long time. He rests his chin on the bow rail and closes his eyes. Again I'm struck by my lack of compulsion. I feel no all-consuming drive to *do*. Sitting in silence this long would have been impossible a week ago. I've wasted the day and I don't care.

Eventually he says, "Tell me your goals, Carmine. What does the future hold."

"That's a big question."

"But a good one."

"Life would be so much easier if I had a clue. I woke up and I knew nothing. The first thing explained to me was that soon Herders would hunt me down because I'd become a mutant. If not the Herders then powerful enemies would enslave me and everyone like me. I've been trying to survive since. That's my answer. My past and my future and my goal is survival. My survival and the survival of others similar to me."

"You feel like a cornered animal."

"Well phrased."

He nods and pats me on the back, a familiar and comfortable gesture. "Your anger is understandable."

"Yeah, well, there's a lot of it."

"You have amnesia?"

"Something like that."

"What do you remember of your former life?"

"Much of my childhood. Very little of my adolescence."

He nods. "I heard you in your sleep. You remember the night the... Cheerleader died?"

"Yes," I say without pausing to consider. "I was a junior in high school. The Outlaw was there," I hear myself say but the words aren't mine. The words just tumble out. Katie is speaking and with each word I feel as though sunlight is bursting through clouds. Rays of hope! "But I didn't know Chase was the Outlaw. Tank was there, and Hannah..."

"Yes?"

"I...I forget the rest..." I jump up and frantically search the horizon for more memories. "That was the most I've remembered in a long time! Hannah didn't die that night, but...I thought she did. And Tank..." Flashes of memories. Of fire. Of the Chemist. "Tank tried to protect me. He was hurt. And Chase...ahhhh! I'm *so* close to remembering."

He laughs as I pace the bow, ducking under the foresail lines, my hands making fists in my hair. He says, "It will come."

"Maybe. Maybe not! Ugh that was painful. Bittersweet. Why can I suddenly remember?"

"Because. You are healing."

"That's Impossible. I've been on this boat for what? Four days? And I've only been awake for two." I lower myself down to the bow again, gripping the rail so hard I leave dents. So close. Katie's getting stronger, even if I haven't heard her much since the explosion.

"Do not underestimate peace, sweet Carmine. The freedom from responsibility. The strain has been removed from your mind. Do not underestimate peace."

"Nor the ocean."

"Nor the ocean."

We watch as the sun burns a hole in the western sky on its way to the horizon, and I think about the people in New Los Angeles.

- 7 -

The Outlaw

Tank's parents were wealthy before the great evacuation. They owned real estate around Los Angeles, and after our confrontation with Tank goes to visit a tower they used to own. His childhood home, not far from City Hall. He stays there all day and night, probably enjoying a long nap, though I don't see how any bed could contain his considerable bulk. He doesn't allow his giants into the building and instead stashes them inside the nearby Emerson's luxury suites.

I don't witness any of this. I go to sleep in Katie's apartment soon after our showdown with Walter and I don't wake up for eighteen hours. But I know it happened because Kayla is sitting on my bed at six in the morning.

Kayla is saying, "…and the giants didn't like being away from Tank and they started to cry. For real, Chase. For real crying. Like babies. Really loud. I was all, shut up giants! But not really because they seem nice. So like around two in the morning Tank finally comes out and walks to the Emerson and tells them all to be quiet and thankfully they all go to sleep. But *then*—"

"Kayla," I groan. "It's early. Please hush."

"Hey dude," PuckDaddy says. "How about some manners."

Puck's voice comes out of the speaker sitting in Kayla's lap. I'm laying on my stomach so I hadn't noticed it. "Don't you two ever hang up?"

"Why would we?" she asks.

I stare blearily at her over my shoulder, and note, "You know, Kayla, fewer people would stare at you if you wore clothes that weren't so tight."

"That shows what you know about fashion," she retorts. "Which apparently is nothing."

"Yeah that outfit is banging," Puck says.

"I haven't sent you a selfie today. How do you know?"

"Puck never spies on you from your own camera. But there are a lot of other camera phones in the world, and even a few working security cameras Puck can access. I check you out."

"You spy on me?" She beams and hugs the speaker.

I bury my face into my pillow. "Go away. Shoo. Get a room," I grunt. "A room that's not mine. Maybe a chatroom."

"This is *not* your room. This is Queen Carmine's. And she's going to be mad when she finds out you slept here."

"Shhhhhh."

She pulls the sheet off my shoulders and draws it down to my waist. "Your back looks good! It's still *ew*, but it's healing."

My voice comes muffled out from the pillow, "It feels much better."

"Your Spartan nurse sent ointment. Want me to rub it in?"

"No," Puck says. "No he doesn't. No touching."

"No thank you."

"Queen Carmine's Devotee got some coffee sweetener from the black market. Would you enjoy some hot coffee?"

"Kayla, I'm surprised my scent doesn't bother you. Especially while I sleep. Don't I smell like...I don't know, like an enemy?"

"Yes, you smell *Augh!* You are super scary. I'm being nice to you so you won't eat me. Plus, I trust Queen Carmine and she trusts you. So that helps." She's poking and prodding my back, and the room smells like sugar cookies.

"Are you bonded to Tank yet? Is that how it works?"

"I feel better now that he's here. But I think I'm less affected by musth than the others," she says. Suddenly my back seizes up as she squirts lotion onto sore muscles. *So cold.* "Oh calm down, you big baby. The nurse said you had to apply it or she'd skin me."

"Kayla. Please go away."

89

She smears the lotion in and says, "Okay, Outlaw. Puck and I are going for a walk."

She gets off the bed and leaves. Despite myself, I miss her immediately. She puts off heat and smells great. Katie's Devotee sticks his head in the room and asks, "Hey. You want coffee?"

"Sure," I sigh. "And tell me about this black market. And put on some pants."

There are a dozen sport motorcycles in the tower garage, keys in the ignition, tanks at least half full. It's good to be the queen, apparently. I steal one and drive to Tank's apartment. My outfit draws too much attention so I wear regular clothes.

I wish Katie would hurry up and return. I miss her.

Tank's apartment looks like something out of a horror movie. Variants surround the building, sitting or laying on the ground three people deep. They cling to the walls. Perch on the roof. This new breed of mutant doesn't like me but they've become slightly less intolerant. As if the Variants know they aren't allowed to attack. But when I try to walk through the crowd to the tower, they rise and snarl. I hold up my hands and back away. "Whoa, whoa. Down boys. Easy."

Infected like me are hard for average citizens to spot. We grew up with the disease, survived its devastating machinations, and now can usually blend in. The Variants find that much harder. The average Variant has a damaged mind, nearly zero impulse control, no self-regulation, and very little awareness of self. They're like doberman pinchers, some of which are well trained and some of which are nearly feral. Mason and Kayla are two of the exceptions, those with sound minds. Kinda. Katie's absence has not helped the collective sanity of this tribe.

"I'd like to speak with Tank," I announce to the sea of Variants staring at the tower. "It's almost nine. His lazy butt should be up by now." No one responds. "Hello? Walter is outside the city. I'd prefer we begin preparing defenses. Anyone?" Several mutants glance in annoyance but that's it. "Have you seen Mason? Hello? Raise your hand if you don't suck." No one raises their hand. I knew it.

I could probably fight my way in. Might be fun. But I'd rather this crew not be more angry with me, so I get on my bike and leave the freak show behind.

It's another perfect day in sunny southern California. I drive south on the 110 through Huntington Park towards the ocean. Unpleasant memories assault me like sour nostalgia as I roll past Compton; I spent far too much time inside Compton in a previous life. The roads are clear and the neighborhoods are largely abandoned but my skin still crawls, and I rev the engine to leave it behind. My destination is Trump National Golf Club, in Rancho Palos Verdes, and I make the trip in twenty-five minutes. The impressive clubhouse is in good shape, apparently inhabited by fastidious squatters, but the fairways and greens are one big untended morass. Without a working sprinkler system the lawn has become brown, overgrown, and weedy. From the clubhouse parking lot I spot three distinct herds of grazing mule deer on the ninth fairway alone.

This is the place. The location of earth's biggest mystery.

This is the spot the Inheritors vanished.

None of us knew the Chemist was infecting infants with the Hyper Virus. Not even PuckDaddy or Carter (a shadowy but knowledgable Infected elder). In retrospect, we should have guessed. Why wouldn't he? If the Variants are super soldiers, then the Inheritors would grow up to be…I don't know, something even more powerful. Even more terrible. Demigods.

None of us know exactly how it went down. Legend has it Carmine stumbled upon the Inheritors in the basement soon after seizing control of Los Angeles, realized what they were, drove them to the coast, and poisoned/slaughtered all five hundred. That's the story Teresa Triplett reported, complete with photographic evidence.

No way. I don't believe it. Katie still survives under the hard Carmine shell, and she'd never let that happen. Those Inheritors still exist, but we can't find them. Carmine doesn't trust us with the secret. Not even me.

I walk down to the ocean from the eighteenth tee box. An infamous photograph circulated of Katie/Carmine collapsed onto the eighteenth fairway, arms soaked in blood, head in her hands, weeping. It's an impressive photo. Genuine anguish. But I doubt the source of her grief is the death of five hundred babies. No way, Katie. You staged the massacre to fool me. To fool Walter. To fool everyone, so those kids could grow up in peace. You knew the truth; every evil force on earth would be after them. So you pretended to kill them and it worked. You tricked nearly everyone. But not me.

The rocks are stained with eight-month-old blood like brown rust. So are the sand dunes gathered up the hill. Closer to the ocean, the sand has long been cleansed by waves. I rest on a boulder and gaze up and down the coast. There is a *lot* of blood.

But no bodies. Swept out to sea, she says. I still don't buy it.

I remain for an hour, absorbing the atmosphere and environs of the coast as a whole. The longer I stay, the more clear her ruse becomes. There's too much blood on the rocks. When I questioned her ability to murder so many people with her bare hands, she privately admitted the poisoned lemonade did most of the work. But then why would there be so much blood? Because she wanted the place to *look* as if a massacre happened. The rocks would hold the stain if anyone wanted to verify her claims. Look, see? See all the red? Believe me.

But I don't. She's trying to keep those kids alive. Of course she is. But where the heck are they?

Puck calls me around eleven. "Dude, what are you doing at Trump's golf course?"

"Looking for bodies."

"Find any?"

"Not a one. Those kids are still alive, Puck."

"Dunno, bro. I track her everywhere. She doesn't visit them. Or if she does, she fools me."

"She fools you," I say. "Those kids are close. She knows you follow her, and she throws you off track. She's smarter than us."

"Whatever. Kayla requests your presence at the War Department. General Brown has called a meeting."

"What the heck is the War Department?"

"You don't know anything."

"I've lived here for, like, two days. Where is it?"

"Puck's talents are wasted. Pearls before swine."

"I am *not* swine."

"The War Department is in Olympic. Move your ass."

The War Department is at the top of the tower, cramped and hot with computers, television screens, and technicians. General Brown is here, and so is Mason and Kayla. Kayla is texting at light speed and Mason twirls a knife between his fingers, which is super cool.

Also the big ugly mountain called Tank is here.

General Brown wastes no time. "Walter's army has arrived," he barks. On screen, satellite pictures show parts of the city I don't recognize. Northwest L.A., most likely. "We estimate he has two thousand mutants and ten thousand armed gunmen. They've taken up residence in Santa Clarita, off Interstate 5. Not far beyond our border."

"Good," Tank grumbles. "Let's go eat them."

Kayla makes pained expression. "Gross."

"Not so fast. We have more company. The President has mobilized and, to be honest, caught us off guard. Troops from the Federal Government are marching down Interstate 15 to the east."

"The U.S. Army?" I ask. "How big?"

"An entire division," he replies. "Fifteen thousand, coming from Las Vegas, where we incorrectly assumed they meant to incarcerate the rampant prison population. But apparently they've been earmarked for us. Our recon suggests they'll set up a temporary outpost in San Bernardino. Make no mistake; this is a coordinated attack. They mean to crush us."

Mason asks, "Can't we drop a bomb on them?"

"We can and will utilize rockets, but nothing in life is easy or simple. Both Walter and the army travel in a widely dispersed formation. Our rockets will inflict limited damage. Plus they travel with missile defense systems. To further complicate matters, innocent civilians live in both San Bernardino and Santa Clarita. I don't like collateral damage."

We silently watch as the video shifts to multiple points of view, showing troops marching, erecting launchers, supply trucks rumbling down the highways. I don't want those soldiers to die; they're just following the sanctions of Blue-Eyes and her presidential toy.

I muse, "Last time, Walter and Blue-Eyes sent small infiltration teams. In November. We expected a full assault but instead they snuck in. This looks like a different tactic."

"Operation crush the infidels," Mason says.

Brown nods, hands on his hips. "That's my guess."

"Puck. Are you listening?"

"Obviously," he answers through the wall-mounted speakers.

"What about Katie?"

"Her name is Carmine, and Zealot says she'll return when she's ready."

Tank asks, "Where is she?"

"In the ocean. Couple miles off shore. It's hard to pinpoint."

"Why in the ocean?"

"The waves," I answer. "They help our minds. I don't know why."

"We're a hard city to break into. My commanders are already reinforcing our positions on both fronts. We are not without resources and manpower. Our military is 35,000 strong. We match them soldier for soldier. The President can't bring his full military to bear because he's dealing with the Resistance on a thousand different fronts. We will not be destroyed easily."

"Can they detonate a nuke?"

"Unlikely. Nukes are being dismantled on both sides. Not even Blue-Eyes wants a nuclear war. This part of the country bristles with surface-to-air missiles, able to shoot anything down. Plus, the Federal Government doesn't want to destroy Los Angeles, or risk nuclear fallout. Much more likely are strategic rocket strikes, but we have warehouses full of anti-ballistic missiles.

As I said, a tough nut to crack."

"They can't lay siege to the city," I say. "Walter's Variants will be too impatient. Too antsy."

"I agree. They don't plan a long siege. They will take the offensive."

"So what should we do?"

Brown takes a deep breath, as though he's standing on the lip of an open airplane door, mustering up courage to jump. "This battle is being fought for the mutants. Walter and the President are here for them." He turns his gaze from the wall and onto us. "The key to this battle will be the Variants. When the Chemist was still alive, his squads of mutants decimated our military. We couldn't shoot what we couldn't see. Nothing's changed since. Victory or defeat rests on their shoulders. Our Guardians. And Walter's. I can resist the President's infantry, and his tanks, and his missiles. But we're ·defenseless against Walter and his paranormal army. You ask what should we do? Here's my answer; figure it out. This war for Los Angeles will be intense and brief, probably less than a few weeks, and it's up to you. You control your own fate."

Tank nods his heavy head with approval. "Damn right."

"The people follow you, Outlaw. But the Variants follow Tank. You two decide a course of action, and keep me apprised."

The door behind us bangs open and a woman walks in. Trim, strong, fiery green eyes, two pistols on her belt. She could be twenty-one or forty, hard to tell. Striking in appearance, like an eagle. "It's been a long two days. Someone point me towards a bed," Samantha Gear growls. "I look like hell and need a nap. Then I'm ready to kick ass."

The legendary Shooter, a pure-born Variant and my good friend, has arrived. Our odds get a little better. I say, "Use Katie's room. Twenty-second floor."

"I prefer being the big spoon. But I need a little. Chase? General Brown? Mason, you look like fun. Want to spoon with me? No? Screw you wimps, I'm going to bed."

- 8 -

Carmine

Another day, another field of blinding golden seas. My spirit rides easy on the swells, but my body grows anxious and cramped within the boat's confines. A larger vessel and occasional storm would be ideal. There's no such luck in paradise, however, so I loop bow lines around my shoulders and I dive in.

Our boat is several miles south of Santa Catalina Island, and the ocean's current is a gradual pull toward the equator. Saul thinks if we dropped sails and raised our rudder we'd eventually be adrift halfway to Australia. I churn northwards, tugging the boat behind me in halting jerks. My muscles stretch and bunch and strain, and the exercise is euphoric, burning off stagnant endorphins and generating dopamine. I kick and pull for hours, long past my estimated point of fatigue, and for the final thirty minutes I'm joined by a social pod of harbor porpoises who think I'm fascinating.

I still haven't said goodbye to Becky. Not really. She died unexpectedly, instantaneously, and I woke up a day later. Instead of dealing with loss in a rational matter, I found a big sword and rampaged; probably not what a counselor would suggest. Becky was the first person to trust me. To embrace me fully. She was so innocent. I don't know how to be sad. I don't understand grief. What are the appropriate coping mechanisms? What is closure? No clue.

Goodbye Becky, I think. I love you and miss you. You died because people hate me. It's not fair, and I'll never forget you.

Goodbye.

Goodbye.

But it doesn't help. I still hurt, still ache. So I keep thrashing through waves. I won't forget. Not ever. I promise.

Finally I release the rope coils and float limply on my back. A porpoise visits me soon after, resting his chin on my abdomen. "I'm okay," I pant and smile. "Just exhausted." He gazes at me a moment before emitting a friendly chattering noise and diving. I coast beside Saul's boat until my heart rate returns to normal and during that time I draw the attention of multiple fish. I think animals like me more than they do normal people. Before climbing up the stern ladder, I open my hand under water and soon a flat fish approaches and rests on my palm. That easy?

"You have caught a halibut," he calls and laughs. "The fish willfully gives himself to you. Your body has calmed and you are in tune."

"In tune?"

"With the world. As you should be." He takes the fish, which does not squirm, cuts the head off, and prepares the grill.

I don't feel in tune. I've begun a trophic tremble so I eat one of our last apples, dipping slices into peanut butter. "How long could you survive out here, Saul?"

"Two weeks," he replies. "Two weeks if I was alone. But you are here. And you are hungry. So we need fresh supplies soon."

We don't address the obvious question: what will I do when we return to shore? He serves us both grilled halibut, which has a clean sweet taste, and we chew in silence. He glances often at the blue sky, the water's surface, the northern horizon, and a glass barometer. His shirt is off, providing me an opportunity to inspect his torso. His skin was probably tighter in his youth and his spine is slightly hunched with calcium deficiencies, but it's obvious he's a powerful man. His sinewy muscles are so hard they might as well be iron bars. His motions are careful and deliberate, as if he's accustomed to breaking his surroundings otherwise. He could be fifty, or he could be a hundred and fifty.

He doesn't want me to go back. He thinks I should find a reservation and hide on some distant corner of the globe. I tell him the good people of the world can't sit by and do nothing while evil rises.

"Ah, but you see. You are cursed, sweet girl. The same as me. We are *not* the good people in the world. Society runs more smoothly if we are removed from it. As you saw with Martin. With the Chemist."

I have no rebuttal.

Last night Saul sat at the tiller without sleeping, as he often does, so now he naps in the cabin. I scrounge through his selection of tattered paperbacks and lower the mainsail to use like a big pile of blankets. Bliss. The sun pauses at the zenith and bakes me, and I'm so comfortable that I read fifty pages of *Lord of the Flies* before realizing I've read this book before. But that's not what's startling. I *remember* reading it. My insides twitch and tug. The facts of the book come flooding back and I recall…images and emotions. Small truths about my past. I close my eyes and tent the open paperback across my face. Remember. Remember, Carmine.

A voice in my head says, *I read Lord of the Flies in the tenth grade.*

Yes. Yes…in Ms. Grant's class.

Ms. Grant needed a makeover. That hair. Yikes.

It was an intense book. Kids trapped on an island. I remember the character Ralph. The good-looking kid. He tries to keep order, to get them rescued, and the kids hate him for it.

Ralph reminded me of Chase. So likable and stout hearted. Naturally does the right thing.

I remember loving the character Simon. Little Simon, always fainting. He was goodness. He wanted peace. And they killed him. He was innocent. Like Becky.

And Piggy. They killed fat Piggy because he was different.

And Jack. A character named Jack. The details are fuzzy…

Jack wanted to control the island, but he wasn't evil. The class thought he was, but he was only instinct and impulse. What little boy isn't?

That's right. Jack had no self-control. But from his impulses came great evil eventually.

Yes. Yes. You remember.

Katie?

Katie, can you hear me?

Silence. What a bizarre, atypical question. I *am* Katie. Kinda. Of course I hear myself. The boat bobs and pitches as the ocean's swell increases. I can't stop thinking about the tenth grade. It's as if I'm in a fog waving my arms and connecting at random with history. The book. Ms. Grant read it out loud. I argued with her about the Jack character. I passed Chase notes.

…Chase was in that class.

Yes, before he changed. That was the year Chase's mom died.

His mom died? I don't remember. Poor guy. But I clearly recollect the note passing. He once asked me to marry him and drew funny pictures…

No. That was in the twelfth grade. Our senior year.

The Outlaw and I had English together in the twelfth grade too?

A sudden swirl of emotion, so strong I groan and curl inward. I want to go back there. I was good at school. I want to be in a classroom. I want cute boys to pass me notes and to not worry about my mind breaking. Maybe it's better I don't remember. The recollections are awful. Because of loss. Because I had Chase…

But. No. I dated Tank. Not Chase. Right, Katie?

Ugh. Speaking of evil coming from impulse.

Tank isn't evil. He's…instinct. He's pride and sadness. Chase spent that year trying to keep me safe. Safe from Tank?

I'm frustrated. Like a puzzle with half the pieces gone.

Chase spent the year keeping me safe while he battled headaches and the disease. I only found out later. He is the opposite of Tank. He is selfless and entirely without arrogance.

Another surge of pain. Or remembrance. Emotions without source. So powerful I gasp. And breathe in saltwater. The scent hits my brain. Salt water. On the beach. A flash on my consciousness, the night I was kidnapped. The whole world was looking for me but Walter got there first. Tank fought for me. Ready to die for me.

I feel as though I'm on the verge of a breakthrough when the craft pitches forward. I remove the book from my face. Back in the real world. Time has passed. The sky blotted out by clouds, and the sea is disturbed. Saul emerges from the cabin, barometer in hand, and announces, "The winds are shifting."

The NOAA's radio service still works. Some brave soul broadcasts weather warnings to a barren coast, probably from nearby Navy ships, but Saul refuses to listen to that channel on his portable radio. He mistrusts governmental systems. I ask, "How do you know the winds shift?"

"The glass and temperature are falling. A cold front blows down from Alaska. I think. Should not be a big storm. God will keep up safe. But we will seek shelter."

I'm enthralled by the possibility of a big storm. Sounds like an adventure. Worst comes to worst, we capsize and swim to shore. Even that'd be fun. But I follow the orders of our boat's captain. I haul on the mast's rope to raise the mainsail, which snaps and fills with air, and the boat heels slightly to the south. Saul spins the wheel and aims our bow into the wind as far as he can.

The next hour is spent sailing north. We cut, or tack, back and forth in a zigzag pattern. I release knots when he calls, duck under the mighty swing of the boom, and fasten knots again on the far side. Over and over. He's right; the squall won't be as severe as I'd like. The waves grow to six feet and the wind tears foam from the tops to throw in our faces, but it's a manageable chaos.

I relent from my position at the bow and return to the cockpit. Saul stands easy behind the wheel, watching our approach. We're still a couple miles from shore. There's a new tone in his voice. It feels like gravity. "It is time you tell me about the children."

"The children?"

"The children Martin injected with the disease. PuckDaddy calls them Inheritors, I believe is the word. You alone cannot bear this weight."

I don't reply. I had hoped Saul was ignorant of the Inheritors. I hoped maybe they were a bad dream which would dissipate as time passed. But they're real. A reality so painful I avoid admitting it exists.

Soon the gale eases as we escape into the protection of looming Santa Catalina Island. There are other boats cowering closer to shore on the eastern side. Saul adjusts the wheel and alters our heading, putting us on a more direct collision course with the uninhabited southern shores and the towering clouds stacking beyond. Sheltering here was a good idea. The sky is grey and we can ride at anchor.

"Carmine. God has brought you to me. Because he loves you," he says in the quiet as we coast. "It is time. It is time to tell me the secret which darkens your heart."

"This is a secret you want no part of, Saul."

"I believe you. But I also believe it is my destiny. I do not run from pain."

I take a deep breath. And I tell him.

- 9 -
The Outlaw

General Brown, Samantha Gear, and I drive around Katie's Kingdom in one of those loud stripped-down green army jeeps with no roof. I'd prefer driving but Samantha and I are in the back and our driver's a kid who won't break eighty.

"Our inland border is a hundred and forty-two miles long," Brown calls over his shoulder. "From Malibu to Newport Beach approximately, and stretching in a half circle inland as far as San Gabriel Mountains. Far too much territory to actively defend, so we're relying on electronic surveillance, advanced warning, and quick responders. Make sense so far?"

Samantha Gear snorts. "Obviously."

"We'll physically barricade the roads, and monitor the rest. The President's army won't be able to breach, not any time soon. It's Walter I'm worried about."

"Me too."

He asks, "You trust Tank to protect our western front? With the Guardians?"

"Not really, no," I say. "But what other choice do we have?"

"Tell me again," Samantha says, "Why you can't lead those Guardian freaks?"

I respond, "The longer you spend with the Variants, the more you realize they aren't like us. They're different than Infected. More...animal and aggression. They only accept Tank because of his genetic connection to Katie."

102

She grins. "They hate you."

"They hate me. But at least they no longer attack."

"You're in love with a girl who controls an army of freaks that hate you." She laughs and claps her hands and kicks the back of General Brown's seat. "Isn't that the best thing *ever*."

"It is exactly and precisely not the best thing ever. Maybe you need another nap."

"Nah, I'm good. I visited your dad on the way. I rested there."

My stomach turns. Samantha has involved herself romantically with my father, a police detective who relocated to Utah. It's an on-again off-again affair which I'm convinced they maintain to gross me out. He's fortyish and she's thirtyish, far too great a difference.

"Though, admittedly," she says, "he didn't let me sleep much. More of a booty call."

The jeep is stocked with supplies, including road flares. I grab a flare, pop the top, and strike the tip's surface in one smooth motion. I'm faster than Samantha and I deposit the flare down the back of her vest. It ignites and sprays molten sparks like a match. Samantha ejects from the back seat as though shot from a cannon. She screeches and rips off the vest before landing on her feet. The flare falls to the road but she dances and smacks at her back; her white tank top has caught fire. The jeep brakes sharply to a halt.

I observe, "Having a hot flash? You must be too old for booty calls, you big stupid prostitute."

"Ouch!" she roars. "That *hurt*, Chase."

"What a shame."

"Do I have a mark?" She cranes her neck but can't get a visual. "Do I? You have to tell me. Or I swear your father will hear about this."

General Brown looks sadly at his confused driver and shakes his head. "Don't tell the others about this, son."

The longer I study Los Angeles, the more I realize it's a city on a plain surrounded by natural barriers. These barriers limit the points of ingress into

Katie's Kingdom. All traffic from the north or west has to funnel between mountains, creating organic chokepoints on either side of the northern mountain range. General Brown is actively demolishing small roads coming over San Gabriel to avoid surprises and to force large enemy strike teams into points of congestion.

We visit these chokepoints one by one. My recognizable outfit creates a stir, turning me into the figurehead of our defense. At least until their queen returns. I shake hands and offer encouragement and let the stronger men heft the three-foot bat I keep shoved down the back of my vest; it's notoriously heavy and difficult to use.

The Outlaw fights with us, they say.

They are right.

Samantha Gear is an infamous warrior for the Resistance, beloved and worshiped by the troops; she reluctantly poses for pictures, and eagerly points out tactical mistakes in defensive positions. She and I are awed by the amount of firepower General Brown arrays across the entire defensive front. Roads are blocked with sandbags, guarded by machine-gun nests, and missile launchers are hidden in a thousand garages. A tough nut to crack indeed.

Elsewhere in the Kingdom, Tank and Kayla and Mason are seeing to mutant affairs. I don't know what that means exactly. Bonding maybe. I'm not allowed because they hate me. The giants dislike the noise of Downtown so Tank took them back to Tarzana in several big eighteen-wheelers, but those warriors won't be contained much longer. They ache and howl for combat.

A familiar stillness settles over the troops as the day wears on. Classic hurry up and wait anxiety, a calm before the storm. Battle looms large and a respectful silence envelops our ranks. Blood will be shed soon. Much of it ours.

To my surprise, the Priest is a constant source of industriousness. That pristine preening peacock is hard at work, distributing Law Keepers to fill needs. He acts as a tireless liaison between civilians and the military, his voice consistently ringing out on the radio. Maybe I judged him too quickly.

For the tenth time that day, I query Puck. **Any news on Katie?**

>> aaaaahhhhh no stop pestering me.

>> **puck will report carmine updates w/out u asking**

>> **puck is busy**

Night approaches and a low ceiling of clouds rolls in, bringing the first precipitation in weeks. Gusts of soft rain whip into our faces. Samantha and I sit under umbrellas on a rooftop in Ontario near Interstate 15, New Los Angeles's bristling border, watching the activity. The President's Federal Army has installed itself into San Bernardino, barely visible on the eastern horizon. Blue-Eyes is not with her troops; Puck reported spotting her in Washington earlier today, and that gives me comfort. She's the last thing we need.

Still. Uneasiness nags at me. I'm worried about something I can't place. Samantha keeps drifting to sleep, her forehead resting on knees drawn to her chest. I text Puck again, **Where is Tank and our Variant army?**

>> **ugh scattered. don't get Puck started.**

>> **a good administrator Tank is not**

>> **kayla is doing her best but they don't listen 2 her**

>> **Tank is in north hollywood at the moment**

>> **variants...everywhere and restless**

>> **Tank doesn't want 2 b bothered until its time 2 fight**

>> **this weather is making surveillance impossible**

Great. Perfect. Our hope rests on the shoulders of an imbecile with attention deficit disorder.

I glance at the black sky. Surveillance impossible. Variants restless. We're vulnerable. I shove Samantha awake. "Come on. We're going."

She's instantly alert. "Where to?"

"We're on the wrong side of Los Angeles. We need to be closer to Walter. He's the danger at the moment."

"He's mobilizing?"

"No. He won't attempt a full on assault tonight. But with these clouds, it's a perfect night for him to do...something." We jump from the roof and climb into a Prius. Gasoline isn't scarce but functional gas pumps are. Electric cars become more handy every day. Samantha throws her stuff onto the back seat. Stuff like two shotguns and a backpack full of shells. She and I are accustomed to acting as free agents in the build up to a skirmish. The journey is sixty miles on Highway 210, skirting the southern side of the mountain range, and we make the trip in forty minutes. Samantha naps and I daydream about Katie. I miss her like I'd miss food. I'm weak without her. In moments of quiet she's all I can think about. I'm addicted.

We arrive at the northwestern chokepoint, a barricade across Interstate 5. It's heavily guarded, but the bulk of our defenses are quick responders sheltering from rain in nearby San Fernando. I check with the commander; all is quiet. Intelligence reports no significant movement in Walter's Santa Clarita outpost, so I let Samantha sleep while I explore. I walk up and down the roadblocks, inspecting the barricades and fist bumping the star struck-soldiers. Everything is secure and sound.

Except Walter's sanity. My skin crawls. What's he up to?

I find the commander and point to a large industrial complex to the south, just visible through the drizzle. Unlike most of the city, it burns bright with electricity. "What's that plant?"

"Water filtration, sir."

"It's operational?"

"Yessir. All the queen's water comes from that aqueduct."

All the water? This close to the border? That's not good. The water filtration plant is enormous, the size of multiple city blocks. Much of the sprawling and towering campus is busy with activity. I approach the eastern entrance and I'm met at the gate by a short man.

There are only thirteen Infected on planet earth (twelve plus me) so at first I don't realize I'm looking at one. He's bald with beefy forearms. His work coveralls are smeared with grease and he's wiping his hands on a rag. "Outlaw," he barks. "Was hoping to run into you. Come out of the rain."

"You're Nuts," I realize. "Aren't you."

"That's what they call me."

Nuts is a legend. The brightest engineer to ever live, and the owner of multiple patents which make him a fortune. He single-handedly keeps the gears of New Los Angeles churning, according to Katie. Most Infected throb with power and strength, but not Nuts. He crackles instead, like an overcharged battery. He leads us into a cavernous warehouse which hums with machinery and hydraulics. I want to ask him a thousand questions about the Infected and our history; he's ancient and he'll have answers, but the first thing that tumbles out of my mouth is, "Nuts, do you know where Katie sent the Inheritors?"

"Who's Katie?"

"Sorry. Carmine."

"What's the Inheritors?"

"The babies the Chemist injected."

Nuts waves the question away. "Bah. She can tell you if she wants. Not my place. I focus on immediate problems."

"This water treatment facility is too close to the border."

"You're damn right. I'm shutting it down. We have other water treatment options."

"How quickly will that happen?"

"I estimate eighteen days for full transfer. Biggest caveat is, we generate thirty percent of our electricity from these water turbines. So I'll keep running them until the new plant has turbines installed, but that'll be a month. Might not sleep until then."

"Do we have water reserves?"

"Enough for several weeks. We're safe long as Walter don't poison it."

"What about—"

"Listen boy. I'm glad you're here. Walter needs killing. Understand? You take care of that. I'll handle water."

"Nuts. You're awesome."

"You here with the Shooter? Always wanted to shake her hand. Strikes me as no-nonsense, the way a woman ought to be."

At that moment, alarms begin wailing. The distinct harmony of jarring military sirens. "Speak of the devil," Nuts says, looking northward through the open door. "I'd wager that's Walter. Get to it, Outlaw. Don't let him destroy our water plant. Not yet." He turns and stalks back into his compound.

Samantha is out of the Prius, slinging a backpack onto her shoulders. The dark night is punctured with search lights, and I can barely think over the din. PuckDaddy calls me. I stick a bluetooth headset into my ear. "Talk to me, Puck. What's going on?"

"Motion sensors picked it up. A force of several hundred incoming mutants. They burn too bright to sneak through infrared."

My pulse quickens. "Is Walter with them?"

"Negative."

Samantha's on the phone call too. Her hand is at her ear. "Several hundred," she repeats. "We're not ready, Chase. They'll shred our defenders. Where are they?"

"Coming through the woods on foot. Halfway down Santa Susana Mountains. Quarter mile east of your position, near O'Melvney Park. You've got five minutes. Maybe."

"Call Tank. This is a paranormal fight."

Puck says, "Kayla is trying to find him. Mason and the Falcons are on their way."

Defensive teams pour from nearby houses. Troop transport trucks roar to life, headlights angry and piercing. I hop aboard the first truck and direct it westward. A caravan of twenty trucks rumbles after us on Balboa Boulevard, picking up speed past the massive water filtration plant. Samantha's voice comes across my headset, "They're coming to destroy our water."

Adrenaline dumps into my bloodstream, hardening soft tissue, accelerating synapses.

Puck orders us onto Timber Ridge and into a deserted neighborhood at the base of Santa Susana mountain. One of those newly built neighborhoods cramped with uniform one-story houses. The weeds are overgrown, there's no electricity, and wild animals scamper in our headlights. Samantha innately assumes command, bawling orders and positioning soldiers into natural defensive position behind houses and cars. She keeps brushing sodden hair back from her eyes. "Shotguns!" she roars. "No pistols! These are *mutants*. You can't hit them with bullets, they're too fast. Throw grenades, and fire shotguns when they get close!"

The looming mountain is wet and black above us. The commander stays by my side, fighting to keep fear from showing. "We have three hundred men, sir. Two battalions en route."

I press my earpiece. "Update me, Puck. Where's Tank?"

He says, "Not close. Mason is ten minutes out. But you don't have ten minutes. Walter's forces are…damn, they're everywhere, dude."

Puck's right; the commander is looking at a tablet indicating tripped motion sensors. The whole screen is red.

"Stand ready!" Samantha calls in her unnaturally loud voice. "Stand strong! Don't leave your shelter! Only fire close range! Don't fight alone!"

"Commander," I say. "Light'em up."

He speaks into a radio and rocket launchers shatter the night. Two salvos streak overhead and punch the mountain. The earth trembles and trees shatter with bright eruptions. Fire uncoils in the forest. Another wave of rockets unleashes and shreds acres of scrub brush.

Out of flame comes the enemy. A host of humanity twisted by hate and sickness, wearing goblin armor. Hundreds descend like a bristling ceiling. They howl and leapfrog rooftops, completely bypassing our foremost positions. Our soldiers fire simultaneously, one loud boom from a hundred shotguns, followed by ineffectual assault rifle chatter.

All is madness and hell. The enemy moves in fast-forward, and our infantry is immediately overwhelmed.

I pull free my bat, nicknamed Thunder Stick, and *Launch* into airborne traffic above. I collide with the swarm. With mighty hacks I fell those mutants closest to me, striking them down midair, before I plummet. I'm slowed by the injury to my back. Again I *Jump*, and again we meet in the rain but this time I'm mobbed and we fall in a writhing clump.

A second wave of enemy rushes from the mountain. These aren't Leapers. They *Move*, scattering across the neighborhood like insects, like Olympic sprinters on speed. The Kingdom soldiers throw grenades, brief detonations of shrapnel, and they fire shotguns at ghosts already gone, and they die. Samantha Gear is a woman possessed, standing boldly at the intersection of Timber Ridge and Golden Valley. The river of mutants meets her and breaks apart, falling to her expert marksmanship. She empties two shotguns into the cracks of their armor, drops the weapons, and pulls a pistol for each fist. Murderous firepower, zero misses.

I surge from the five person dog pile clawing at my face and I crush them with vicious blows. Even injured I am too powerful for them to contend with. Their bodies yield and surrender, hurled into nearby houses. Panting, I survey our battlefield; we're losing. The neighborhood is infested and I'm surrounded by dead soldiers. The thrust of the swarm passes us, moving east.

Samantha and I give chase after the enemy, which moves unrelentingly towards the water plant, but there are far too many. The rearguard mutants engage us on sight, clawing and screaming, and prevent us from stopping the wave.

"Trucks!" Samantha calls, and she points north to the long line of approaching headlights. But they're too far. The water plant will be destroyed before reinforcements arrive.

Suddenly Samantha and I both feel the earth shake. A low tremble in the ground, and a deep moan fills the air. Like an earthquake or an avalanche. From a distance I hear Puck in my headset exclaim, "Holy smokes, dude…"

"**Aaaaaaaooooooooooooooooooooo!**"

A great thundering herd of giants erupts from Mission Tierra Way, the final row of homes before the water treatment facility. The herd stampedes out of the darkness, clubs lofted and swinging like wrecking balls. Travis leads the charge, muscles bunched and bulging with anger. The deep moan is a battle cry. All things disintegrate before them; even houses collapse from their pure might. The fifty giants meet the two hundred remaining enemy Variants, a collision which I feel in my bones. As an iron tsunami meets an unmoving sheer wall. Like rocks breaking.

"What the *hell*, Outlaw!?" Samantha cries. "This is new! Are they friendly?"

Travis wields a great cast-iron pipe like a hammer and his victims are pulverized, bodies cast upwards and cartwheeling out of sight. The enemy Variants launch themselves onto the towering giants as wolves onto bison, attacking with pack mentality and long wicked knives. More than one titan bellows and falls. The giants momentum carries their bodies deep into the neighborhood, huge feet stomping cars and mutants alike. Kingdom soldiers cower and run, and I don't blame them. The fury and fight is terrible to watch.

Samantha uses her pistol to pick off enemy Variants clinging to Travis, and I use my bat. We mow them down until Travis spots me. In a fit of rage, he grabs my neck in a colossal fist.

"**Outlaaaaaw!**"

"Travis," I squeak, but he flings me into a nearby house. I plunge through the front wall and into the rear bathroom, landing heavily inside a busted fiberglass bathtub. He squeezed so firmly my nose bleeds and ears ring. For the space of twenty seconds, I lay quietly, trying to re-inflate my lungs. "...not cool, Travis..."

By the time I emerge, choking and coughing, the fight is over. Walter's forces are broken and retreating into the dark forests above, which are still tinged with fire. Giants bellow and raise their weapons, a celebration of victory and battle.

"**Aaaaaaooooo!!**" Our water is safe, but the first battle was a costly one. We pay for the water with too much blood.

Soldiers pick themselves out from rubble. More trucks arrive, bringing medics and late reinforcements. I wave the medics away and sit on a decorative iron garden bench, and I brush drywall dust and stucco chunks off my vest and pants. I cough, producing a faint mist of sheetrock particles.

Travis leans heavily on his pipe and pants, loud heaves of air. Blood runs from multiple wounds. He snarls in anger when Samantha approaches. "Friend!" she shouts. "I'm a *friend*. A friend of the queen." She places her hand on his exposed abdomen and Travis is pacified. This one is not an enemy. She pats his thigh experimentally, as though she can't believe he exists. "What a tall handsome boy you are. Look at these muscles. Big beautiful muscles. Want to give me a ride on your shoulders?"

I'm too exhausted to laugh.

- 10 -
The Outlaw

The following morning General Brown convinces Tank to take up residence in San Fernando, closer to the western front, closer to Walter's unnatural army. He refuses to hear Samantha and me, but begrudgingly he listens to the General. By noon he's found a mansion worthy of his bloated butt, and Katie's Variant army follows him.

Fat load of help they were last night.

Samantha and I move to the eastern front, giving the mutants space; they don't like either of us. The infantry here is abuzz with stories from last night's skirmish. They've heard about the nightmares falling from trees, the mutants which fly through the air, impossible to target, and the arrival of the thunderous giants. The Ride of the Behemoths. Somehow grainy video footage already exists on the internet, captured from helmet cameras. The soldiers want to extract further details from us, but our grim faces dissuade them. We lost fifty friendlies, plus another fifty in the hospital. No reason to celebrate, especially since the hostilities have only begun.

At three in the afternoon General Brown finds us in an open carport playing cards. He sits in an adjacent chair, and through his professional exterior I spy signs of frustration and anger. He grumbles, "If that boy was not crucial to our operations, I'd haul him out by his ear. Double-time."

"Tank? He's a big stupid thug, isn't he."

"Not a grown man. Not at all. He is an arrogant and entitled and defiant adolescent."

112

"That he is." I fold my cards, surrendering the pot to Samantha, and I grab an orange. She's on a hot streak; I owe her twenty-two million dollars now.

"Got another one?"

Samantha tosses him an orange.

"I miss the old days when we ate things other than fruit and chicken," I say.

All our cellphones ring at once. It's PuckDaddy on conference call. I put it through my speaker and his voice is shaky. "I'm pushing a video to your screens, amigos. You need to watch."

We do. And it's a nightmare.

The city of Denver is gone.

Helicopters are filming at a distance but the city is an unrecognizable mayhem of smoke and debris. There is no metropolitan skyline. The news report displays a map indicating current estimates of damage. Downtown Denver is entirely demolished. Destruction spreads as far as Lakewood and Aurora, and citizens are fleeing beyond Highway 470. Hundreds of thousands dead.

There's a close up of a little girl running. She's no more than four, and she's wearing pink socks. In one hand she holds onto her mother, and in the other is a doll. The mother appears to have second degree burns, but they are the lucky ones; they're alive. For the moment. I don't know enough about radiation exposure to know if it's fatal.

"That's a nuke," Samantha observes. Her vision is filled with war and she gazes past the screen to the hurt and battles beyond.

"Thermonuclear," General Brown agrees. He removes his camouflage cap and wearily leans back in his chair. "The B83. Has to be. General Isaac Anderson worried about them. Seventy-five times greater yield than the damn bomb dropped on Hiroshima."

But this wasn't dropped on another country. This wasn't dropped during a world war. This is three states away. Unthinkable. "Who did this?" I wonder.

"Both Resistance and Federal Armies had gathered there," Brown responds. His words are heavy and slow. "Was about to be conflict."

"No way Isaac Anderson drops that bomb."

"No. He would not."

I ask, "But would the President set off a nuke in his own country?"

"That ain't his own country anymore. Colorado's governor declared independence and martial law months back. But to more directly answer your question, young man, the President wouldn't. But the Blue-Eyed girl would." He slowly stands and walks from the room, looking ten years older. Already his radio has begun to squawk.

Samantha and I watch video footage for the next hour as word spreads of the nuclear attack. A lot of people within earshot are making calls to friends or family in Denver.

"Carter used that airport," Samantha says. Carter's an old acquaintance, not exactly a friend. Nor an enemy. A powerful Infected mercenary prowling the globe. "Last I heard he was in Texas, though."

"Did you and I ever go to Denver? I can't remember."

"What are we going to do, Chase? She's dropping nukes now. Do we just watch?"

"I don't know."

"There's gotta be something…"

"I'm staying here. Waiting for Katie. Where she goes, I go."

"Ugh. Unconditional love is so weird. And the rest of the world? What about them?"

"There's only two of us," I say. "You and I can't fight every battle. Maybe Katie's got the right idea. Pick one part of the world and make it safe."

"Safe? You call this safe? We're surrounded by pissed off Infected. Walter to the north, Blue-Eyes to the east, and Russia to the south. They can't stand each other, but one thing they have in common - they all hate your girlfriend."

"Which is dumb because she's great. And super cute."

"It's not dumb. She seized control of the most powerful army on earth. Not to mention the most expensive real estate. They're terrified of her."

"I remember the first time I met Russia. Such a cold man. So dead inside and indestructible. And so eager to kill. It's hard to imagine he fears little Katie Lopez."

"She's not so little anymore, dummy. Katie hasn't been *little* in over a year. Now she's...I don't know. Fierce. Strong."

"She's still kind."

"Maybe."

"She's still smart."

"Very."

"Do you think she's gotten even hotter?" I ask.

"Oh hell yes. She's taller, stronger, *and* curvier. It's not fair."

"Yeah. It's awesome."

"You're a moron."

"I wish she'd come back."

"Me too." She nods and looks towards the unseen ocean. "Me too."

The President of the United States (or what's left of the States, which is only the east coast) addresses the nation on every channel that evening at six. Samantha and I watch in a rowdy movie theater, along with three hundred others. He's a handsome, square-jawed man, gray around the ears, but he's aged two decades during the previous twenty-four months.

"My fellow Americans. Today we mourn the loss of far too many countrymen and women, as well as the loss of our safety and security. We have been attacked by cowards who seek to end our way of life and our trust in each other.

"Never before have nuclear weapons been used on our soil for sinister purposes. But today, that unthinkable act of war occurred. Terrorists possessing a B83 thermonuclear gravity bomb took off from the Lackland airstrip in Texas..."

We can't hear for several seconds as our troops revolt and cry him down. It's a lie, provably false. Lackland is an Air Force base in Resistance territory. No way the plane left from there.

"...under direct orders from the Resistance general, Isaac Anderson, the bomb was dropped at 1:15 PM central time, extinguishing the bright life of so many hardworking and honest Americans. We call upon your prayers and your resources to aid those in need, especially in the great state of Colorado.

"Although we are shaken and scared, we shall never alter course. Our enemies will not escape justice for this act of mass destruction. The mutinous Resistance will be held accountable. I call for the immediate arrest and trial of the Resistance generals, especially the war criminal Isaac Anderson. I also call for the immediate arrest and trial of the criminal Carmine, an ally of the terrorists, and one who was recently recorded savagely attacking innocent citizens in San Diego. Finally, I call for the immediate arrest and trial of the criminal Chase Jackson, known as the Outlaw.

"Due to the grave nature of these threats, we will provide no period of respite for our enemies. No chance for them to plot further evil. The three culprits I named have until 11 PM eastern to surrender, after which time we will bring them to justice with aggressive force. Pardon will be extended to any solider of the Resistance who lays down his or her weapon and submits to the Federal Government."

At this, the President glances off screen and his stern face cracks into a faint smile, barely visible. Samantha and I know he's looking at Blue-Eyes, an Infected woman who's bent the President to her will. He says, "Our Secretary of State will work closely with the Department of Defense. She and her tribunal will see that justice is served and the traitors crushed under the mighty glory of the United States."

This is too much. The President bombs his own citizens, blames it on us, calls for the arrest of the Resistance leaders, and then brags about his girlfriend. Soldiers near the front open fire with pistols and perforate the movie screen. Sergeants call for order.

General Isaac Anderson himself texts me.

>> **He's given us two hours.**

>> **What do you say? Want to surrender?**

I smile grimly. **You go first.**

>> **Nah. I look terrible in orange.**

Agreed

The prison jumpsuits would clash with my red mask.

>> Nice of him to offer though.

>> I call dibs on cutting his throat.

I put the phone away, in no mood to laugh. Where is Katie? The call for her arrest makes me nervous.

Thirty minutes later, Isaac Anderson issues his own address. He displays evidence proving the President's claim about Lackland airstrip is false. He encourages citizens on the east coast to overthrow their puppet President and especially his girlfriend, and he tells the President that the Resistance fighters are prepared to sacrifice their lives to end his regime.

General Brown also speaks, specifically to the troops in Katie's Kingdom. He rallies them to the queen, to the cause of freedom and independence. We are protected by warriors and a net of surface-to-air missiles, he reminds us. Not only that, but also by innovative directed energy weapons. Lasers, in other words, capable of shooting down any explosives the President launches our way.

It's a nice theory. I hope it works.

Samantha and I meet with the Variant Mason McHale, leader of a small elite group called the Falcons. We're not simply going to sit around and wait to be smashed under the President's glory. Starting tomorrow night we begin infiltrating the enemy's camp. With only a few surgical missions, we should be able to cripple the Federal Government's army, allowing us to focus more directly on Walter. With Puck on speakerphone we pour over maps and make plans until alarms begin to wail. I check my watch; the President's early.

The campaign against us begins with a bang. Our radar detects inbound missiles launched either from the ground or distant aircraft. Samantha and I rendezvous with Mason in Pasadena at the Rose Bowl Stadium, a good halfway meeting point, and from the top of the press box we have an expansive view of the city. We listen over the radio as General Brown and his commanders do what they've trained for: engage in warfare.

The night is dark and clean for several minutes as sirens howl. Citizens have been instructed to get underground, inside nearby commercial basements. We probably should too but self-preservation is not a trait common to those with the disease. We lean against rails and search the stars for incoming death and wonder how things got this bad.

"Puck," I say. "Any sign of movement from Walter?"

"Nope. I think he and his goon army are sitting tight, waiting to see what happens."

Our rockets flare in the east. Rapid fire launches, hissing off into the night behind coils of dark smoke. These are anti-ballistic missiles, and we track their trajectory out of sight. Soon additional rockets take off, so bright and angry they look like minor explosions, and then suddenly the first salvo meets their target. Brilliant eruptions high above the mountain, followed by sounds of the sky shattering. Incoming death impacting defensive shields.

The northern launchers issue rockets to intercept danger from a new direction. Soon the entire horizon begins to detonate like remote popcorn, and Los Angeles echoes with the cacophony. Samantha's face is set hard against the east, illuminated by bursts of light.

Some incoming missiles sneak through the fragments and get much closer before being detonated by directed energy weapons. These eruptions are violent and loud and leave afterimage trails in our vision, and we feel the concussion.

For an hour the stalemate rages, billions of dollars exhausted. The nebulous of combusted warheads descends as fog, bringing a smell like burning sulfur. A stray missile impacts high on the San Gabriel Mountains, causing a brief fountain of fire. Near 9:30 PM, there is a noticeable slackening of pace. My ears ring after hundreds of explosions but now the intermittent activity is distant, almost unnoticeable.

Mason laughs and pumps his fist. It sounds like he's under water. We survived. Very little harm done. Take that, Witch.

However, the radio bursts to life again. Frantic yelling. Something's wrong.

"Look," Samantha warns. I can barely hear her over the tinnitus. She points east and south. Moving so quickly they're hard to spot is one final incoming wave. I count eight pinpricks of light streaking across the stars. Incoming.

"Where is our defense?" Mason asks. "Fire, General. Fire! Come on, launch, dammit."

The enemy rockets scream overhead, a wall of noise, traveling over a mile per second. They strike south of us, just beyond the Downtown tower cluster. The earth shudders and kicks up debris. Clouds of smoke and brilliant flame. We feel eight impacts in our feet, as though the planet's being struck with cosmic hammers.

"Where is that?" Samantha calls. "What got hit? I can't tell."

"Looks like USC," I say.

"Yeah man," Mason agrees. He words are heavy and full of sorrow. "Blue-Eyes just took out the entire college. Why didn't we shoot'em down? I was gonna enroll there one day."

- 11 -
Carmine

We are halfway between Santa Catalina Island and Long Beach when the fight starts. The battle in our atmosphere is thirty miles away but we witness flashes and hear the vague retort. Almost like watching fireworks when I was a kid.

"So it begins," Saul says, and he doesn't try to hide his tears. He hates violence.

There is no wind so we bob in circles. I keep changing position on his boat to get the best view. I'm enraged. The bitch and her inculcated President are coming after my people with explosives. For no reason other than hate. Saul closes his eyes and prays.

Eventually the attack ceases, but not before one final surprise; a handful of rockets touch down unscathed. This explosion is much closer and I see the plume of fire. Sharp cracks reach us over the water. Each one is a blow to my heart.

Something went wrong. Some system failed. People just died. The metal rail I'm holding crumples in my fists.

"It won't end," he says, a man full of sorrows. "There will always be another war to fight. Ever it is so."

"Somethings are worth fighting for, Saul."

"I do not argue. But to return is to lead a life of struggle and strife. The cost will be great. Is it yours to bear?"

"I won't abandon them."

"I have lived in peace for over eighty years. It is possible."

"Maybe you shouldn't have. Perhaps you should've intervened earlier," I snap.

"Perhaps. Or perhaps I would have made things worse, despite my good intentions. The way Martin did. With you, there will be wars. Without you, there will be wars. It is a dangerous thing to predict what might be. You can stay. With me. Or elsewhere, beyond the fight. You can save yourself."

I don't care about saving myself. Saul places a much higher value on my life than I do. I cannot leave the people. I cannot leave the Variants. Or leave Chase. Or Tank. Or Kayla.

"Saul."

"Yes, little one."

"You have saved me. So now I will save others. Take me home. I'm going back."

Part Three

The earth is beautiful, and bright, and kindly, but that is not all.
The earth is also terrible, and dark, and cruel. The rabbit shrieks
dying in green meadows. The mountains clench their great
hands full of hidden fire. There are sharks in the sea, and there is
cruelty in men's eyes. And where men worship these things and
abase themselves before them, there evil breeds.
- *The Tombs of Atuan*. Ursula Le Guin

- 1 -

Carmine

As dawn breaks clear and golden, Saul guides us without effort into a berth at the California Yacht Marina inside the East Basin. I make our mooring lines fast to the bollards and we disembark. After days at sea, the ground feels hard and cruel. I want to move unobserved, so we raid houses in Long Beach until I find a crimson Angels baseball cap and pair of discarded Prada sunglasses. Who throws away Prada? Even I know that brand.

It's strange moving north through the city as a vagrant instead of a queen. I have no money, no phone, nothing to barter with. We pass markets full of scavenged goods and food but those are luxuries beyond our means, unless I want to reveal my identity. We walk miles, hungry and thirsty and footsore, until discovering a working electric bus moving people into and out of Downtown. Thank you, Governess, for your managerial acumen. Eagerly we board and are whisked north on Interstate 110. The other travelers are tired and scared and quiet. The scraps of conversation I hear are about last night's attack.

I notice for the first time that clothing inside our Kingdom is wearing thin. For months we lived wild, wearing new designer outfits every day, lavish in our abundance. But apparently the surplus has run dry and citizens now wear clothes in need of washing and patched knees. "Seamstresses," I muse under my breath. "And seamsters. That's a good job for Workers."

Saul looks up from his book, the New Testament, and arches an eyebrow.

"Just talking to myself," I explain.

We plunge into shadows cast by the towers and soon unload near the Cafeteria on 8th. Breakfast has already been served for Farmers, Shepherds, Scavengers, and the rest but I talk the suspicious Cooks into handing over plates of cold biscuits and a block of cheese. Better than nothing.

We walk and eat. My joints ache again, and I experience the familiar rumble of a headache. Saul earns a few second glances but I'm ignored. Our situation is reversed now; I'm the host and he's my guest. "There are no Guardians," I observe, scrutinizing the city for any irregularity. "I wonder where they are."

"Guardian is your term for teenagers injected at the age of eighteen by Martin?"

"Correct. Now they're turning twenty."

"Do you call them all Guardians? Even Walter's?"

"No. He calls his mutants or Variants, I assume. I prefer Guardian."

"Me too." He nods with satisfaction. "A good name."

"We need a car. Follow me." I lead him to the Olympic tower and down inside the dusty garage. We're in luck! My beautiful Land Cruiser sits in my parking spot. Saul deposits his satchel into the back and opens the passenger door. There's no key in the ignition or over the visor. Darn it. Must be in my room. "Wait here. I need to run upstairs—"

"Hey! The hell you think you're doing. Get away from my truck!" Dalton, beautiful angry Dalton, storms out of the stairwell. His boots echo in the empty garage.

"*Your* truck? How about our truck," I say.

"How about I throw you out this garage by your neck. This area is off limits." He's about to grab me by the back of my shirt so I remove the hat and glasses. His eyes get big and he cries, "Oh…oh damn, Carmine! Hah!" He wraps his arms around my neck and squeezes. "It's about time you got yourself back here, kid."

I hug him in return and compress his ribs until they crack. "Good to see you too. Now leggo."

"Not yet. Thought maybe I'd lost you."

"You're sweet. But I have a lot to do. Give me the keys."

"No. Who you got with you?" Finally he releases and peers into the truck.

"That's Saul. My friend. What do you mean no? I need the keys."

"Get in the back, then," he says. "I'm driving."

"Why would you drive?"

"Because you took off once on me. Now I drive. Just us brothers in the front, me and Saul." He steps past me and gets behind the wheel. He and Saul shake hands, and he says, "I'm Dalton. The queen's bodyguard."

"I am Saul. How did you burn your face, Dalton?"

"Long story," he chuckles, and he guns the engine. I have to hurry into the backseat before he leaves me. "You wanna go find the Outlaw? Or Kayla?"

"Not yet. A few things I need to do first."

Dalton drives us into Glendale, turns left into an overgrown vacant neighborhood, and parks at the first building on our right. He looks at Saul and says, "So you're trying to tell me, Saul, that Carmine is at risk of completely losing her sanity and the rest of her memory if she's too connected with the Guardians?"

Saul nods. "I believe so, yes. That is what happened the night she fled into San Diego. They steal her spirit. Her recovery required several days."

"And the more she remembers of Katie, the healthier she'll be."

"That is my hope."

"I'm right here," I grumble from the back. "And I wish you jerks would quit talking about me."

Dalton blows a blast of air from his mouth and shakes his head. "I should never have left the SEALs. Crazy ass stuff."

"You two wait here," I say and shove open the door. "I've about had enough." We're at Katie Lopez's old apartment building. I've visited only once since waking up in the hospital, and it helped. I walk through grass and weeds to the back sliding door and I open it. A mouse is startled and he runs under the bedroom door, vanishing beyond.

My room. My bed and my desk. I miss this place.

That's the first I've heard from Katie in a couple days.

The atmosphere is heavy with silence. I pull the dusty desk chair out and sit. There are hearts and names drawn in pencil all over the distressed wooden desk top. I see Chase Jackson written in cursive. And Tank Ware. And Katie Lopez, and Cory, and Lee, and Hannah, and others I don't know. There are pencils neatly sharpened and arranged in the top drawer. Notebook paper in the second. Wax in the corner where I played with candles. A sudden flashback, pouring hot wax onto the desk absentmindedly while I talked on the phone. There's a jewelry box fallen behind the dresser. I retrieve and open it.

Not much here. I don't wear jewelry and neither did Katie, based on photographs. A couple earrings. And a diamond pendant necklace.

The necklace.

That was Chase's favorite. He used to play with the chain when he came over.

I wore it during my final homecoming.

Yes. That was the night. My favorite night.

The night I kissed Chase. He went home, and I snuck inside his bedroom and... A sudden blush creeps into my cheeks. Sneaking into boys' rooms to make out - naughty naughty Katie. She snickers and warms with pleasure. I remember that night like it's a movie. I experience it from a distance. I latch the chain around my neck and keep looking.

The closet has mirrored sliding doors, which means I can only see half the clothes at a time. So I break both doors off their track and set them aside. Anything here that will help me remember? The shoes might have belonged to someone else. I'm too tall to wear most of this stuff now. I can reach the top shelf, which was always a struggle before. A lot of the clothes are from when I was younger. But not this, what's this?

"Tank's sweatshirt," I realize. He gave this to me the winter we began dating. Smells like his cologne. It was a chilly night in January and we were going somewhere and he had this sweatshirt in the back of his Hummer. I pull it on, like if I dress like Katie then I'll remember her.

Tank had his moments. Sometimes I forget that.

128

I don't want to go into the rest of the apartment. Katie and I have a mom and I'm not ready to deal with that yet. Would be too painful. But this bedroom holds nothing else for me, an exhausted resource, so on a whim I leave out the back and hurry to a nearby townhouse Mason once pointed out for me.

Chase Jackson's childhood home.

I enter cautiously, as though it's hallowed ground. The front wall is a pile of rubble on the main level. "I remember cooking in this kitchen," I announce into the looming silence. The smell of peppers. Drinking iced tea. And that couch!

We would sit on that couch and share a blanket. I tried to pretend I didn't notice our legs touching. We watched Natalie North movies.

There's a tug at my heart, a real emotion. A deep ache, like being homesick.

Muscle memory guides me upstairs, anticipating the squeak of the final step. His room looks as though a stampede trampled it. The window is broken. But it's still his room.

I LOVED this room.

It's small. Blue carpet, blue bedspread. Rarely used desk. His closet is a disaster, but I rifle through. I recall this Calvin Klein shirt. Kinda. And these football uniforms. I lay down on the bed, and it's as if I've been struck by lightning. That night, after the Homecoming dance. I surprised him here. I told him I would break up with Tank. I told him we couldn't kiss yet, but we did, and—

I press the heels of my hands into my eyes. More emotions. A sense of lost joy, so sweet it hurts. I was wearing the necklace I have on now. My throat throbs and clenches. Hot tears spill into my ears.

He skipped school once and I found him asleep in here. The disease almost killed him, but I didn't know it at the time. On his bed. He couldn't move. Poor thing.

What about Tank? No pity for him, Katie? He had the disease AND you dumped him. AND he was thrown in prison and starved. How about that?

Thirty minutes later I climb back into the Land Cruiser. I'm still sniffling and the two men don't speak. Neither of them mention the sweatshirt I'm wearing, or even look at me. This visit was a success; it hurts but I feel more grounded. More sure of myself.

Finally Dalton says, "Okay, Saul. Let's say you're right. But there's no way he could walk on water."

"Why not?"

"Because that's crazy as hell."

"A deity cannot walk on water?"

"I still don't buy it. No offense. Maybe healing people through prayer, sure, whatever. But people don't just run around on lakes." Dalton turns in his chair to look at me. "Where to, now?"

"One more stop. Hidden Spring High School."

The school. The halls. My halls.

Katie guides me to my old locker. To my English classroom, which shows signs of being used as a drug den recently. Katie chatters non-stop about memories. I sit down at a table in the cafeteria, a room redolent with powerful memories, and *know* this was my seat. I always ate here, with Chase beside me, two friends across but I don't recall their faces. I smell unwashed bodies in the kitchen, probably vagrants sleeping. I visit the impressive football stadium and sit in the stands and watch cows munch lazily on the grass in the end zone. The two Shepherds wave at me, but I'm lost in that Homecoming night, standing on the field with Chase while the crowd raved.

I am Carmine…

But I am awash with swirling memories. Recollections which usually don't connect with me emotionally.

I *am* Carmine.

And I am Katie. I've found as much of myself as time permits. And for the moment it has to be enough, because I have work to do.

- 2 -
The Outlaw

General Brown's technicians pour over missile launchers arrayed in an Ontario neighborhood. Those are the weapon systems that failed, resulting in the destruction of USC's sprawling campus. Even PuckDaddy assists, desperately searching for the flaw. I text him, **Having any luck?**

>> **puck is searching thru lines of code**

>> **specifically inside the patriot's fire control**

>> **so unless u know about antenna mast grouping…**

>> **or high performance radar sets…**

>> **shut up and let me work**

I know very little about fire control and antenna mast grouping and radar sets.

Before long, rumors begin to circulate - sabotage. Someone manually disabled the launchers. Someone with access to the radar trucks. There is a traitor in our mist, probably one of Brown's officers. That's the last thing we need.

Samantha and I finalize our plans. At midnight we will set off through Riverside, infiltrating the Federal encampment from the south. We're going to destroy equipment including radios, radar, and gasoline supplies, and then abduct their commanding officers. We can't drive away the Federal Army in a single night, or even in a month, but we're going to make their life hell. We're not taking Mason; he's an elite warrior but he'd slow us down.

Satellite intelligence indicates the size of their infantry is about to double. Reinforcements are en route from New Mexico, withdrawing from all engagements with the Resistance and traveling across Interstate 40. We want their army spooked and shaken before the new troops arrive, so she and I will travel with backpacks stuffed full of explosives. It's going to be a long, cathartic night.

At dusk I can't wait any longer. I text Puck again. **What about Katie? She still at sea?**

>> no

>> zealot came ashore

>> i assume he brought carmine with him but his phone is off now

>> dunno where they went

Find her

>> use ur manners

Please.

>> puck is gracious

>> puck will try

>> puck is also sleepy

Samantha and I wait and doze inside the Prius, something we've done a lot of in the recent months. We have no home. No place to permanently keep our stuff. It's a restless and tiresome existence. Our favorite vehicle to sleep in is a Honda Odyssey because of the backseat and comfortable captains chairs and extra storage, but it's hard to inspire our allies when we roll up in a minivan.

Supply trucks roar past on Interstate 210, often being driven by the Priest himself, bringing food and water to the front lines. We have enough protein but fruit and veggies will become an issue after a few weeks. The siege prevents us from reaching Katie's orchards and farms. After a short nap, Samantha wakes up and watches another episode of *The Walking Dead* on her phone. She's convinced she'd be an elite zombie hunter.

Near dinnertime, the back door opens and Kayla scoots in. She pushes aside our packs and closes the door. "Ew. It smells like feet in here."

"Holy crap you're sexy," Samantha says, turning in her seat and gaping.

"Good gosh, am I sharing one of Chase's dreams or something?"

"Thanks! I'm real, but I only eat lean meat and I *always* exfoliate."

"Is all of you real? There's no way."

"All of me, but let's talk about something else now because this is weird kinda. I brought you Pepsi and pizza." She opens the sack she has on her lap and pulls out two cans of Pepsi and two slices of hot cheese pizza.

I take one of the cans and almost drop it. "This is cold!"

"Yes," she says simply.

"Where'd you get it? I assumed soda ran out months ago."

"You have to know where to look. And I do! There are still some refrigerators working."

I pop the top and suck down froth. It's intensely sweet. And cold. And delicious. Samantha groans as if she's getting a deep tissue massage, and drains half the can. I say, "Kayla, I can't remember the last time I drank something cold other than water. Thank you, this is the best."

She blushes with pleasure, which looks so good on her I avert my eyes to maintain focus. "You're so welcome! PuckDaddy told me you're going across the enemy lines tonight, so I thought you deserved a treat."

Samantha eats the pizza and noisily licks the grease off her fingers. Kayla makes a pained expression and extends her a napkin. "The last time I saw you," Samantha says, "we'd just fished you out of a lagoon, half-dead."

"Yes, that was unpleasant. I got seaweed in my ears."

Samantha asks, "Did you bring chocolate chip cookies too?"

"No."

"Yes you did. I smell them."

"But I didn't. I promise."

"Don't lie to me. I'll frisk you."

She hesitates and says, "You're just smelling me," and her blush deepens.

"What, like a perfume?"

"No… And stop staring at me."

"I don't believe you."

I laugh around a bite of pizza. "She smells good, Samy. It's as simple as that."

Samantha wears a blank expression. "You smell like cookies?"

"Sometimes, but you're a very blunt person."

"Do you taste like cookies? Can I lick your hand?"

"Samantha! Jeez, get a grip."

My phone rings. It's PuckDaddy, and I put him on speaker. "Heads up, dummies. Walter is inbound."

I share a glance with Samantha. We knew he'd attack soon. For Katie's Kingdom to survive, Tank and the Variants need to defend the northwest. Samantha and I can't fight on both fronts, and Tank has double the amount of mutants as Walter, plus a large number of General Brown's soldiers. He should be able to hold the line. He needs to. He has to.

"Tank has Mason with him," I say, which is something I've reiterated ten times already that day. "They should be fine."

"Yep," Samantha nods. "Probably."

"There's no way Walter can break through. Right?"

"Right."

"Right," I repeat.

Kayla sits in the back and wrings her hands. Puck's breathing is loud. We're betting everything on Tank and Mason and their untested army. If they fall, the Kingdom is lost.

I ask, "Puck, do you have good intel? Is Walter bringing everyone?"

"Everyone, bro. He emptied his entire camp. Maybe twenty-thousand, including his freaky mutants. Coming straight down Interstate Five."

Samantha sucks at her teeth and I stare out the windshield. Should be fine. Our lives are in Tank's hands and he's facing a better trained army. No sweat…

I say again, "Should be fine."

Kayla suddenly shouts, "I don't understand why you aren't driving and please hurry because I'm *so* stressed because we're definitely going to die if you don't!"

"For real, homie. Get your ass over there."

I start the car and gun the engine, which is not very dramatic or effective in an electric car.

We have a battle to win.

A convergence of major roads is set like a wide river north to south through our western barricade. Interstate 5, the Golden State Freeway, San Fernando Road, and Foothill Boulevard combine for a twelve-lane super highway along the bottom of a series of shallow canyons. Walter to the north, and the Kingdom to the south. It's an excellent choke point, and General Brown's troops have it expertly barricaded under the Balboa bridge; no heavy machines are getting through anytime soon. Trouble is, Walter doesn't plan on moving heavy machinery.

We arrive in our red-lining Prius as the sun sets on the western rim of the battlefield, and the attack begins on cue. An avalanche of hate descending from the north. In addition to his mutants, Walter gathered a collection of mercenaries. Gunmen, Herders, escaped convicts, all sorts of scum. He comes on foot and motorcycles. Thousands of motorcycles, in mimicry and defiance of Katie's armada. They ride two to a bike, wearing grisly iron helmets. His army and cavalry move like a heavy blanket two miles wide over the hills. They launch RPGs (rocket propelled grenades) which are too small to be shot down by our technology. Explosives fall like thick hail and rupture the defensives. Our troops duck behind armored jeeps and dive inside the Cascade houses as a thousand grenades burst. Gas tanks blow, townhouses crumble on Nicholas Drive, and men fall. General Brown's commanders return fire, a violent volley of unguided 70mm rockets. The dusty hills belch dirt and flame, but Walter's forces aren't fazed. They are spread too thin for the rockets to inflict significant damage. The descent of the horde is unchecked.

We park at the Rockwood condos, a quarter mile from the front lines. I tie the red Outlaw mask around my face while Samantha stuffs ammo into a hundred pockets.

More RPGs land. Our temporary command post, the former county assessor's office, shatters and falls apart. The Balboa bridge staggers from multiple impacts, chunks breaking off and falling onto the interstate.

"Look!" Kayla cries, and she points to the north. Walter's mutants climb the steel lattice of tall electrical towers and begin *Sprinting* across the dormant power lines, hundreds of feet in the air. More climb the southern towers. The whole of our horizon is dark with the enemy.

I hear Tank's voice. He's bellowing orders I can't decipher.

Our forces fire more 70mm rockets, breaking apart the interstate and slowing the foremost motorcycles. They're within extreme machine gun range and we release a murderous rain of fire. Still they come. Our troops stay in defensive positions, mostly hidden.

"They're afraid," Kayla says. She stands on the curb of Foothill Boulevard. She closes her eyes and inhales the breeze which tosses her hair. "Our forces are terrified. I smell their fear."

Samantha Gear chambers a round into her powerful rifle and announces, "We've already lost. Unless the Outlaw can change our fate. Give us hope."

Kayla's eyes are still closed. "I wish the queen was here."

I finish pulling on gloves, now dressed in the entire outfit. "Stay alive, Shooter. And I'll see you on the other side."

"Good hunting, Outlaw."

I *Jump* onto the third-story condo building, take two steps and unleash my power upwards, three hundred feet into the dusk, and engage my wing suit. The wings catch wind with a snap and I surge forward. Gathering speed. I am a human missile. The planet rotates below and I soar past our defenses. A black specter in the sky, streaking towards Walter alone. I am spotted by our Variants and our troops, and a great rallying cry is raised.

The Outlaw fights with us.

We will not run.

We will not fight afraid.

We will meet our enemy head on.

My muscles are rock. My reflexes are lightning. My skin impermeable hide. Laser focus. Fury a hot oven. Death in my fists.

I duck under a barrage of gunfire and RPGs. My altitude reaches zero and my speed hits a hundred. I collapse the wings and barrel through motorcycles, breaking apart the tip of their spear. These aren't Variants; they are men with soft flesh, and they die upon impact. In the middle of the interstate, two hundred yards beyond our defensive line, is the battle begun.

The wave of enemies washes over me as I climb to my feet. The battle is too large for me to fight all of it, or even a large part. Therefore my contribution must be significant. Instead of a mound of sand before their tide, I will be a boulder.

The motorcycles seek to trample me but I unhorse the drivers. Gunmen open fire and miss, instead carving holes into their own ranks. I hunt the bravest, the biggest, the boldest, and I end their war with hands like hammers. The enemy is wise, though. Walter instructed his mutants to stay away from me and I cannot find any.

Instead his Variants run across power lines in the sky and scamper over hills. With my enhanced eyesight I see them, wearing metal helmets and armor. Samantha's heavy rifle booms over and over, blasting the Variants clean off their perches but she can't staunch the flood. There are too many.

Around me the enemy gunmen waver and break, fleeing to far parts of the interstate. There are other battles for them to fight, where they don't have to face the Outlaw. I find myself in a clearing, surrounded by bodies, and the river of motorcycles keeps its distance. How do you defeat the Outlaw? Minimize him. Stay away from him and kill his allies.

"Walter!" I scream. My voice bursts nearby eardrums. "Show yourself, Walter!"

The road is wracked with detonations as our military commanders open more salvos of rockets, anything to halt the advance, flinging dismembered bodies upwards. Leapers begin *Jumping* our defenses. They block out the stars, numbers uncountable like leaves swirling on the wind in autumn, and touch down in the neighborhoods and vacant studios beyond, where Mason and our Variants wait. Their crusade begins, thousands of bodies colliding.

Chaos reigns, and we fight in the purpling blue of dusk.

Tank and the giants are within protective fortifications in the west, guarding the water plant. The enemy crawls the mountains and assails their position. Others drop in from power lines above like jungle cats from vines. Tank is a fearsome combatant, his mighty axe sweeping and chopping. He and the giants are outnumbered ten to one but the battle favors them. Our behemoths stomp and crush and absorb damage like heavy earth-movers. Enemy mutants soon break ranks and flee from their rage, unable to resist such force.

We are engaged and overrun across a three mile stretch. Our military defense is in place but ineffective. The battlefield is too large, the fighting too personal and too fast. You can't shoot what you can't target. You can't target what you don't see.

Puck is yelling in my ear but his words are fuzz. The Thunder Stick sings in my fist, felling riders and infantry men alike. I am a force of nature and they run from me.

The ground shakes. It's not another rocket strike; the vibration is different. I turn in time to glimpse a titanic fist, which crushes and casts me to the ground. A hand the size of a large microwave. "**Ooooutlaaaaw!**"

A nightmare towers above. Finally I hear Puck's voice: "Walter has giants too! Move!" A dozen armored beasts. Their forearms are covered with iron, and they wear helmets of beaten metal. I roll out from under a huge stomping foot which cracks the pavement.

Some genius military commander sees the giants and orders a strike. Unguided rockets scream in, but the giants are ready. Two of them raise large, three-quarter-inch thick sheets of steel. Rockets erupt against the barrier. The two giants are blown backwards but alive. The impact nearly bursts my ears, only ten feet away, and my skin is singed. Shrapnel digs deep.

I feel nothing. Hear nothing. Just my heart throbbing.

We need to regroup. We're lost if we don't. I'm grabbed again by the giant. With one violent twist, I free myself and scramble onto his hulking shoulders. Swaying to keep balance, I *Hack* my bat down on his skull. The thick helmet punctures inward, breaking into his cranium.

He falls slowly like a tree and I retreat, *Sprinting* back to our defense. The Balboa bridge has been captured and I'm forced to reclaim it, throwing wild men aside. A pack of Walter's Variants storm up the ramp from the west. I raise my hand and shout, "**Get *back!*"** They scatter and fall as though blasted by a firehose.

Samantha was right; we've already lost. Our enemy's strategy is to lengthen the battlefield and engage us in a thousand individual skirmishes, and it's working. From my vantage on the bridge, I spy fighting from the far Granada Hills Recreation Center all the way to the Saddle Tree Ranch neighborhood, a distance over two miles. The enemy is too well-trained, too vicious, and our Guardians are disorganized and cannot use superior numbers to their advantage. Tank is no leader. He fights an insular battle, no thoughts for others. The enemy's courage grows while ours seems to diminish.

"Walter!" I cry, but he won't face me. He doesn't need to. He'll wage warfare in secrecy and shadow, and he'll win. His soldiers are bound to him in hate and violence.

Mason and his Falcons are the only valiant soldiers in sight. They soar in formation on racing bikes and cut down gunmen and goblin, for that is what Walter's mutants look like - goblins. As I watch, Mason is surrounded and stalled by a wall of flesh bristling with swords and spears. The Falcons will soon fall, crushed under a concentrated surge. I hurl myself upon the reeking foe and fight towards him, and the rod in my hand heats red from hammering armor and deflecting bullets. Time and again it falls, cleaving a path. Gunmen fire but they cannot hit Mason, winnowing their own numbers instead.

These are Variants falling under my fury. Their enhanced bodies are hard and they fight back and the work is hot.

"Outlaw!" Mason laughs when I reach him. He's panting and bloody, and he's missing two comrades. "You fight like el diablo. Thanks for the help. I owe you one."

"Perhaps before the night is over you can repay the debt." "This night will never be over. We've been at it an hour, but it feels like five minutes."

"Five minutes? More like an eternity," I say. Our intersection on Foothill is temporarily clear, but sounds of warfare ring from darkness around. Samantha's rifle maintains a continual roll of thunder, each burst indicating a fallen enemy. "We're losing, Mason. We're scared and in disarray. We need to regroup, otherwise we'll lose the entire Kingdom. From here they'll pour over the military and leave us defenseless from missile attack."

"Aye amigo, I agree. Our fallback position is the Allied Beverages warehouse."

I put my hand to my ear. "Puck, are you hearing this? Can you alert the military commanders? We'll round up the Guardians."

"Hang on a sec, dummy. Help is on the way."

"What help?"

"Carmine! She's back, baby."

Mason is staring east. He feels her before I do. A buzz builds, like an electrical hum inside the Guardian's flesh. Their queen has returned. Walter's mutants sense her too and the attack falters. Our enemies on San Fernando cease pushing inwards and they look for help, seeking guidance from Walter who was so sure of easy victory. Their courage and confidence wavers, and that is enough; the atmosphere of the battlefield shifts, like a sudden reversal of wind. First one, then another of Walter's forces turns and runs; they don't know what, but *something* is coming. Soon there is a stampede from the east, foes streaming in reverse. Even Walter's giants, who were busy smashing the Sylmar Juvenile Courthouse, begin an uncertain shuffle back to the Balboa bridge and the farther safety.

Onward comes our swarm of Guardians, a shocking and haunting sight. Once meek domesticated dogs, they fight now as wolves, a cleansing flood, fighting as one. I can't see Katie but her presence is obvious; her wrath and determination has been imputed to those who follow her. The slower enemies are *consumed* by the avalanche. Walter's gunmen flee, outpaced only by the goblins who often as not scamper on all fours. They trample across neighborhoods and reach the interstate. Those enemies who can't make it through the chokepoint are forced into the hills to survive.

The fight is over within ten minutes, so devastating is her counter-attack.

Desperately I seek Katie, and I spot her atop the Balboa bridge glaring north as her adversary retreats. She is surrounded by an ocean of clamoring Guardians and sudden celebration. We crossed from death to life, from defeat to victory. Some of the more vigilant military gunners discharge a final wave of rockets to chase them up the distant rise.

I only have eyes for Katie. She is flush and breathing heavy, a pillar of strength and authority, silhouetted by the ruptures of orange fire beyond. She is Katie and she is Carmine, the warrior queen. As I get nearer, I hear Tank calling, "Let this war be ended now! We should chase them to their homes and crush their skulls!"

"No." Katie's voice is soft but sharp, cutting across the noise. "This fight is enough. Let them limp home."

Tank is too caught up in battle lust to heed her. He calls, "I go to remove Walter's head! All warriors brave enough will join me!" He begins trotting north on the wide interstate, beyond the cones of our searchlights. Several hundred Guardians follow, ignoring their queen. Refusing the chance for adventure and further victory is difficult for those fueled by adrenaline and arrogance and glory.

"Tank!" she calls. "Do not chase the fox into his own lair. It's suicide."

He won't hear. He refuses the caution, and so do his followers. I care not. It wouldn't be the worst thing if he got his foot shot off. I'm pressing through the crowd to reach the queen. In the midst of the maelstrom, she searches for me too. Or so my hope makes it appear.

We finally lock eyes when suddenly Walter's rearguard opens fire. Tank and his small overeager army crest the hill a mile north on the interstate and charge into an ambush. Our friends are strafed and mowed down from all directions, and they're beyond our help. My stomach turns into a cold knot, and our victory party quiets. Katie drops from the bridge and strides north, weaving around the field of death.

The guns fall silent.

We wait in silence. It's too dark, and even my enhanced eyes can't pierce the smoke of spent artillery. Haze drifts across the battlefield and Katie stops near the giant slain with a crushed skull. Mason somberly signals his Falcons and they turn to search for fallen companions.

Katie's voice pierces the dark. "Saul. I need you." A man I don't recognize steps from the crowd. He wears a cowl to hide his face.

Tank is limping home, along with half his forces. *Half.* Saul reaches Tank as the big man's strength gives out and he surrenders to blood loss.

- 3 -
Carmine

Tank will live. His wounds are many but not grievous. I *Feel* his health.

I *Feel* them all. They hurt, I hurt. They rejoice, and so do I. My head is buzzing even though I force them out but one cannot hold back the ocean. If I close my eyes I can even see what their eyes see, thousands of view points. Hands clutch me, and for the brief moment the world fades.

Los Angeles is gone. Time collapses. I'm in a black room, a dark chamber far away. A woman with blue eyes watches me. I can't hear. I can't move.

Yes, she mouthes. Yes. Very good, she says.

What is this...

She touches my face and I feel her finger.

No, I say, and suddenly I return. The solid world resurfaces, hallucination evaporated. Once more I smell gunpowder and hear laughter and crying, and I'm sweating. I force the Guardians and connections out of my mind with a tremendous act of willpower. Like shoving boulders. I would be overwhelmed and crushed without Saul's training.

I select a home in Chatsworth as an improvised headquarters, several miles west of the military's ineffective barricade on Interstate 5. The house is like a vast estate from a fairy tale; Cinderella could have lived here, a thought which brings me a small amount of pleasure.

The homeowners are survivalists, and they lovingly maintain their residence. As we arrive, they rush from their basement shelter to help move

142

our wounded. They are a handsome Portuguese couple and both husband and wife are physicians. An unexpected blessing. The rooms are high-ceilinged and richly furnished, and the dark hardwood floors gleam. Manoel helps Dalton walk Tank inside to a king mattress, and he sets to disinfecting and cleaning the wounds. His wife, Jovita, acts as a point of triage, sending injured Variants to specified corners of their grand home.

I love this place. I want to live here. Forever. So many bookshelves.

Not now, Katie.

The Outlaw and Saul have a fascinating and intense greeting. They seek each other out and grasp hands, a handshake which lasts and lasts, each searching the other's face. Chase says, "Zealot. Thank you."

"Outlaw. So it's true. I feel it." His voice is faint and wondrous. "You have a gravity. No wonder they hate you."

"My natural charm."

"We will talk later. We must. I can find you with closed eyes," Saul says, and he turns to me. "Little Carmine. You did it again."

"I didn't intend to, Saul," I snap. "I got mad and they connected to me without asking first. Besides, it worked."

"And had you died? So would they. Learn to protect yourself, for the sake of us all." But he smiles and leaves to tend the wounded. The Variants are suspicious of him and angry until he lays hands on their skin. Just a touch, and they quiet. His hands are medicine.

Chase. I could look at him all night. In a grimy world of shattered hope and gloom, he shines like the sun. He watches me like I'll vanish if he's not careful. I place my hand on his face, cradling his cheek and strong jaw. As our skin touches, my headache dims. "Chase. You have been busy. The Kingdom only stands because of you. I am in your debt."

"Your friends are high maintenance. You're lucky you're cute."

"You love me."

"I do. Always. You're recovered from the bomb?"

"Yes, and I've recovered more memories. I remember Homecoming."

His face reddens and he flashes that smile. "That was a night worth remembering."

"I'm finding more of you. And more of Katie. Like old movie footage. You have sacrificed much for me."

"You're wearing her necklace. *Your* necklace, I mean."

"I found it behind her dresser. My dresser. Whatever."

"Did you find the tiny pajamas that went with it?"

That was NOT a modest outfit. I'm mortified I wore it when we made out. But. He obviously remembers. Boys are so simple, it's a little embarrassing we get fixated on them.

"You wish." But I smile. The whole house is watching and I don't care.

"I'm glad you're back," he says.

"Me too. Thanks for staying."

"For you, Katie. Anything."

"My name is Carmine," I answer on reflex. "But. Katie's not so bad."

We work hard for an hour, getting our wounded situated and stable. It's only midnight but our troops are dead on their feet. I order a skeleton crew left at the borders for defensive surveillance and everyone else to their beds. Tomorrow we bury the dead. Chase and Samantha Gear (whom I admire) are outside meeting with military commanders and discussing ways to improve our disaster of a chokepoint. Clearly we need upgrades, and we need them yesterday.

Despite the violence, we suffered few casualties. Perhaps because we were too defensive and cowardly, but nevertheless most are still alive. Our Guardians bear signs of shocking damage but they'll heal. Walter returned with most of his army intact also, other than those the Outlaw and Samantha destroyed.

The rear lawn was once a paradise of cozy landscaping, replete with evergreens, pool, and gazebo. It's remains lovely but now also contains a water well and solar panel bank. I walk the stamped concrete patio and let recovering Guardians touch my hand, offering encouragement and praise. Many are still jumpy from battle and suffering from adrenaline sickness, myself included. Some are asleep on the lawn, some are fighting nausea, and some are euphoric. I missed them, and they missed me, and I'm lightheaded from the connections. I catch myself looking for Becky.

Suddenly I'm wrapped in a fierce hug. A woman, slightly taller than me. Samantha Gear. *The* Samantha Gear. Her arms go around my neck, and mine go around her waist.. She's thin but she's also wearing a tattered ballistic vest and various battle equipment, including a rifle across her back. My hands barely touch. "Katie. Carmine. Whoever the hell you are. It's good to see that beautiful face."

The Shooter thinks I'm beautiful.

I say, "I saw you work tonight, Shooter, and I'm glad you're on my side. We are grateful."

"Bah. Only got forty-two. I think Chase beat me." She releases, grabs my chin, and kisses me loudly on the cheek. "Don't run off again, gorgeous. He's insufferable when you're gone."

My heart skips a beat. He misses me when I'm gone.

Speaking of Chase, I find him in the small guest bedroom where Tank rests. The walls are rich mahogany paneling, lit by candles. The Outlaw's impressive arms are crossed over his chest, and he and Tank are in the midst of a glaring contest. "You got those people killed, Tank."

"It's war, little hero. Risks are inherent, and fortune favors the bold. Get over it."

This is the first I've examined the Outlaw in the light. His hair is caked with dried blood, a bullet is lodged in his shoulder, his skin is lacerated and punctured by shrapnel, and the wounds on his back have opened again. Goodness. I say, "Chase, you need to let Saul examine you."

"The Zealot?"

"He doesn't fight. He heals."

Tank grimaces and shudders. "Man's spooky. Felt like he was inside my brain."

"A unique sensation for you, the feeling of having something between your ears other than air," the Outlaw comments.

Tank is pale and clammy. He laughs to cover his anger. "That's cute, pajamas."

Jovita, the beautiful homeowner, severe with dark hair and dark eyes, brings juice for Tank. I thank her and place the cup on the floor next to Tank's mattress. Squatting next to him, I grasp his hand. "I'm finding more memories, Tank. I remember the night on the beach when Walter came. You were ready to die for me. In case I didn't say it at the time, thank you."

His eyes pool and redden. He nods and looks away, and the pressure on my hand increases.

Chases asks, "What's this about a beach?"

Tank sniffs. "See, little hero? Told you she can't keep her hands off."

"It's called pity, you oaf. She's wearing *my* necklace."

"And *my* shirt. Which looks sexy as hell."

"So? It's a stupid shirt."

I say, "Okay, boys. That's enough pre-pubescence for one night."

Chase grumbles under his breath, "Might want to clean the shirt. He sheds."

There's a knock. Manoel stands in the doorway, holding a small boy by the hand. "Do we interrupt? Little Mariano wants to meet the heroes."

"I'm not little." Mariano is a sleepy duplicate of his father, and he can't take his eyes off the Outlaw. Chase's mask is tied around his neck like a bandana at the moment, but the infamous costume is hard to miss. Chase slides free his Boom Stick or whatever he calls that rod of death, and he crouches to the boy's level.

The father nods to me. "You and your forces may stay as long as you need. We are appreciative of you, Queen Carmine. We feared we must move until you arrived. We love our home very much."

"Did your neighbors stay too?"

"Some. Yes."

"We won't burden you long, Manoel. But tonight you are a godsend. We will regroup and be gone as quickly as possible."

"My wife and I tonight sleep in little Mariano's bedroom. You will honor us by taking the master."

"Absolutely not. We impose too much already."

"Surely you and the Outlaw need somewhere to sleep," he protests.

"Thank you, but I won't get any rest tonight, and…and…" I stammer when I fully grasp his words. "…and the Outlaw and I don't sleep in the same bed."

146

"You do not? I apologize. I believed the rumors foolishly."

"The rumors? What rumors?"

Mariano tugs on my pant leg, earning a sharp reproof from his father. Mariano says, "Miss Carmine, where is your red silk?"

"I've lost it," I grin. "Hopefully I can find more soon, because my elbows hurt."

"Did you kill Walter?"

"Not yet, little Mariano. We will catch him soon."

He says, "Walter killed my uncle and aunt in Oregon."

"And my parents," Tank says from his mattress. He's drained the orange juice, but he could use several gallons. "We'll get him, kid."

"Are you a giant?"

"Do I look like one?"

Mariano nods. "Your feet do not fit on the bed. Are you injured, giant?"

"Not for long."

The father asks, "Is my family safe here? Do you think?"

"There are few safe places at the moment," I answer. "Denver is destroyed. So is Las Vegas, and much of northern Texas. The east coast is calm, but under the control of a mad woman. Maybe try Canada or Alaska if you want safety."

"We do not fear hardship. We are willing to work, and we take our shifts at the hospital. But the bombs sounded close."

"You're near the border. Closer towards the ocean or Downtown would be safer until this storm abates."

Chase grabs my hand and pulls me into the hall. Just the two of us. He says, "I need to go."

"Go? Where?"

"To meet with General Brown. Tonight's engagement did not go well," he says.

"But first, want to engage with me in the master bedroom?"

...

Oh my gosh. What?!

He's too stunned to respond. But not nearly as surprised as I am. "Holy sweet sugar," I groan, and I smack my forehead. "Ugh. That was Katie. She says stuff without asking permission first."

"Wow."

"I know. Sorry."

He's smiling. "What a potty mouth."

"Shut up."

"I kinda like it."

"You should go now, Outlaw."

"Tell Katie I'll take a raincheck."

"No. Leave."

What?! We just got Chase back. Don't send him off.

I'm not. He has to leave anyway, so I'm saving face. You humiliated me, Katie, and I don't know how romance works. I'm doing my best.

"I'll come back when I can," he says. We walk outside. Samantha Gear is waiting for him by a car. A Prius, of all things, hardly befitting the two most fascinating people I know. He winks as he slides behind the wheel, and they motor north into the black.

You're terrible at this.

This neighborhood is swarming with Guardians. I *Feel* them pressing into my consciousness, invading my spirit. The sensation steals my breath. Many of them crowd the exterior walls of Tank's bedroom. He has devoted followers now, drawn to his power. They watch me with curiosity and shame, wondering if I'm angry at them for swearing fealty to another.

I couldn't care less, kiddos. I don't even understand it.

Despite the exhaustion, there is an ebullient glaze on what's become our village. Part of it radiates from my relief at discovering so many survivors. A sense that finally we're all together again, and my emotions are contagious.

Kayla finds and hugs me. A long time. "Don't you ever leave me again, my queen."

"It's nice to see you, my Kayla."

"Come look. Mason wants to show you something." She pulls me towards a neighboring house. "By the way, Carmine. I watched the Outlaw fight. It's like…it's like…I don't even know. He's like Superman, but with a stick. He beat up so many people. All the soldiers are talking about it. He's *a-mazing*."

"Did you see his arms? I'm fond of his arms. And of his face."

"I rubbed muscle ointment on him, just because I wanted to touch him. I liked it," she says and a pink patina settles into her cheeks, and she smells of smoldering marshmallows.

"That's sweet, Kayla, and if you do it again I'll break your pinky fingers."

Mason and the Falcons have commandeered a neighboring house. Inside the grand foyer is an orc on his knees. Or at least that's how he looks. And smells. The stench is awful. His nails are overgrown and so is his hair. He wears rags and a battered chest place, which appears crafted from the bowl of a metal birdbath. His need for a shower and toothbrush is desperate. To my eyes, he emits a faint sick-green bioluminescence. He doesn't actually glow; it's part of our disease interaction.

"Caught one of the rats," Mason announces. He holds a leash connected to the mutant's collar and chain. "Thought you might like to meet, Queen Carmine."

Fascinating. I lower to his level. His eyes are balls of chaos and pain. The man (or boy) twists away. His neck is striated with quivering muscle, and his wrists strain until they bleed. I pity him; he is not so far removed from us and what we could be. He chose to follow the wrong leader, and now his life is misery. "Can you understand me?"

He scoffs, and spittle lands on the polished floor.

On a subterranean level, I'm aware of Mason and Kayla and the Falcons. Their biotic essence seeks mine, constantly reaching for connection. It's corporeal fulfillment transacted without touch. They don't even know it's happening, but thanks to Saul I'm aware now. The boy on his knees, though, does not have a searching spirit. His soul throbs and shoves. He reacts as though scalded when I examine his mind. He's not a part of my hive, so to speak, not attuned to my frequency.

"You were after our rocket launchers tonight?" I ask. "To deplete our defenses?"

No response

"Why do you follow Walter? Why not me?"

"Isn't it obvious," Mason snorts. "Because he's degenerate."

"No. No he's not. He's ill. He's like…an addict."

The orc-boy's head swivels back to me. Sunken haunted eyes. He makes a gurgling sound in his throat. "…master Walter is a god…"

"Walter is a man. A thug and a terrorist. I want you to leave him. And join us."

Our eyes are coupled. I wonder what he sees? Because he's scrutinizing my face like I'm an alien. The garbled humming in his chest strengthens. "…cannot…"

"Yes you can. You will be fed and clothed. We are your family."

"…we *hate* the queen!" Before I'm ready, he explodes upwards, his legs pumping like pistons. He goes through the ceiling sheetrock as though it's soft, hands suddenly free, squirming like a maggot. Mason brings him crashing back down with one mighty haul on the leash, and ends his life by a well-placed knife thrust. Hot blood spurts.

I'm sick of violence. I almost vomit.

Kayla's face twists in disgust. "That is legit nasty. Someone clean him up." Three Falcons jump to obey her. "But don't use the cashmere throw."

"What were you *doing*, Carmine?" Mason asks me. "You had me worried."

"What do you mean?"

"You and this disgusting rat were…talking without sound."

"Yeah, and I started sweating, and I never sweat," Kayla says.

"Noetic wrestling," I say.

"No-what?"

"Humans can communicate in ways other than vocalization. Especially us. We're human and we're something else. I was convincing him, but he didn't like it. I want to try again. Catch me another, Mason."

"I'd rather simply cut their throats."

"If they can be restored then it's worth the effort."

Kayla takes my hand and squeezes. "Okay, Queen Carmine. Whatever you say. But now? Let's find you some soap. And a razor. And shampoo. You smell like fish."

"Kayla—"

"And some girl clothes."

"Kayla—"

"And earrings to match your darling new necklace."

Mason groans and he leaves.

She continues, "And makeup, and please don't bite me."

- 4 -

Carmine

Other than smoldering craters in the hills, the night appears like every other in southern California. Warm, starry, and idyllic. I'm standing on Northridge Road, off Devonshire, surrounded by bustling manors lit with electric lanterns, and I can't get the swarm out of my head. I'm hearing voices and hallucinating no matter what I do.

I'm still amped - refreshed and clean and well-dressed thanks to Kayla. No sleep for me tonight. Tomorrow we bury our dead, but what to do until then?

The answer comes in the form of thunder. Giants have arrived. They clomp into view off Winnetka, fifty strong, dragging weapons that throw sparks.

Dalton is in our Land Cruiser, on the radio. I tell him, "Wake up the Governess, and request more food. We have big mouths to feed." He grumbles something unpleasant.

I go meet the incoming horde. Travis leads the way, and his face cracks into a big smile. "**Queen!**"

"Welcome, brave giants!" I call. I heard Walter has a few giants of his own, but tonight the tons of flesh never clashed. "You deserve food and rest, mighty warriors. Here you will find both. I've sent for more supplies to meet your large appetites."

A colossus in the rear of the procession takes me seriously, and he promptly drops with a thud on the adjacent lawn and closes his eyes. Travis says, "**Tank. He is here.**"

"He is sleeping."

"We will too. Near him."

"Pick an empty house and find a floor big enough," I say. His friends charge into nearby homes and smash things in their search for rest. I place my hands on Travis's abdomen to halt his progress. "Travis, I stole Hurt. Your sword."

His face brightens with childlike joy. **"You haave it still?"**

"It's on a boat. I'll bring it to you soon. I'm sorry for stealing."

"Thank you, queen. Forgive you."

Travis chooses to sleep outside, his head propped against the exterior wall of Tank's bedroom. Such devotion is admirable. And a little worrisome.

I'm about to check on our order for additional food when I detect a familiar scent. An aroma which triggers internal alarms, though I can't identify it. I have the olfactory abilities of a predator so the source of the odor might still be distant, but it's not wholly disagreeable, like the tang of car exhaust...

Gasoline and perfume. That's the scent of the Cheerleader. She's nearby. A woman about my age who lives in the lonely places of our Kingdom, she possesses the gruesome combination of insanity and combustion. I twist in a circle, triangulating her direction. She's south and east, near the Chatsworth Reservoir and Bell Canyon. I'd guess a mile distant; the breeze must have shifted, bringing her biological fragrance. I'm already sweating. The last time I saw her she was engulfed in flames and ready to bake me alive in her arms. Maybe now—

"Queen Carmine? Do we interrupt?" Manoel and Jovita are on the side lawn with me. Both are drying their hands on a towel, and they have crimson stains on their clothes. A busy night for all the medics.

"No, I...no, you don't interrupt."

"We are going to bed now. All the injured are stable." Manoel smiles. He's exhausted, indicated by the bags under his eyes.

"Your soldiers demonstrate remarkable vitality," Jovita adds. "They should each of them live through the night. But nurses will monitor."

I'm trying to pay attention, but Katie Lopez is shifting nervously between my ears. She says, *Hannah Walker. Hannah Walter, the Cheerleader, is here for Chase. Or maybe me. If I leave, these people should be safe.*

"You are okay, Queen Carmine? We will see you in the morning?"

"Yes. Yes, thank you Manoel," I say. "And you, Jovita. You are miracle workers."

"You should rest now," Jovita adds. "Because you are very pale. Good night." She takes her husband by the hand and draws him away.

I'm struck by the tenderness of their fingers interlocking. Momentarily I forget the Cheerleader and watch the two physicians. Before they disappear around the corner, she leans her head wearily on his shoulder. A hollow ache opens in my chest, or maybe it's always been there but I've ignored it. Holding hands. Off to bed with a lifelong companion. Perfect.

I feel isolated by comparison. Alone. I have no right to self-pity; even now my skin prickles with the awareness of watchful Guardians. I'm surrounded by them, and they stare at me. I'm very much not alone, but that doesn't prevent the ache. Kayla is nearby. Mason is grabbing a few hours of sleep in the adjacent house. I could go find either of them? Or even Tank, a man who adores me. Anything to stop the sudden awful hurt. Most likely the despondency is a side effect of remembering Katie Lopez. She had family and boyfriends and a full cafeteria table. Carmine has...needy acolytes. Carmine has responsibilities only. Carmine has nothing.

I'm being unreasonable and I know it - this is the corresponding depression following battle. However, it's never been this crushing before...

Carmine.

I'm at the door to Tank's bedroom, my hand on the knob. How did I get here? The house is quiet, except for me. I'm gasping for air and leaking hot tears.

I'm not alone. I'm not. I'm not.

You're not alone, Carmine. Get a grip.

I'm a warrior. A queen. I shed blood tonight. A lot of it. I am above petty human desires and needs.

Except that I don't feel above anything.

Don't. Go. Into that room.

Why not?

You're being selfish.

I'm entitled to a little selfishness, Katie.

You had a week on a private yacht!

Alone! Totally alone, except for Saul!

Tank will solve ZERO problems! Trust me. He'll create new problems. Bigger ones.

I only want someone to hold my hand. I'm finding more of you, and this is the price to pay. Suddenly my need for companionship is stronger. This is your fault.

You don't want to hold Tank's hand anyway.

You have no idea what I want.

Yes I do. And he's not in that room.

Ugh. She's right. Now I'm sitting in the hall, hugging knees to my chest. Keep it together, Carmine. Hold onto your sanity. I feel madness at the fringes. I'm not yearning for companionship as much as I'm yearning for a person. A certain person.

Chase.

I don't want to be like that orc. Broken. Mad. Lost to myself. A slave devoted to the disease. I need to keep myself intact, retain humanity. I need to love. And to be loved.

But I will not throw myself at the feet of any man. I can be strong and still have desires. Can't I? I can. I must. Where is Saul? I need counsel. I need help.

Outside, supply trucks rumble into the neighborhood. Fresh food and drink and medical supplies. Something to occupy my mind. I unlimber and stand to greet them, and I'm surprised to see the foremost truck is being driven by the Priest, the leader of our Law Keepers. A man too pretty to do hard work, usually. Maybe I was wrong about him.

And that's when the military alarms begin wailing.

- 5 -

The Outlaw

Samantha and I meet with General Brown on DeVry University's campus, a temporary command post, until two in the morning. The mood is somber and quiet. Missile strikes against Walter's mobile infantry units aren't effective, so what should we do? We don't have an endless supply of ammunition. Electricity? Fire? All options are open, especially because reinforcements appear to be en route for both the Federal Army and Walter. The size of our enemy will double.

The Priest is here too, the Overseer of Law Keepers, about to leave and deliver fresh supplies to Katie. He's essentially our police captain, and he's working hand in hand with the military. Normally a picture of pristine self-possession, tonight his clothes are disheveled and his hair's a mess. My opinion of him rises a few notches.

"Now the queen's back, our defenses should hold," Brown says, leaning over a digital map on a dusty table in DeVry's former English department.

"For how long?" I ask.

The Priest answers, "Couple more weeks. Then supplies run low, according to the Governess."

Brown says, "We can't reach the outside world. Cut off."

"Will we get help from the Resistance?"

"Should. But they're doing no better than we are." Brown lifts his eyes from the map to Samantha and me. "We gotta make our own magic."

Samantha snaps a nod. "Understood. I got magic coming out my ass, starting tomorrow night."

I explain, "We're going into their camp and dragging the commanders out."

The Priest looks relieved, like a dead man given hope.

Brown says, "That's what I like to hear. Now the queen's back, we'll run our plans past her first. This is mutant stuff, her territory. Now get some sleep. Military housing is one street to the south."

DeVry's campus is adjacent to Bonelli regional park, which is now an enormous chicken coop. Outside the building we hold our noses; the stench is brutal. We stroll across DeVry's extensive parking lot (packed with M860 semi-trailers and jeeps) to our Prius. I snatch Samantha's elbow, stopping her mid-stride.

"Leggo."

"Someone's here."

"Who?" She withdraws her sidearm.

"Dunno. Don't shoot them, though."

"Don't tell me what to do. I shoot who I want to shoot."

A shadow detaches from the nearby parking lot lamp post. A man wearing a cloak. The Zealot. I feel his deep strength like a dormant volcano, and I cannot begin to guess his age. He asks, "May I join you?"

Samantha holsters her pistol. "Zealot. Don't be so creepy."

"Why are you quick to shoot strangers, Samantha?"

"Because it's a strange world, old man."

"Come, Zealot," I say, and I pop the Prius's trunk. "We getting our stuff and sleeping in those houses on Kellogg Park."

The three of us cross a dormant highway to the charming neighborhood taken over by the military. A man with a flashlight and radio directs us to a vacant house, because the others are full of sleeping soldiers. Samantha inspects the backyard and announces, "I'm sleeping outside. M'tired of being indoors and cramped." There's a pool but it's evaporated halfway down and thick with leaves. I fetch blankets and toss them onto reclining lawn chairs. "Hell yes," Samantha says, stretching out. "This is so much better than a Prius."

"Before you sleep, Samantha," the Zealot says, "may I hold your hand?"

"By all means," she yawns. "You can sing me a lullaby too."

He sits next to her and takes her hand. Suddenly, at skin contact, she gasps and closes her eyes. Her back arches slightly. "What are you doing?"

"I am looking at your pain."

"Why? How? It's like our lungs are touching."

His smile is apparent in the dark. "Our bodies and spirits can talk. Did you know this? I want to help."

"But—"

"Do you remember when last we met, Samantha?"

"Of course," she murmurs. "Five years ago. I was in Libya on a job."

"I held your hand then too. Such violence." The Zealot's voice is soft, and his words are clipped, as though English is his second language. Or third.

"…yeah…well…"

She doesn't speak for a few minutes. Because, I realize, she's fallen asleep. The Zealot lets go and chuckles, "She is wound tightly, this little one."

"What did you do to her, exactly?" I ask. I ball a blanket for a pillow and drape another over my body.

"I gave her peace. And forgiveness. By connecting with her."

"The rumors about you aren't exaggerated, Zealot."

He laughs. "That is good to hear! Yes. Please call me Saul. Neither are the stories about you exaggerated, Outlaw."

"What stories are those? The paper gets most facts wrong."

"I do not read the papers. I talk to friends."

"Friends like Carter?" I'm tired and I yawn so big my jaw cracks.

"I know Carter, yes, and we spoke. And others. They are right: you have the ability to lead us. A dangerous gift, and one they very much fear."

"I've heard that. Samantha explained it once. That the Infected cannot endure one another, except for me. Like alpha predators who refuse to share territory."

"I do not use the term Infected, because I prefer the Cursed. But yes, you are correct. I feel your influence too. As does my friend PuckDaddy. As did Croc, before his death. So does the girl called Blue-Eyes. She could have killed you, but she did not. Yes?"

"True. I was helpless."

"That is your gift."

"I wish it worked on the Variants, but the Chemist did something to their biology."

"The Variants are the dangerous outcome of playing a deity. Victim and villain. But the Cursed? We are proud. We do not wish to be led. So for hundreds of years we lived in shadow. Alone. But now the world has shrunk and technology speeds us up and brings us together, and so we clash. But they have heard of you. We know your influence. Your enemies have been warned and will not parlay with you. Russia and Carter, they both did wish you dead but could not. Because they were unable. Because of your gift."

"Do you believe I'll become like them as I age? Angry and power hungry?"

"No. I do not. You have the inner fire. You have a purity. Which is why you must lead the young. The young will follow you. The young like Samantha and PuckDaddy. There is a girl in China, too. In Hangzhou. One day she may need you. I hope you will help her, if the need comes."

I nod, sleep becoming a heavier need.

"May I hold your hand?" he asks.

"Sure." And he does, and suddenly we fall into each other. He's everywhere in my world, down to the tectonic plates of memory. My emotions are magnified and my thoughts race. I'm dimly aware I possess the ability to resist, but why would I? It's an exhilarating sensation, like a free fall and too much oxygen is rushing through my nostrils. Then he releases.

"Whoa," I wheeze. "Is that what Katie's Guardians feel when they connect?"

"Possibly, yes, a little." He's giggling. The sound of a child laughing with untainted joy. "You are a delight, Outlaw. You bless me."

"That was weird, Saul."

"You have so much love. And loyalty. And determination. So rare, and I am blessed. The girl, though, Carmine. She will need all of it."

"What do you mean?"

He waves his hand towards the west, and he settles on his lawn chair, facing me. "She is troubled. Much is asked of her. Great trials and responsibilities. One day she may lose herself to violence."

"The same way the Cheerleader is lost?"

"I do not know. I have not met her. Perhaps it is as you say."

"Did she mention the Inheritors?" I ask.

"The children?"

"They're alive, Saul. I know it."

"Our future. Our hope and our destruction, I fear."

"Exactly," I say. "I want to help her. The burden is too great, and those kids are paramountly important."

"One day the children will need guidance too. You must help."

"She won't tell me where they are."

He shrugs and gathers a blanket. "I do not know either. We must trust her. Perhaps, for the moment, she knows what is best."

And suddenly the sirens begin to wail. I'm jolted upright, disoriented. Missiles inbound, death from above. No sleep tonight.

- 6 -

Carmine

Once again Federal fire rains from the sky, and once again our rockets rise as an umbrella shield. Bright thunder echoes across the Los Angeles basin. The forces of good and evil clashing in the atmosphere, neither giving an inch. I return to Northridge Road on the western side of our Kingdom and we watch the light show until six in the morning. Helpless. Powerless, safety entrusted into the hands of technology and military might. The Guardians watch too and we connect so strongly that I'm disoriented, dizzy and motion sick.

Katie Lopez feels the intrusion too. She groans between my ears and says, *I'm going insane. I always knew I would.*

Our shield cracks and fails as daylight dawns. Missiles touch down two miles distant. Tufts of earth erupt in sequence, and a larger explosion uncoils upwards. Fire and sonic shockwaves, which hurt our ears. Something *big* blew up.

"Fuel depot," Mason guesses, rubbing his weary eyes. "That secondary explosion. In Panorama City, I bet."

More missiles rupture the horizon, too far for us to determine targets. Why are these weapons getting through?? I want to call Brown or PuckDaddy and demand answers, but I know they're busier than I am at the moment. Doing their best. As frustrated as we are. They'll update me later, and in the meantime I can best serve them by shutting up. Trust people to do their jobs.

Kayla is sitting crisscross in the grass crying. "Why? Why are they doing this? We've done nothing to them!"

We live, Kayla. We threaten them by our existence, because they are afraid of what they can't control. Of what they don't understand. They fear. They hate. And we suffer.

The Guardians are excited, and my head buzzes. I cover my ears and close my eyes. "Get out, get out," I repeat over and again, but they're everywhere. Pressure builds, a star going supernova between my temples.

Katie Lopez is panting and she says, *I can't stop it! What's happening??*

All of a sudden, my vision shifts. Los Angeles is gone. I'm in a dark room, and the sound is distorted. Large blue eyes peer intently into mine. A face so beautiful I want to cry.

Where is she? she says.

Los Angeles, I reply. But I'm not in Los Angeles. I'm in a temple or a chamber or some black place I've never seen, except in these hallucinations.

Where? the girl with blue eyes asks.

I—I'm not sure. There are rockets…what is this? Where am I?

Are you in there, little queen? Can you hear me?

Yes.

The beautiful face smiles, a cruel twist to her lips, and she raises a pistol. A burst of brilliant light.

My face breaks, and the supernova star collapses inwards, a black hole of agony, and I scream. I scream and scream.

And I'm rolling across grass.

"Carmine! Queen Carmine!"

Kayla's voice. She's here. The black chamber is gone. My hands clutch my face and I'm relieved to find it's whole, unbroken, no gunshot wound. What *happened.*

I don't know! I was somewhere else. And it hurt.

Kayla holds my hand and peers into my eyes. "Sweetheart? Are you okay?"

"Kayla?"

"You were talking to someone. Where are you injured?"

"It's over. I'm fine." Although I don't sound fine; my voice shakes.

Dalton helps me to my feet and he says, "Bedtime for you, kid. And I won't hear any arguing."

"Dalton, I'm okay."

"You want me to carry you? Or you want to walk?"

Carry me, please, Katie responds.

Dalton and I glare for a tense moment but he's not giving in, and I cannot let the hundreds of Variants see me carried. "Walk. Big bully."

Twenty-two Guardians and three hundred soldiers. Those were our loses from the battle last evening. And an additional nine killed at the fuel depot explosion this morning. Far too many. We bury our dead at the San Fernando Mission, an elegiac gruesome process. Turkey vultures descend from the angry sky north on the Interstate, towards the massacre of Walter's forces.

Fresh provisions have been brought from Downtown, including crates of fruit and chicken, and barrels of water mixed with juice. Our forces and giants have plenty to eat.

I listen to Kayla's report from Manoel and Jovita's king-sized bed. I slept for three hours and my strength has returned but Dalton growls any time I attempt to rise. One would think the queen would have more say-so over her own life.

PuckDaddy rings my phone around noon.

"Sabotage," he says. "Again."

"Explain."

"Two more Patriot missile systems went offline during the night, leading to the defensive collapse. That's how the Federal rockets got through. Some jerk is visiting our trucks and physically breaking the radar. It's not electrical, otherwise Puck the Almighty could prevent it."

"Any leads?"

"Zero. General Brown's investigating but this is looking for a needle in a needle stack, you know?"

"I'm assigning two Guardians to each of our trucks. We can't allow this. I'll send them shortly for his dispersal."

"Good idea. I'll alert him. How's everything on the western front?"

I hesitate. If Puck knows about my collapse and the visions, he'll inform Chase and Saul, and those two have enough on their hands at the moment. Besides, I don't really know what happened. Probably just sleep deprivation messing with my brain. Kayla thinks I should tell him and she's glaring at me.

"We're all good over here, Puck," I say.

Liar! We are NOT!

- 7 -

The Outlaw

Midnight. A MH-6 Little Bird helicopter warms its engines at the Ontario International Airport and the pilot gives me a thumbs-up. We're good to go.

General Brown grabs my vest and yells in my ear, "You won't have long. Once the pilot hits eight thousand feet, he's coming back down, double-time. If they launch Surface-to-Airs, he's coming back no matter the altitude. Roger that?"

"Yessir. We'll be quick."

The Little Bird's rotors begin throwing air wash across the tarmac. Samantha and I salute the General and run to the aircraft, ducking out of habit. It's a tiny chopper, barely big enough for the two of us. We put on headsets and the pilot calls, "Ready, Majors?"

"Take us up!"

"Yes sir! An honor!"

He increases the throttle and engines scream. Our landing gear lifts gently off the concrete and we hurl into the stars. He's gaining altitude as fast as the machine allows. He flies north, getting us closer to the target. The metal shakes and I hold tight. It's been a while since I've done this, and my stomach flips and flops as Los Angeles diminishes. Sixty second later and the airport is a distant prick of light.

Samantha laughs and screams in pleasure.

Voices blare in my ears.

"Five thousand feet."

"We got a radar lock."

"DEW standing by."

"No launch. Weapons hot."

"Six thousand feet."

Samantha and I crowd the door, ready to jump. Our toes hang over nothing, facing east. The rotors beat us senseless.

"Seven thousand feet."

"We have enemy ignition! Inbound!"

"Two rockets, Riverside!"

The helicopter jolts violently and the pilot yells, "Times up! Good luck, Majors!"

Samantha and I leap into roaring black. We tumble apart, gaining distance from the Little Bird. The air is hard and cold and I steady myself, bringing order from chaos. The horizon partially stabilizes. I clip my gloves onto pant hooks and haul my arms forward. The air hits with a snap. Instant wings. I fasten the leg webbing into place and I rocket forward, flying on a hard surface that slices through the night like a glider.

To my right, enemy SAMs streak for the Little Bird. Nothing I can do to help, but the Directed Energy Weapons can. Friendly lasers find the rockets and ignite their payloads. An eruption of light and fire behind me, loud in my ears despite the wind. A wave of superheated air passes under and thrusts me higher into the atmosphere on my journey westward, out of the Kingdom and into foreign territory.

Fifty feet to my right, Samantha is a black phantom. She's a hundred feet below and she crosses enemy lights as I watch.

Her voice crackles in my ear. "With me, Outlaw?"

"Above you. Pick a spot and I'll follow."

She twists her shoulders and banks left, following Interstate 15, barely visible around the foot of mountains. Flying with the wing-suit is like free falling downwards AND forwards, an amazing rush; I can't catch my breath.

Puck's voice pumps into our ears, "The almighty and handsome PuckDaddy recommends the San Manuel Amphitheater, at the highway intersection. Big landing spot and it's abandoned."

We are mere shadows, infiltrating enemy territory in secret. Our parachutes open with a crack, and I'm nearly yanked out of my vest. We touch down on a grassy field and retrieve the chutes. Nearby Interstate 215 is busy with jeeps and trucks operating sans headlights.

Puck whispers, even though no one else could possibly hear him, "First stop, amigos. The Glen Helen Raceway, a mile south, home of Federal gasoline tankers. Get started, because PuckDaddy needs a nap."

Samantha and I move south on Glen Helen Road through low scrubby hills in total isolation. We could be on Mars, talking to Nasa. This part of the city is dust and brush, and we run through dirt racetracks after leaving the hills. The Federal gasoline tankers are a half mile off 215, around an old track. They sit quietly, awaiting use; only one tanker is drained at a time. Destroy their fuel, destroy their spirit. This is one of three large fuel depots, but we cannot visit them all in a single night. Guards patrol on jeeps with searchlights but we're quick and invisible. We hold our breath and plant small packets of C4 in vulnerable spots and hope they don't blow. Receivers switch on and Puck confirms he's getting a signal. We set six and move parallel to Institution Road, away from the racetrack and into the heart of the enemy's camp.

Much of their infantry has hunkered downtown in San Bernardino, but the command posts are in Shandin Hills and Ridgeline. Puck directs us through the California State University San Bernardino campus and student housing, south to the Shandin Hills Middle School. The adjacent neighborhoods are crawling with trucks, artillery, and ordnance. Radios squawk everywhere. We set more C4 charges on stacks of crates and vehicle gas tanks.

We've used up half the night when we finally arrive at their HQ, tired and cranky. We rest a moment on the roof of a 7-11 and shove chocolate granola bars into our mouths.

"This is not a lot of fun," I note.

"I haven't shot *anyone*."

"Listen, dumbasses. The middle school you're looking at is the Federal command post, but, this late, most military leaders are asleep. Housing is on Sheridan Road, that street in front of you. I don't know who sleeps where, though."

"Kidnap the commanders in their sleep. I love it when a plan comes together." Samantha grins.

"First things first," I say. "Secure an egress."

She whispers, "I got my eye on those FMTVs," and she indicates the parking lot with her chin.

"The camouflage cargo trucks?"

"Yes, the FMTVs."

"No one knows what that means, Gear."

She scoffs. "It's a disgrace you were awarded the military rank of major."

"Shut up and let's go."

"Roger that, stupid."

Six big trucks are lined up, ready for use. Keys in the ignition. Gas tanks over half full. Samantha sets charges on two of them and climbs into a third. She slides into the passenger seat, a pistol in her fist. I fire the engine, which is the loudest thing I've ever heard. It's a wonder Blue-Eyes herself doesn't hear us in Washington. I ease the truck into gear and lurch out of the parking lot and onto Sheridan. I stop a few houses in. She holds up two rolls of duct tape.

"You hit," she says, "and I gag."

"Roger that, Shooter. Puck, you plot us a way out of here."

"Roger that, dummies."

The houses are stucco ranches, once pleasant but now overgrown and militarized. We hustle through a garage and into a kitchen. We're surprised to find a lamp on and a man working on an iPad at the dining room table. He's wearing a crisp brown uniform and going gray at the temples. I don't know much about ranks, but he appears important.

The officer glares. "You're not authorized to be here, soldiers."

Samantha says, "Hit him. Duct tape's ready."

The man's eyes widen at my mask and he stands. "Outlaw. Shooter."

"I told you to lose the mask," she hisses. "Now hit him."

"I can't hit him," I say. "He's looking at me. It's weird."

"Who sent you?"

"We sent ourselves, old man." Samantha cocks the hammer of her gun. "Let me see those hands. Who else is in this house?"

"I am Colonel Wallace of the United States Army, and I request asylum."

A moment of silence.

I say, "What's that mean?"

"It means, I'm coming with you. Sir."

The three of us stare uneasily.

I say, "I hear someone snoring, in the back of the house."

"My aide. The rest of my staff is next door."

"Why would you request asylum?" Samantha demands.

Puck notes, "This feels atypical."

"The military is being ordered to enforce sanctions which are unconstitutional and unlawful. A third of the brass I know is considering resigning. There is no more America," Colonel Wallace says. "I'm going with you. You have something worth dying for."

Samantha and I share a glance — do we trust him?

"Additionally, I request you bring two other officers," he says. "And we need to hurry. Reveille is at 0500."

Thirty minutes later, we're rolling down windy Little Mountain Road. Colonel Wallace rides with us in the noisy cab, and two Brigadier Generals ride in the back with their aides. Samantha has one pistol pressed into the Colonel's kidneys and one pointed backwards through the rear window into the cargo area.

"You act funny," she growls, "and I'll shoot your teeth out."

"Yes, ma'am."

"Outlaw, ditch the mask."

I pull the red mask from my face, grind the gears, and drive westwards on Highway 210 towards home. We've got fifteen miles to freedom, and ten thousand troops in our way. But Colonel Wallace should be our golden ticket.

"It's hard to believe," he half laughs. "It's really you."

Samantha says, "The cameras make us look fatter, but we're thin. You can feel my abs."

"I wouldn't dream of such an honor, ma'am."

"Go ahead. Pure muscle. I won't even suck in. Or shoot you."

I ask, "So there's unrest in the Federal military?"

Colonel Wallace nods. "Unrest and damn near mutiny. Majority of the officers are loyal to the office of the President, but the troops are divided. Some defect to join the Resistance, and others talk of finding Queen Carmine. We hear the rumors. General Adkins has begun shooting deserters himself."

"And you side with Queen Carmine?" Samantha asks.

"I side with the Constitution. Seems to me, Queen Carmine is the only leader in sight offering true freedom. You wouldn't believe what the President and his Secretary of State are asking the military to do to citizens."

"How soon does the military attack Los Angeles?"

He gives a crisp head shake. "We don't. No such orders."

"I'm confused. Then why the show of force? It's not easy to move an army that big."

"Our orders are to prevent your escape eastward. The President expects the mutants to eradicate one another," he responds.

"He's talking about Walter?" I ask. "In the north?"

"And the southern mutant, codenamed Russia. We're simply a barrier to the east, witnesses to the coming slaughter."

Samantha and I are grim. It makes perfect sense. Russia plans to join the fray. He and Walter will coordinate attacks and crush the Kingdom on opposing fronts. They've joined in an effort to capture or eliminate Carmine's Variant army, and I don't see why it won't work.

Samantha asks, "When does Russia attack?"

"Unknown, ma'am. He isn't our ally, but for the moment he isn't our enemy. His purpose aligns with the President's."

Puck has been listening from my earpiece and he says, "More accurately, it aligns with Blue-Eyes's purpose. She hates Carmine."

We roll through two checkpoints easily. Colonel Wallace flashes his identification and no questions are asked. At the third gate, however, the guard takes his ID card and walks into the small outpost.

"Potential trouble," Wallace mutters under his breath. "Get ready on the gas."

"Oh gosh I hope there's trouble," Samantha sighs.

The guard comes back and returns the identification. "Negative, Colonel Wallace. You're entering a restricted area without authorization."

"General Adkins—"

"I spoke with the General's aide, sir. You're not authorized. Use the junction to turn your truck around, Colonel."

I'm holding my breath, but I know the moment has arrived - we fight our way out. Quietly, I put the truck into first gear.

Wallace says, "Pass a message for me, Corporal. Tell General Adkins that the Outlaw and Colonel Wallace requests he blow it out his ass."

Samantha grins and raises her pistol, aiming between the guard's widening eyes. "Double-time, handsome."

There are two other guards nearby who've taken an interest in our truck. Time to go. I mash my foot on the gas and we lumber forward. In my sideview, I see the guard bolting for his outpost and radio.

"It's about to get loud," I note.

"Scuse' me, Colonel," Samantha says and she climbs lithely over him, through the window and onto our roof. I hear her screaming with delight.

In my ear, Puck says, "Oh heck. Shooter lost her mind."

"Puck, alert General Brown that we'll be coming in hot with precious cargo."

"Roger that, Outlaw. And I like that we all say 'Roger' now."

Colonel Wallace retrieves a radio from the truck's dash and says, "I can help the cause."

"Do it."

He turns the device, on, depresses the talk bar, and barks, "Four-eight to forward base. We have insurgents in-wire, moving east on sixty-six. Recommend immediate action." He releases the bar and grins. "That'll play hell at command."

The radio squawks, *"One-one to four-eight, say again."*

We max at seventy miles per hour and the Colonel keeps conveying false information. But we're not free. At least one more checkpoint lies ahead and I see oncoming headlights in my side views. Samantha bangs on the ceiling.

"I see them!" I call. "Can't go any faster!"

In my ear, "Outlaw, Puck suggests we ignite the fuses."

"Good idea. Set us on fire, Puck."

"Boom, baby." Even though we're ten miles distant and inside a screaming truck, the explosions are audible. The fuel trucks detonate one by one, a staccato of eruptions, and the northern horizon glows red.

"Wow. Nice work, guys. I'm watching on satellite. You may burn down the west coast," Puck hoots.

We're being trailed by four jeeps so far. Samantha's pistol cuts loose, and the headlights behind us shatter in succession. Eight shots, no misses.

"She's doing that with a pistol?" Colonel Wallace asks.

"Wait till you see her mad."

She fires again and the foremost truck's tire bursts. Brakes scream and the driver overcorrects, and for a moment the jeep rides on two wheels, verging on flipping.

"It's going to get dicey in a half click," Wallace warns. "The final outpost will have their hydraulic barricade raised. Our truck will have the guts ripped out if we don't stop."

"Puck, you hear that?"

"The almighty PuckDaddy is on the job, homie! The barricade is on a simple circuit, and can be activated remotely. Child's play."

The highway curves slightly south and the checkpoint comes into view. Blazing lights across the wild cloverleaf interstate junction.

I bang on the ceiling. "Eyes front, Shooter!"

Colonel Wallace yells into his radio, "Highway 210 outpost, hold your fire! Hold your fire!"

But they've been alerted to his machinations. Semi-automatic weapons unleash and chew into our heavy armor. Fortunately they haven't been able to point the heavy guns inward.

Samantha opens with a pistol in each first. We can't watch her work but we see the results. Spotlights extinguish. Sparks fly. Men fall from their perches. The checkpoint is being disintegrated with pinpoint accuracy.

"Hot damn," Colonel Wallace shouts.

Samantha and I see the anti-tank rocket launcher at the same time. A man stands on the Interstate 15 overpass, bracing an AT4 on his shoulder. Its heavy warhead will punch through our vehicle and detonate.

"Samantha! Rocket!"

"I see it!"

Everything happens at once.

The soldier fires the rocket propelled grenade.

Samantha fires.

I swerve.

There is a violent eruption in front of our windshield. We're bathed with fire, shrapnel puncturing the hood, and something heavy penetrates the road under our tires and lurches the truck to the side.

"I shot it!" she screams, and the truck's sudden jolt tosses her backwards and onto the canvas ceiling. "I shot the rocket!"

"I think she actually did," Wallace says. He's sweating and cursing. "That's impossible. I didn't even see it."

"Puck, how about that barricade? We're about to connect."

"Dropping now."

The barricade is built like a heavy steel ramp, set reverse in the street. Before the truck is eviscerated at seventy miles per hour, the barricade lights flash once and the mechanism flattens. Our truck passes safely over top.

"Who the hell is this Puck?" asks Wallace.

"A friend."

"Well, he's got serious pull."

We roar under the cloverleaf junction and into the darkness beyond. Our headlights are broken but I don't need them. Highway 210 runs straight as an arrow for ten more miles, taking us home, and our pursuers have stalled at the checkpoint. They won't chase us into our Kingdom.

I take a deep breath and inform my passengers, "We're free. Nothing but clean air."

"Step on it," Samantha says in my ear. Her voice is weary. "That shrapnel about cut me in half. I need a nap."

"You require medical care?"

"Send that good looking Colonel up here. He can unzip the vest and see my abs for himself."

I debate telling the Colonel this, but he seems discombobulated enough as it is. My foot mashes the pedal further into the deck. "Almost there."

"Chase, now that the action's over, we need to talk about Queen Carmine," Puck says. His words sound hesitant and worried, and the hairs on my neck stand on end.

"What about her? What's wrong?"

"She's sick or something, but she's hiding it. Kayla told me. She's hallucinating."

I'm on the way.

- 8 -

Carmine

Nuts has worked overtime to install new water turbines at a secondary aqueduct, so if Walter breaks through and destroys our water filtration plant in Sylmar then we won't lose total power. The little man is exhausted, and he talks about a nap for the first time since I've known him. He gives me a piercing final inspection and stalks back to work without another word.

If I had an army of Nuts, I could take over the world. He is never a problem, only a solution.

After my meeting with him, Kayla and I invade an abandoned Denny's off Interstate 5, near our western border. Dalton stands out front, arms crossed. No one gets in.

"There are three hundred thousand people in the Kingdom," Kayla says. "And only fifty thousand are combatant. The rest are families and people trying to survive."

"I know this."

"They need to hear from their queen." She sits beside me and adjusts the red silk compresses on my elbows and shoulders, fussing about finding a more flattering pattern. As usual I look like a sweaty warrior and she sparkles and smells like frosting. She's focusing all her energy on my mood, trying to cheer me up but it's not working. A Chic-fil-A breakfast sandwich would do the trick, but we're fresh out of functional chain restaurants.

"Why? What have you heard?"

"They're scared. The Kingdom doesn't have a news channel so they only hear rumors and lies on CNN. Rumors that they're going to die or be enslaved."

I lower my head onto the table and sigh. "Everything was fine until that stupid bomb. And then Walter decided to attack. Saul is right, Kayla, people hate without reason. Walter hates and attacks because he has nothing better to do. It's his religion."

She remains silent.

"Are the people correct? Will they die because I promised I could help them start a new life and I was wrong?"

"They have faith in you. I have faith in you. Even if we fall, I will *still* follow you."

I bang my head slightly on the table. The Denny's restaurant is surrounded by hundreds of Guardians, maybe thousands, peering in through the windows. Looking for their leader. Looking for hope. And their combined interest makes my concentration swim. "Issue a statement, Kayla. Tell the people that I will not rest until they're safe. Our entire planet is in danger and powerful people hate us without cause, but we won't give in. We cannot. Each of us will do his or her job, and we'll work hard, and we'll be the light this world needs. Stay together. Stay with me. Stay alive."

"Yes Queen Carmine." She types into her phone at light-speed and she's so happy she turns pink.

I take a deep breath to steady my nerves. This place smells like spoiled cooking grease and rat urine and mold.

And gasoline.

Katie Lopez shifts uneasily between my ears. I feel the same way, Katie. We know that scent. The Cheerleader is nearby, lurking. I've detected her several times in recent days. That crazy woman is the last thing we need. Kayla and I should relocate before nightfall.

The bell over the entrance jingles. The Outlaw is there, filling up the doorway. He's vastly different than pictures I've seen of his youth - now he's a thick warrior wearing a tattered vest, the dirty mask hangs from his neck, his arms are crisscrossed with scars and tattoos, and his knotty muscles flex as he makes anxious fists. He's twenty-one, or close to it, and in need of a shave and trim. He used to be a boy, a lifetime ago, but now he's the people's champion, the man our world demanded, the man who suffers so others don't have to. What is a man? I read in one of my leadership books that a man exhausts himself in service to a cause greater than himself, and that he can be judged by his relationships. What is a man? I know it when I see it, and it's Chase Jackson. He's the one thing that might cheer me up, and I wonder if I'll always have such an ardent reaction upon first glimpse. His eyes are wild and feverish and they don't leave mine. Samantha Gear enters with him, wearing heavy gauze taped across her midsection and shoulder. Saul comes after and closes the glass door.

Katie Lopez hums happily.

Kayla smiles and claps. "Gang's all here!"

"Except for Mason," I reply. And General Brown and the Governess, but I don't want to ruin her moment.

"Mason and Tank are patrolling the border," she says.

Chase Jackson slides into the booth next to me and takes my hand. The distant rumble of headache dissipates and the swirling steadies. He says, "What's a good-looking girl like you doing in a dump like Denny's?"

Katie Lopez smiles, and it's such a warm emotion that I smile too. "I'm not dressed for the fancier restaurants."

"I have it on good authority that leggings and red silk are fashionable now."

Kayla calls PuckDaddy and put him on speaker. Samantha slides into the booth next to Kayla and Saul gets a chair. Our war council would be better with Denny's pancakes, but we don't live in a pancake universe any longer.

Samantha Gear takes a deep breath and says, "This Denny's has been abandoned for months but something smells delicious. Like...frosting."

Kayla's face reddens, and she chirps, "Who knows! But isn't this fun? We're all together! Talking!"

The Outlaw squeezes my hand. "Tell me about your hallucinations."

"Who tattled on me?"

"Everyone. Saul believes it's related to the Variants."

The wise old man nods and comments, "I too sometimes feel overly connected with others, and I feel what they feel. This is why I taught you, Carmine, to detach them from your mind."

"I know. You did. But there's thousands of them."

"Tell me about the hallucinations," the Outlaw says again.

"First, give me details from last night."

He does. He tells me about the helicopter jump, the fuel trucks, the defecting military officers, and their harrowing escape. "Here's the most important detail we've learned so far: the Federal military isn't planning an attack. At least, no attack other than missile strikes, which are being launched out of state."

"Why no attack?"

"Because the commanders worry your Guardians will cut them into ribbons. The President ordered the army to simply keep us in place and let the mutants kill each other," he says.

"His plan might work."

"It gets worse. The Colonel we spoke to says Russia will coordinate with Walter. They plan to attack simultaneously. Soon."

The news crushes me. I feel air leak from my spirit. Hope fading. We were already outnumbered, and now the warlord from San Diego is joining the fray.

"The whole world is arrayed against us," I mutter.

Samantha Gear gives a short nod. "Just the way I like it."

"They hate us because they don't trust me."

"They hate you because they *hate*," Saul says. "It is simple. And the virus provides the means to act."

"Tell me about the hallucinations," Chase says. "Please."

"Why are you so worried?"

"Because I love you."

"Awwww," Kayla says.

"And because I don't think they're normal hallucinations. Eyewitnesses say you acted like you'd been wounded. Saul wonders if Walter is somehow using the connection to hurt you."

"How could he do that?" I ask, but there's an immediate ring of truth to his statement. My skin crawls.

"You feel what the Guardians feel. If he's captured some of your Guardians, perhaps he can hurt you *through* them. Hurt them, hurt you."

"Or perhaps, see what you see," Saul notes. "If you have visions of what others see, perhaps the reverse is also true."

"Spy on me? Or maybe I should say, spy through me?"

"Maybe," he says. "As far as I know, nothing like the strength of your connection has existed before. And I'm old."

"It's not Walter." I shake my head, but I dread what comes next. "My vision isn't of him."

"What, then?"

I take a deep breath and slowly release. This news won't be received well. "I see a woman. With blue eyes."

Stunned silence. Chase tightens his grip on my hand. No one speaks, so I continue.

"I'm in a chamber, or a dark room. I can't move and she is there, asking what I see."

Chase's voice quavers. "Do you answer her?"

"Sometimes I do, and sometimes someone else does. A masculine voice. The last time it happened, the woman with blue eyes called me 'little queen' and asked if I could hear her. I said 'yes' so she raised a pistol and shot me."

Kayla gasps, "That's why you started rolling on the grass, holding your face."

Yes!

"Yes."

They look at me as though I might implode at any minute. As though I'm weak. Or a liability.

"So," Samantha Gear says after a long pause. "It's Blue-Eyes. And the bitch can hurt you. Maybe kill you."

I say, "I don't know. It's all so strange. It only happens in moments of extreme excitement. The connection has to be strong and buzzing. My head feels light and the visions start."

"Puck, are you listening?" Chase asks.

PuckDaddy's voice rattles from my phone. "Of course, dude. Totally freaked."

"Where was Blue-Eyes yesterday?"

"How should I know that?"

Kayla answers, "Because you know *everything,* my dear," and she turns red again.

"Well. That's only partially true. But I'll check. Blue-Eyes is really good at hiding. She left Washington a few days ago and I had no idea," the phone says.

"Where'd she go?"

"Atlanta."

Saul asks, "What is in Atlanta?"

"The CDC," Kayla responds. "The Centers for Disease Control. Someone spotted her there and posted it online."

Chase is squeezing my hand tight. "Is she still there?"

"Dunno. Like I said, she's sneaky." We can all hear Puck clicking on keyboards and drinking something. I realize I'm famished.

Saul asks, "This CDC. What does it do?"

"Studies disease," Chase says. "Like the Hyper Virus. I have a theory. Do you remember last year when the Herders captured handfuls of the Guardians and took them away in trucks? I think the abducted Guardians were taken to the CDC, and now Blue-Eyes is there. When Katie and the Guardians are excited, the connection is strong and I bet mutants feel it everywhere. Even in Atlanta. And Blue-Eyes discovered the connection and is trying to kill Katie through the connection by executing captives."

That woman is the worst. I do not often promote violence, but someone needs to remove her head.

I'm having a hard time focusing with Katie yammering in my ear. "Blue-Eyes's plan won't work. Guardians die near me often. Sad, but true. It hurts, but I'm okay."

"Yes, but Blue-Eyes is drawing you *inside* her captives before she executes them. She talks to you first. Somehow she summons your mind to her room, using the power of influence."

"That's not possible."

"But it's happening."

Samantha says, "And if she kills you, we're all dead. The Guardians rampage and Walter collects them."

Puck's voice buzzes, "Okay. So. Check this out. I think she's still in Atlanta, and I can confirm the CDC has incarcerated mutants. I'm browsing their secured servers."

Chase says, "That's it. That's what she's doing. She's going to break your mind from long range."

Not if I don't let her.

"Not if I don't let her."

"I wonder when the next flight to Atlanta is."

Samantha Gear has a dangerous glint in her eyes. "I was just thinking the same thing, Outlaw."

"Puck, find me a plane," he says.

I sputter, "You can't simply fly to Atlanta."

Don't let him go. Don't let him go.

"Sure I can. We'll fly low, under the radar, and jump out if they try to shoot us down."

"That's insane. You'll get hurt."

He laughs, one of my favorite aural sensations. "You expect me to let you die? I'll jump from a thousand airplanes and burn down a planet full of CDC buildings before that happens."

"No."

He grins. "I'll be back in twenty-four hours. Shooter will come to keep me company."

"Shooter will come to burn that bitch's ass," she mutters.

"PuckDaddy found you a plane," the phone says. "Fueled and ready to go."

"Excellent." Chase stands up. "I'll sleep during the ride."

Kayla's eyes are huge. "This is all happening so fast."

"Wait," I growl. Loudly. They wait. "We have one more thing to discuss."

"What?"

I blurt it out, because the longer I wait the harder it'll be, "The Inheritors."
Chase slowly sits back down.

The Inheritors, the children infected with the Hyper Virus at birth. Five hundred of them. They'll grow up and break the earth's crust, and I've done my best to shelter them but it's not enough. Time to come clean. "You were right," I tell him. "They exist."

"Where?"

"I know these kids are going to change everything when they reach eighteen. I know we'd be better off if they didn't exist. But we're not going to execute toddlers. Understood?"

Saul nods gravely.

Puck says, "Duh."

"Where are they?"

"They're hidden inside a monastery. South, between Los Angeles and San Diego. Directly in Russia's path. If he comes north in force, he could discover them."

"So," Samantha says, and she starts ticking her fingers. "The Federal Army is on our doorstep. Walter hangs over our heads with a pack of mutant freaks. The President is nuking cities. Russia will attack soon. Blue-Eyes is trying to kill Carmine with telepathy or something. *And* we have to protect a pack of babies."

Chase's head slowly swivels to examine our motley menagerie, beaten, tired and filthy. "And we're going to handle it. All of it. But we need help."

"Who?"

"Colonel Wallace, a defector from the Federal Army, says there are mutinies among the Navy ships parked off the west coast. Some of the captains have seceded from the Federal Government and declared loyalty to Queen Carmine. Many of those ships are transport ships. Let's radio one and have them pluck the Inheritors from a beach."

Kayla squirms nervously in her seat. "Do we trust them? I don't know much about those little gross kids, but yikes that sounds sketchy."

"Nothing about this is optimal," Chase says.

"I'd rather the Inheritors be on a Navy boat than with Russia," I say. "We could bring them into the Kingdom, but we're already dealing with sabotage, and I don't know how the Guardians would react. We're running low on options."

Puck rattles from the phone, "PuckDaddy doesn't hate that Navy plan. I can remotely monitor the boat, too."

I glance at Saul, who takes a deep breath and says, "Anything is better, I believe, that entrusting priceless lives to Russia. The man has a black heart. And I agree - a Navy boat would be better than inside your Kingdom at the moment."

I say, "Very well. Kayla, call General Brown and get us a boat. I'll get him exact coordinates soon. In the meantime, Chase and Samantha will fly to Atlanta and kill the witch. She dies and many of our problems go away. The rest of us will stay here and keep this city intact." I pause for contributions or objections but there are none. The die has been cast. "Good. Let's do it."

"But first!" Kayla cries, and she sends a text message. Immediately the front doors are thrown open and trays of food brought in. Sizzling hamburgers with real cheese on fresh buns, and freshly brewed iced tea. Real ice. My stomach gives a jolt.

"Kayla. How on earth?"

"It pays to be my friend!"

"Yeah, but how did you do this?"

She winks and giggles. "You can get anything on the black market. Even ice." Succulent food is set in front of all of us, and Samantha has to wipe her mouth. "I thought we could use a pick-me-up."

"Hell yeah we can," Samantha says.

The Outlaw raises his cup of iced tea, and we all follow suit. "A toast. To peace in our future."

"I'll drink to that," I say.

We clink cups and Kayla says, "Cheers!" and we eat the best hamburger of our lives, and we laugh together like we aren't about to die.

The meal ends too soon. I give coordinates and instructions to General Brown, and tell him I'll personally oversee the Inheritor-removal process. Samantha goes to find more weapons, in preparation for her flight. Kayla leaves to help the Governess deal with a food supply issue. Saul and Dalton climb into my Land Cruiser to debate theology.

In the Denny's parking lot, Chase and I embrace and he says, "If that woman gets into your head again, kick her out. No games. Give me twenty-four hours and I'll release her hostages. If things go well, I'll bring you the witch's head."

I have faith in you, Chase.

"I have faith in you."

He says goodbye and the distance spreads out between us like a gulf. I'm hit by some spasm of premonition - he'll be across the country, and if he dies I can't even bury his body. A sudden grief opens in my stomach, horrible fear.

He turns to leave and I catch his hand. "Chase. Before you go… I-I'm remembering more and more. I don't know you as well as I should, but I have these strong emotions, and… Just stay alive, okay?" I nod towards the city, and pretend my eyes aren't pooling with tears. "None of this will be worth it without you."

He nods slowly and his eyes are alive with pain and fiery determination. "I'm not going to leave you, Queen Carmine."

I try to smile but I can't. It hurts too much. "You can call me Katie. I'm her. She's me. More each day."

Suddenly he's wrapped me up, an intrinsically perfect embrace, and his scruffy face is pressed against mine. A sad desperate kiss which ruins me. Queens shouldn't be devastated by goodbye kisses but I am, and not only because Katie Lopez is weeping. I'm wrecked. He says, "You've always been my Katie. And you always will be."

Then he's gone.

Part Four

"To sleep, perchance to dream - ay, there's the rub,
For in that sleep of death what dreams may come
When we have shuffled off this mortal coil
Must give us pause"
- Hamlet

- 1 -

Carmine

General Brown calls my cell. He's exhausted and grouchy, likely running on three hours of sleep a night. "Explain this to me, queen. You want a Navy transport ship to fetch a pack of kids. That's a hard ask."

"Not only that, but I need it done in secret. Probably shouldn't even tell the crew."

"I need more information."

"Put me on the phone with the ship's captain," I snap, irritated. "I'll tell him what he needs to know. Those kids are the most important factor in your grandchildren's future. Trust me. Tomorrow morning I'll drive down and meet the ship myself. Get it done, General." I turn off the phone and debate smashing it on the street.

I miss Chase already.

I tell Dalton we're traveling south tomorrow to oversee the transfer of precious cargo. In typical Dalton fashion, he spends a couple hours overpacking the Land Cruiser like we'll be gone forever.

The day's wearing on, so I commandeer a motorcycle and drive to the frontline. Hundreds of Guardians follow, some on bikes and some *Running* and *Leaping* through the parallel neighborhoods. Their anger and thirst for battle pull at the edges of my consciousness, like stimuli on the periphery. It's as though I'm developing a sixth sense - I can't control them through my mind, but I *Feel* them. To my eyes they glow and the glow has spread to my inner sight, which means I'm able to locate Tank and Mason by following the buzzing and glow of their Guardian contingent. They're on the Balboa Bridge.

There is a difference between my Guardians and Tank's. He has a following of Variants who find their identity in him. I *Feel* his mutants but there is no strident connection. My strength is significant but nothing compared to his, and the Variants are drunk with it. Perhaps this betrayal of loyalties should bother me but I don't have the energy to be affronted.

Much to my surprise, Tank observes my approach with sad eyes. For the moment, his bravado and arrogance are dimmed and as I greet them on the bridge he says, "Too much is being asked of you, Katie."

"It's war, Tank. Too much is asked of all of us."

"But it's killing you."

Mason stands with his flight of Falcons, arms crossed over his chest. His comrades lean against their black bikes and sharper knives. Mason says, "I feel it too, Queen Carmine. The battle inside you rages."

"I'll survive," I say. "I have to."

Tank places a hand on my shoulder. He wears white gloves to hide his misshapen blocky fingers. "You're too good for this, babe. None of these people has ever deserved you. Let me take you away. I don't like watching you break."

It's an affectionate gesture, and he's trying to help, yet it won't work. I remove his hand; the Guardians can't think me weak. But I squeeze it to mitigate the rebuke, and say, "Keep us alive a couple more days, boys. Then many of our problems should go away."

"What's changed?"

I don't want them (or the Guardians) to be over-burdened with worry so I relate the highlights. "We know where Blue-Eyes is. The Outlaw and Shooter are flying to kill her. Plus, we received good news — the Federal Army isn't going to attack. They expect the mutants to kill each other off. We only need to resist Walter, and remove the mutant warlord Russia from power."

They are silent, digesting the changes in battlefronts. I stare north to the horizon and the hidden community of Santa Clarita. Walter's camp. I long to attack, bring death crashing around his ears, but he has thousands of innocent hostages. If we endanger their lives then we're no better than he is, but we can't delay much longer.

Dusk falls and, like grisly clockwork, alarms begin wailing. More incoming Federal missiles. I grind my teeth in frustration and watch our military scramble to action. Secure our defenses. Get the civilians underground. The President is going to pound our defenses *every* night? We don't have an unlimited supply of intercepting rockets.

The giants hate the noise and threaten to bolt into the forests so Tank stays with them at the water plant. He walks circles around their hulking, shivering forms, packed together for comfort, and he calms them.

Mason, Kayla and I gather on a roof in Granada Hills and watch the show. The black sky breaks and cracks in the distance, and it would almost be pleasant if not for our radios. General Brown and the Priest shout orders on different frequencies, organizing resources, a reminder that this isn't a simple fireworks show.

Once again the defense systems fail. Federal missiles get through and slam into our Kingdom. Burbank is perforated with mushrooms of fire, a half dozen strikes that we feel in our bones. The flashes light up Granada Hills like the sun, and it is during one of these flashes that I realize the enemy is among us.

A surprise attack! I watch in horror as wretched goblins secrete from sewer drains and manholes in the street.

"The sewers!" I scream, loud enough to be heard for miles. "Walter comes through the sewers! Protect the defenses!"

They pour from every street, slithering loose like demons. I land beside a manhole near our house and slam the heavy cover home, severing a mutant's arm. Mason and the Falcons tear down the road, heavy knives carving through enemies crawling from below. In a matter of seconds we're overrun, the neighborhood and the entire northern section of our Kingdom.

Walter and the Federal Army are collaborating. They have to be; the attacks are synchronized. He knew the rain of missiles would begin and planned accordingly. It must've taken an entire day to move this many fighters through the sewers, and they waited for the noise before spewing forth.

The Guardians are scattered but follow my voice, arriving in waves. Quickly the infestation in Granada Hills is staunched, making me realize the neighborhood isn't their target; they're after our missile defenses. For confirmation, there is a deafening eruption two blocks over at an anti-ballistic missile nest. Four patriot missiles self-destruct, flinging bodies into the sky and incinerating nearby houses.

"Protect the launchers!" I shout and we surge north. My impulses prod the Guardians in the right direction without vocalization.

Suddenly, the nightmare worsens. Like my eyes are playing tricks. A flood of wolves comes snarling from the west. Wolves?! They're so thick I can't see the ground. Like every wolf pack in North America combined into one master pack. Gray wolves, Great Plains, Rocky Mountain wolves, all of them. They loop into battle and attack our Guardians, driven to frenzy. A haunting and horrible sight, as endless as the Pacific.

I surge into the tide, opening their flesh with fingernails, and my connection to the Guardians strengthens our resolve. They subsume and magnify my anger. We fight east towards Mission Hills and San Fernando and the bulk of our missile defense, but the wolves are too thick and wretched Variants fall on us from above. Mason and the Falcons try to ride motorcycles but the wolves wash over and drown them.

There are so many that they form a floor of furry bodies, and other wolves run overtop. They loop across one another, snarling and slashing and hurting their own kind. Our Leapers *Jump* from the mire and land on roofs to get free.

This is impossible. There *can't* be this many.

Kayla is safe above and she's screaming, "There! Queen Carmine, look!"

I follow the direction of her finger.

A man stands in the distance on the roof of the LA Fire Department Station 18 house. Half man, half beast, highlighted by the brilliant eruptions. He is dressed in layers of raggedly cloaks, and his black hair touches his shoulders. I zero in. He's filthy, covered in grime and fleas, but he points his finger and the wolves obey. He howls and they respond.

He can communicate with animals, the same as Saul the Zealot. Walter has tricks up his sleeve. I need to get there but I can't break free and the wolves are cutting me to ribbons.

The Guardians are panicking. How do you fight an ocean of teeth? Our connection makes my head rattle, and I taste their fear.

Another battery of patriot missiles detonates, this one farther north. The eruption echoes the cracks in the atmosphere above Los Angeles. All is chaos and death.

All of a sudden, help arrives. A pair of thousand-pound tigers! I don't know where they came from but they *Launch* into the fray, jumping thirty feet at a time. Their claws are swords, teeth cages, muscles engines, and the air thickens with fur confetti and blood. The male tiger closest to me snaps spines with each crunch of his jaw. Pack mentality forces the animals to hurl themselves against the tigers but they're brought down three at a time with great sweeping paws. I smell musk and copper.

Finally I'm free and I *Leap* to the roof beside Kayla. My head swims and swirls. "Where? Where is the wolf man?"

"I lost him. He's running between houses on all fours."

"Okay...I'lll..."

I can't think. There's too many Guardians inside my head.

My consciousness spreads too thin. I feel what they feel, see what they see. "Carmine?"

The world dims. Los Angeles fades.

I'm gone.

The sounds are gone. Time collapses.

Replaced by a dark chamber. Like inside a temple. A beautiful voice drawing me.

A woman watches. A beautiful woman with blue eyes.

What do you see, little queen?

The wolf man, I say.

The wolf man. Interesting. I haven't had the pleasure.

What else do you see, she asks. What of your cute Byzantine empire?

No, a voice murmurs between my ears. Katie Lopez. ***Don't tell that witch a thing.***

The woman with blue eyes squints at me.

Are you resisting?

I'm pinned. Can't move. I try to shake my head but I cannot.

She touches my face.

Can you feel that?

Yes.

No. Shut up. Close your mouth.

Little queen.

Get us out. Fight this, Carmine.

I strain, and sweat streams down my face. Helpless.

The woman with blue eyes holds a flame to my skin. It burns.

Can you feel that, pretty little girl?

YES!

Don't answer! Resist!

My skin melts.

Katie rages and roars and I do too.

What…what are you doing? Stop that!

The vision of the temple rings, as if struck by a hammer.

Calm down, little queen. Just…relax.

I want to. My whole body wants to obey her.

NO!

But I won't.

I fight her, I push her out like Saul taught me.

Come back this instant.

A voice. Kayla's. "Queen Carmine! Wake up! Come back to me!"

The temple fades. Sounds rush into my ear canals. Los Angeles solidifies. I'm on the grass. Kayla holds my head in her lap and tigers prowl circles around us, primal chuffs. Dalton is here too, pistol drawn and ready to shoot anything that moves.

Katie Lopez pants between my ears.

I pant too. Or maybe it's just me I'm hearing. Katie's voice is becoming mine.

"Okay," I groan. "Okay, Kayla. I'm here."

"Are you sure? That was super scary. And what happened to your neck?"

I raise a hand and touch my throat gingerly. The skin is hot and tender, the skin twisted.

Blue-Eyes burnt me. In some dimension not quite epiphenomenal.

"It's war, Kayla. It happens. I'll survive. How long was I out?"

"The battle's over. They destroyed as many batteries as they could and retreated," she says. Even after battle Kayla looks beautiful. She's too good for this carnage, too sweet and innocent.

I ask, "And the wolves?"

"They ran. There are hundreds of dead carcasses, though, which is yuck. Your pet tigers fight like orange-striped death."

One of the animals stops near my face and nuzzles my ear with a heavy head. His breath is hot and sweet. I scratch the soft underside of his jaw, which is wet with blood, but I'm bleeding from a thousand cuts so I don't mind.

Slowly my pulse returns to normal.

I look past Kayla to the stars beyond. The battle in the sky is still furious. The smoke of spent artillery will arrive soon, and I feel the impact of enemy ordnance. The very ground moans in torment.

"We're going to lose, Kayla. There are too many of them, like an inexhaustible machine. And their weapons too terrible."

"Don't say that, sweetie. You're exhausted. I'll get help. I'll fetch Saul. I'm sure he's healing the Guardians. He will help you."

"Don't you ever feel like we're simply exiles, pretending to be saviors?" I know it's the trauma and fatigue, but I'm emotional. I can't staunch the words. My hope is ossifying. "Like we're faking all this?"

"Carmine…"

"I'm sick of the violence. We're going to lose. Unless we change the war."

She manages an ersatz smile and points to the east. "That's what the Outlaw is doing. He's going to change the war."

Yes.

Maybe.

But it might not be enough.

- 2 -
The Outlaw

Thirty minutes after lunch at Denny's with Katie, our private jet screams down Van Nuys Airport's runway and banks west. We skim the rooftops of Hollywood and punch into clean air over the Pacific.

Samantha and I sit in the cockpit and hold our breath. Not only because of the gasoline fumes we brought with us, but also because the Federal Army may not register our takeoff but the Navy certainly will. Their orders might be to shoot down anything that moves. However, there are no radio calls, no warnings, no incoming surface-to-air missiles. We arc north above the blinding ocean and re-enter California halfway to San Fransisco, far removed from hostilities.

Puck engages the autopilot and drops us low. If we're lucky we might pass the entire trip and never blip anyone's radar. After weeks spent sleeping in dusty cars inside the husk of former Los Angeles, the pristine luxury of the jet is jarring. But welcome.

We're exhausted and in desperate need of a short nap but we stay awake long enough to see Denver. Or what used to be Denver. Through our side windows it looks like a miniature garbage dump. Parts of the earth still smoke. Surviving structures are blackened. Hastily erected tent cities circle the southern neighborhoods. Fortunately it's not winter, else the people would die of exposure soon.

"This all goes away," Samantha says, her breath misting the window, "if I get one clean shot."

I lay one of the jet's leather chairs backwards, pull a blanket to my chin, and am asleep in seconds.

I dream of Katie. Of high school. Of fire.

Of jet fuel.

Judging by the sun and shadows, I don't sleep long. But I wake suddenly with the impalpable conviction that something is horribly wrong. I feel the dread down to my bones.

The door to the rear compartment of the Learjet, which neither Samantha nor I bothered to check, is ajar and a girl stands there. A stowaway. Her blond hair is short, a pixie cut like Tinker Bell's. In fact, the girl reminds me a lot of Tinker Bell, down to the legs and short skirt.

She's the source of the gasoline fumes and jet fuel dreams. Only one girl on earth issues that aroma.

"Hello Hannah," I say, and my voice wavers. Samantha Gear's eyes snap open but she remains still. No sudden movements, don't spook the she-devil.

"Hello boyfriend," the Cheerleader replies. I don't know whether she followed me to the jet and boarded when our attention was diverted, or if this is simple bad luck. Sucks either way. "Where are you taking us?"

"On vacation. Like you asked."

"In our own private jet?"

"Of course. Nothing but the best."

I'm making up lies as fast as I can. Hannah Walker is undead, or as close as it's possible to get. Even more combustible than the average twenty-year-old girl, she can set herself on fire and survive. Impossibly strong, impossibly stark raving mad. And in love with Chase Jackson.

Hannah lowers into my lap, like she used to when we dated. She's still pretty but now it's more the way a mannequin is pretty. The reek of gasoline invades my nostrils, and she's warm to the touch. "Well. Isn't this the perfect surprise," she coos.

I point across the aisle, where Samantha pretends to be asleep. "I brought…a…bodyguard. To keep us safe."

"What a good idea. We can never be too careful."

"You remember what happened last time," I say, but regret it immediately. Maybe I should shut up.

"Last time?"

"Well...actually, I'm not sure—"

"Do you mean when the blue-eyed girl tried to steal you?" Hannah asks.

"Yes. That's it."

"Do not worry about her. If she interferes with vacation, I'll burn her alive. Just like that," she says and she snaps her fingers. The nail of her middle finger scrapes her thumb and a small flame appears there, held suspended in her hand. Fed by the fuel and fumes she secretes.

I take her hand and the flame extinguishes. She squeezes in response; it's playful but it's strong, probably breaking the bones of a normal person.

"Hannah, I was just taking a nap. I'm still very tired. Do you think we could sleep?"

"Of course, boyfriend. But first." She kisses me on the lips. The way girlfriends sometimes kiss boyfriends. Her febrile mouth feels rubbery and thick. The dress she's wearing is obscene and I don't know what to do with my hands, and the whole thing is so weird I'm about to freak out, but I kiss her back. The last thing we need is a human bomb throwing a jealous temper tantrum midair inside a small jet.

She twists on my lap so she can unzip my vest, but Samantha Gear shifts and makes a sleepy murmur. Hannah glances at her, annoyed with the intrusion.

"Maybe we should wait," I whisper. "Till we're alone."

"Okay," she whispers back. "But I won't wait forever. You've always taken care of me, Chase, and I want to take care of you."

She slides into the adjacent chair, leaving her calves in my lap. I lay the blanket over her and she smiles, a dreamy look in her expression. "You're the best boyfriend. Do you have anything to eat? Like chocolate?"

"You stay here. I'll see what the jet has," I say in a tone coaxing her to sleep, and I extract myself from her limbs.

"I love you," she whispers. "Soon we'll be together. Forever."

Samantha peers sideways from the corner of her eye. She's trying not to laugh. In comparison, Samantha Gear isn't far less crazy than Hannah, because she thinks dying is hilarious.

I raid the flight attendant's station and return with chocolate bars and peanuts near expiration, but the Cheerleader is asleep. Something happened in her when she died and came back which causes her to require sleep most of the day.

Samantha hisses, "I can't *believe* you brought a girl."

"I'd rather bring a crate full of badgers than that freak-show in a skirt," I whisper.

"That is quite a skirt. I'm going to text Katie a photo." She raises her phone.

"No. Do not."

"Why not? You feel guilty about something?"

"No. Kinda. But it's not my fault. Katie is finally remembering herself and I don't want you to worry her."

"Ugh. Fine. I'll send the photo to Puck. He'll get a kick out of this," she says.

"You two are the worst friends ever."

"I know, it's great."

Before I sit back down, I glance through the cockpit door. Whoa. "Samantha. Come look."

We both enter the small cockpit and sit in the pilot chairs. The jet is on autopilot so we're careful not to touch anything. Two fires burn on the vast horizon. I'm no aviator and cannot judge distance accurately, but to my eyes the remote fires are enormous.

"Where are we?" Samantha asks. Her voice has fallen to an awed whisper.

There's a digital map on the display between us. I scrutinize it a moment. "Oklahoma. One of those fires is Tulsa." We don't speak as our jet approaches and passes north of the infernos. Like Denver, it's a sight too colossal for words. Our minds can't grasp the loss and damage, not fully. It looks like videos I've seen of forest fires, except those are houses and schools and Starbucks burning below us. Not trees. We scan the planet's surface and spot another column of smoke far north. I call PuckDaddy.

"What's happening, homie."

"We're passing Tulsa," I say. "It's on fire."

"Yeah man. A lot of cities burn. The bands of high-spirited mercenaries, the released inmates, the lack of order, and the rampaging Variants take their toll."

"Is anywhere safe?"

"Sure, lots of places. Oklahoma City, Dallas, Indianapolis. They have powerful militias. Most of the major farms took on big security forces in exchange for food and shelter. Tulsa was abandoned weeks ago."

Samantha asks, "What about Atlanta?"

"The closer you get to the Atlantic Ocean, the safer. Well, kinda. I mean, the President and Blue-Eyes are in total control of the military and police, and they run a tight ship. Citizens are executed for treason every day, which keeps the masses in line."

Thirty minutes later we jet over a major interstate, one that runs north to south like a silver ribbon. An enormous amount of construction vehicles, materials, and manpower are gathered there. This doesn't look like simple road repair. I call Puck again.

"Puck, we're in…Mississippi now. Near the Tennessee border and Memphis. We spotted something unusual."

"Ah yes," Puck says. "Most likely you've spotted the Great Wall."

Samantha says, "Explain."

"The Great Wall of Interstate 55. The President is erecting a wall to follow 55 across the entire country, north to south. On his side, the eastern side, America. The safe zone. On the far side, lawless country."

"Why weren't we told?"

"You've been busy, Shooter. And what could you have done to stop it?"

Not a thing. The battlefronts are too numerous, and I've never felt like such a pathetic little aspirant hero as I do right now. All our hard work, and have we accomplished anything? I lean back in my chair, eyes closed, despondent. A Great Wall in America. Burning cities.

"Keep that chin up, Outlaw," she says. "We have hard work ahead of us."

"I know. Sometimes the light at the end of the tunnel grows dim, that's all. Like we'll never reach it."

She doesn't respond. She feels it too.

Night settles over the land as we descend toward Fulton County Airport, a private strip ten miles outside Atlanta. Air travel is nonexistent and all small airports like this have shut down, so there's no runway lights or personnel to guide us in. We land dark. Tires scream and thrust reversers howl, and we stop at the end of the runway.

"I see no reason to taxi near the concourse," I say. "Let's point the jet back down the runway, refuel, and leave it on the strip. We might need a quick exit."

"Pretty good idea coming from a kid who didn't graduate high school." She grins.

"I had enough credits. I can't help it if the city shut down before graduation, and also shut up."

She turns the plane around, kill the systems, and make ready to open the hatch. Samantha stands with her hands on hips, inspecting Hannah Walker as she stretches and murmurs in her sleep.

"She's going to wake up, soon. We should leave her here."

"I agree," I whisper.

"An even better idea would be if I put a pistol into both her eyes and pulled the triggers. I'd be doing her a favor, you know. She lives in torment."

"You're disgusting. I can't believe my father lets you touch him."

"That's not all he lets me do."

"Hannah saved my life last year. We can't just execute her in her sleep," I say.

"Wuss."

We grab our backpacks, full of food and gear, and quietly pop the hatch. The steps unfold into a dark and vacant airport. The air is thicker than in Los Angeles, a damp humidity even at night. We leave the jet's hatch open, so maybe the Cheerleader will wander away and out of our lives.

From our place on the tarmac, we see several nearby neighborhoods aglow with electricity, and a large distribution center.

"Civilization," Samantha notes grimly. "Happily burning energy to remain comfortable. How I've missed it."

I find an old fuel truck. The dials indicate it's half full, so I drive it to the rear of the Learjet and insert the hose. Hopefully we've got enough to get home. "You think the people in those houses have any idea what we're going through on the west coast?"

"I doubt it. But even if they did? They wouldn't care. What matters most to a person is her own safety and comfort." She takes out her phone to use the map app.

I want to argue with her, but she's probably right. Instead, I note, "I could really do with a Chipotle burrito."

"Got any cash?"

"No. I forgot the rest of the world uses money. How tedious."

We set off for the concourse, and she says, "And I'm used to taking any car I want. But that won't fly here. Cars have owners in Georgia. It's a ten-mile walk to Atlanta, and then ten miles farther to the CDC. We don't have that much time."

"We can't walk in public with you carrying that ridiculous gun anyway."

"It's not ridiculous. It's beautiful. Map indicates a U-Haul half a mile west."

"Let's steal a truck."

Samantha falls asleep in the U-Haul's passenger seat en route to the CDC.

Two nights ago, Walter attacked and Katie returned. I got no sleep that night because missiles began falling soon after.

The following night, Samantha and I raided the Federal Army and kidnapped Colonel Wallace and his cohorts. Zero sleep.

My brain is too fuzzy to add up the days, and I'm not positive my memory is accurate, but I think I've run through seventy-two hours on half a nap. Whatever it is, I'm running off the road with exhaustion.

South of the Centers for Disease Control is Emory University, a sprawling and active campus. I find a strip mall near the Village with a large parking lot. I nestle the truck into a spot in the back and I'm almost asleep before turning the key off.

- 3 -

Carmine

We're gone at first light. I drive. Dalton grumbles in the passenger seat.

"Considering you're an ex-Navy SEAL, you whine a lot."

"Fallujah was a lot more stable than your driving," he barks.

The trip from San Fernando to Long Beach takes an hour. The markets are opening. Shepherds lead their herds to new pastures. Farmers carry water to crops. Cleaners are moving rubble out of USC. Our infrastructure holds. I'm surprised the people aren't more rattled, but Kayla reports that spirits aren't as low as she feared. Surviving bombs has bolstered their temerity.

"I love this place, Dalton. I know we've only been at this a year, but I do. The people here are brave and hardworking. We *must* provide protection, because the future of New Los Angeles could be brilliant."

"Whatever, just keep your eyes on the damn road."

Saul wanted to come on our trip to meet the Inheritors but I need him at the northern wall in case Walter attacks again. He calms and heals the Variants, a priceless commodity. Besides, this should be a short trip. If everything goes well.

Which it won't. Who am I kidding.

I get the phone call as the Pacific Ocean comes into view.

"Queen Carmine," General Brown greets me over speaker phone. His voices sounds like a tree bark being crumbled.

"General, when was the last time you slept?"

"Been a while. I'll hop in the rack later this morning. Our enemy don't sleep, we don't sleep. Listen. I have two pieces of information that will infuriate both of us."

"I'm ready. Spill."

"We discovered the source of our missile defense malfunctions. Or at least, the hacker PuckDaddy did. That boy is on a different level, you ask me," he says and he pauses to yawn.

"What's the source?"

"Treason. The Priest."

"The *Priest*," I hiss, and the steering wheel bends slightly in my shaking fists. "I *knew* I couldn't trust that prissy little…ugh."

"Little bitch," Dalton says. "That's what you're trying to say. He's a prissy little bitch."

"You have the Priest in custody?"

"Negative. He and his inner circle responsible for the malfunctions went AWOL as a group. I expect to apprehend them soon."

"That's why it felt like he was working so hard. He was running around breaking our systems. Using chicanery to weaken us."

"Gonna break that kid's neck," Dalton mutters.

"PuckDaddy is looking into phone records. Determine if he's collaborating with anyone."

"Gotta be Blue-Eyes," I say. "He'll hitch his wagon to the highest bidder. What's the other piece of bad news?"

"Complications with the Navy. Your transport ship isn't ready," he says.

The steering wheel bends further and I grind my teeth. "Get me the captain on the phone."

"Captain Steger is sympathetic to your cause, but he's putting down a second mutiny. Those sailors been at sea for a year. Calling him won't help. They're fifty miles offshore, and he hopes to be ready to assist within forty-eight hours."

"Keep me updated, General. And thank you."

I punch the Off button.

My mind churns with options. The biggest factor is time. How soon will

Russia attack from the south? I have to get those kids out of his path somehow.

Dalton asks, "We going back? That boat ain't ready."

"I can't go back."

"Why not?"

"Because of my connection with the Guardians. Anytime they get excited, my mind gets highjacked. I need space."

He nods. "Makes sense. No actually, none of this makes a hell of a lot of sense, but still."

"You're a good man, Dalton. Thanks for sticking around."

He grunts something unintelligible.

I ask, "Are you dating the reporter? Teresa Triplett?"

"None of your business."

"I'm the queen."

"Don't care," he says, and I grin.

"Teresa is super pretty."

"Fly as hell. And that's all you get out of me."

"I'll sing at your wedding."

"Won't be a wedding, you don't learn to drive."

Even stolid Dalton enjoys the views along Highway 1. My heart is warmed by the children running through the golden surf and by the families at picnic. We wave to the stunned security guard at Dana Point and race down our slice of the western coast, the very edge of our former great country.

Soon we're in no-man's land. Lawless country. Only survivalists live here, neither under my authority nor inside Russia's fist of terror. However, maybe even the stout-hearted have now fled, because there are no indications of human life.

At Lawrence Canyon we turn onto Route 76. Dalton watches our course with interest; the Inheritors were a secret from him too. The Prince of Peace Abbey is not visible from the highway, but it's not well-hidden either. There are signs of habitation which could draw interest from Russia and his mercenaries. I scrutinize the campus entrance, and I come to the absolute conclusion that those kids cannot remain here. There's no ability to camouflage and no way to defend.

The Abbey's grassy fields are kept short by cows and goats. Chickens roam in pens at both the front and rear of the campus. Additional wooden structures have been raised to augment the original pristine buildings; a large dining hall, by appearances, and bunk houses.

Toddlers are everywhere, like one of those hectic crowded *I Spy* picture books. There were five hundred children in the Fall, which is the size of an enormous elementary school. A few of them monitor our approach but quickly lose interest. The mothers, however, in desperate need of news and excitement, swarm the Land Cruiser before we even step out. I'm recognizable and they greet me with enthusiasm, not all of it positive. To some of the women, I'm the source of their grief. I symbolize the genesis of this primitive lifestyle they never wanted. To others, I symbolize hope and their only chance of safety. I am hugged and glared at.

Dalton, a well-assembled, well-groomed, and muscular man, is fawned after, which he deems understandable yet creepy. It's not a pathetic show from the women, it's human nature; they're lonely. The monks at the Abbey are sweet, hard-working men, but chaste and over the age of fifty. Old enough to be the women's fathers. Dalton represents cake to starving women. So to speak.

He disentangles himself and follows me inside. Father Frost is there, a white-haired man with sharp blue eyes. I note he's aged two years in the last six months. He beckons us into his office.

"Queen Carmine, it is pleasant to see you again." He smiles and the three of us sit around his desk.

"Your Abbey appears functional and healthy. Do you have enough supplies?" I ask.

"We have a surplus, yes, thanks to your generosity."

"How are your charges?"

He pauses and drums his fingers on the chair's armrest. "That is an interesting question. Do you mean the mothers? Or their children?"

"Let's start with mothers."

"The women are…bored. And irritable." Father Frost says it frankly and with undertones of frustration. He is seventy-five and has been cooped up with five hundred young mothers and their babies for a year. Any other man would have killed himself by now. I essentially wrecked his monastery and lifestyle. "After growing up in the razzle-dazzle of Los Angeles, I'm afraid they find our simple way of life…difficult to adapt to."

"I understand your point of view. And theirs. You've been through a lot, and we're grateful for your service. More grateful than we have the ability to express. How are the children?"

"Happy, I think. And also…something else."

"What do you mean?"

"Well, statistically speaking, there are fewer of them than when you last visited. Two children died of unknown causes, and three mothers ran off, taking their children with them. But that is not what I mean. The children show signs of being, perhaps you would say, extraordinary."

Dalton rubs his forehead and mutters, "Oh, damn."

"Extraordinary," I say.

"Yes. You won't notice it as first. But. Sometimes I get the impression they are all in one accord, so to speak. They share a common personality, or mind. And what is more, some of them exhibit peculiar gifts."

Dalton and I exchange a glance. Exhibiting abnormalities already? I assumed that wouldn't happen until late adolescence. "I told you they were special children, Father Frost. I wasn't joking. Tell me about the peculiar gifts."

"A handful of them seem to have an affinity for animals. The children are barely walking, yet the local wildlife…*obeys* them, for lack of a better word. They are followed by stray dogs and cats, and even birds. Two of the girls display enormous strength for such a young age. And extreme speed and agility are evident in others."

He doesn't glare at us, but that's what it feels like.

His tone isn't accusatory, but that's what it feels like.

Dalton and I sink lower in our chairs out of reflex. We've displeased the Father.

"The monks at this Abbey have given their lives to service and to sacrifice." Father Frost smiles. "And to God. And nothing will cause us to break our vows. But perhaps it would be better if you explained exactly who or what the Prince of Peace Abbey is sheltering. Children who will grow up to be like you?"

I swallow and clear my throat. "Worse."

"I see."

"But. I've come here to remove them from your custody. You've kept them alive for a year, which is over and beyond what anyone else could have done. Tomorrow, I hope, they'll be leaving."

He is quiet a moment, regarding us behind the cool blue eyes. "Is there danger?"

"Yes. The criminal warlord in San Diego is threatening to come this way. With his army."

"I see."

"I would suggest you and your brothers retreat into the safety of our Kingdom's borders, as soon as possible," I say.

"We couldn't possibly. This is our home, and we will die here. Our Eden, which we've been given to tend. We will truly be sorry to see the children leave."

"I relate strongly to your sentiment, but I cannot protect you here, Father Frost."

"I understand. And I'll present your option to the brothers, but… I know what they will say."

My phone begins to ring. It's PuckDaddy. Dalton and I excuse ourselves and walk to the side lawn.

"This is Carmine," I say into the phone.

"What's up, girl. PuckDaddy the Magnificent intercepted texts out of San Diego. Big movement going on. Looks like Russia intends to lurch his way north tomorrow morning. Moving his army of mercenaries should only take him the day."

"I don't have a boat yet," I growl.

"I heard. I eavesdropped on your phone call with the general. Don't be mad at Puck."

"Have General Brown demolish large stretches of Interstate 15. And Interstate 5. Especially the bridges."

"Good idea," he says into my ear. "But your Abbey is halfway to San Diego. Brown won't get that far, right? You're still in harm's way."

"So Russia is going to get here before the Navy, no matter what we do," I realize out loud.

"Appears that way."

I pace back and forth across the small grassy lawn, brainstorming options with Puck. Our problems are too compounded for us to find a simple easy solution. No matter what I do, people will die. Russia arrives in less than twenty-four hours. Even if he doesn't discover the Inheritors, our Kingdom will be doomed.

Dalton waves to get my attention, so I say, "I'll call you back, Puck."

"Roger that, homie."

I hang up. "Yes?"

He nods to the open campus behind me.

The lawn has filled with toddlers. Dozens, maybe a hundred children, Black, White, Asian, Hispanic, have slowly made their way to us. Mothers left far behind; they arrive independently. They stand. They sit. They crawl. They chew on pacifiers or their fingers, or they breath through their tiny mouths. And the children are preternaturally silent for their age.

They are drawn. Pulled forward by biological and chemical imperatives, moths to a flame. They made their way here without knowing why.

They watch me with curious unblinking eyes. I feel the combined weight of their gazes like a heavy blanket. The minuscule hairs on my neck stand. I stop pacing and their eyes settle.

"What are they doing?" Dalton whispers.

"I don't know."

"Creepy as hell," he grumbles under his breath. "One day I'm going to write a book."

"They shouldn't be like this," I say, and half of them smile at my voice. "Not so young."

"That bastard Russia's going to turn them into an enhanced army," Dalton says. "Right?"

I stare at them, deep in thought. They stare back. They smell of diapers and powder and lotion, a pleasant heart-breaking scent. We can't let him, Dalton. It can't happen. It can't. It can't. It can't.

"Not if we stop him," I say.

"What do you mean?"

"Call Kayla. Get her here."

He pulls out his phone. "What do I tell her?"

"That the three of us are going to kill Russia."

He nods slowly, a grim smile on his face. "Yes ma'am."

"We go tonight. And I need Kayla to pick up my sword on the way."

- 4 -
The Outlaw

Reality scratches at my eyelids until I surrender, and rays of light shoot to the back of my skull, waking me like an alarm. My back and neck are stiff, and my mouth tastes like metal.

Sometime during our slumber, Samantha laid down across the bench, her head in my lap and partially pinned between my vest and the steering wheel. "Wake up, you weirdo," I yawn.

She sits up and stretches as best she can in the cramped space. The pistol in her fist clanks against the window. "I need water. And your vest smells terrible."

"It's never been washed. And it won't be needed much longer."

We use restrooms inside the nearby Panera to drink water and wash our faces. The blaring electric lights hurt my eyes. We keep our heads down to avoid attention, but we're not entirely successful; Samantha and I stand out. These are college students from Emory, my age, but we're nothing alike.

Compared to us, these kids are spongey and limp. Samantha and I have been in combat, off and on, for three years, and these college students sleep till ten every morning. They drink sugary coffee and talk Netflix while we sleep in cars and run through battlefields. Samantha's shoulders are broad, her back straight and powerful. Her legs move with purpose and muscle. Our skin is crisscrossed with scars, and we have gunpowder burned indelibly into our pores. It's not just the disease which makes us dangerous; it's the work. The suffering and the drive.

They are marshmallow. We are tempered steel.

Their clothes are bright and smooth.

Our's are dark, torn, and greased by machinery.

They're pasty, and we're black and gold.

And yet I envy them. I envy their innocence, their arrogance, the lack of responsibility. They're soft because they've lived in peace. Their hands aren't calloused because it's their minds which are being trained, not their bodies.

This is the lifestyle Katie deserved. She was the smartest girl at our school, and she should have attended Stanford, talked science with other brilliant students, and gone on to do anything she wanted.

In the parking lot, outside again, Samantha says, "Did you see those kids? They look nothing like the citizens in Katie's Kingdom. They're all fat."

"Was thinking the same thing." I check my watch. "We slept most of the day, which is infuriating. I didn't mean too. Katie's in danger and I *sleep*."

"You needed it. I'm sure she's fine. Sundown is in two hours. Let's wait till ten o'clock and we'll move."

The CDC is less than two miles away. An easy jog. So we sit in the U-Haul's cab and eat stale chocolate granola bars. I can't help thinking, one way or another, this will be my last granola bar for a while.

The Centers for Disease Control and Prevention would look like any other towering commercial office park on the East Coast if not for the eight-foot-high black fence surrounding the campus. The security fence is no trouble, but the new additions give Samantha and I pause. Search lights have been installed. Armed men pace the roofs and dogs patrol the parking lots. We survey the scene from a large copse of trees, located on the southwestern corner. We're beyond the railroad tracks and fence, perched on a thick branch of a sycamore tree. A crisp night has fallen, the kind of black which feels infinite and imminent.

Puck is in our ears. "So, listen homies. Puck is burrowing deeper through encrypted files. There is significant research being done on a cure for the

Hyper Virus in the western wing of the main building. Can you see it? It's gigantic and made entirely of glass, greenish in color, and it's curved like the top left quarter of a circle."

"Affirmative, we see it," I say.

"PuckDaddy advises you ignore all buildings except that one. There appears to be an impressive underground infrastructure, and that's where Blue-Eyes's classified project is located. Puck's looked everywhere, but I can't find a map of the subterranean facility. All documentation about this project is extremely vague, referring to 'patients' and 'supplies' in general terms. The term 'Washington Researcher' is mentioned several time, and Puck assumes that refers to Blue-Eyes herself."

"Copy that, Puck. We'll get inside and head straight down," Samantha says. "We don't need a map. We have grenades."

My body is so engorged with adrenaline that I taste it in my mouth. Blue-Eyes is in that building. I know it. I *Feel* it.

"CDC's servers indicate the Washington Researcher has an impressive security detail. Including mutants," Puck says, his voice rattling out of the blue-tooth speaker inserted deeply into my ear. "And PuckDaddy bets you anything, they're former Guardians she's brainwashed."

"Makes sense."

"I'd prefer not to shoot them," Samantha says. She's double-checking her pistols' spare magazines. Including the black backpack, and an assault rifle slung around her neck, and her sash of grenades, she's a walking armory. "But I will."

"Ready to go?" My blood is steaming, like a pressure valve which needs release.

"One more thing," Puck blurts. "Inside the encrypted data, I've come across a handful of files mentioning something identified as the Federal Weapon. No clear definition. Very fuzzy, very shadowy. Keep your eyes open for something Blue-Eyes might be planning on using to…kill all of us, maybe? I don't know."

"Roger that, PuckDaddy. Eyes open for a weapon. By the way, what's Katie doing right now?"

"*Carmine* is…safe."

"Why the hesitation?" I demand.

"PuckDaddy does not hesitate."

"Puck. Tell me."

"There's nothing to tell! She's safe. She's…busy. In no immediate danger. Perhaps you should *focus*, Outlaw," he says. "Big night ahead."

"Keep Katie alive, Puck," I say. "Please."

"Puck is trying," he mumbles. "She's high-spirited."

Samantha grins and pats my knee. "Let's go, Outlaw. We have a witch to burn, and a world to save."

Samantha descends the tree, skips over the tracks, vaults the fence, and climbs the side of the CDC's David Spenser museum. So much work. Instead, I *Leap* the distance, an exactly plotted parabola, and land deftly beside her. She scowls. An old spine injury is aggravated by the stress, but my pride is worth the pain. "You're an ass," she says. "And put your mask on."

We scurry across the museum's flat bitumen roof while I tie on the red scarf, lining up the eyeholes. The infamous Outlaw should really have better gear than this old rag. We steer clear of the searchlights and gunmen on patrol, and slip over the far parapet.

"Straight ahead," Puck whispers. "See the door? It'll be unlocked for the next fifteen seconds."

Eyeballing the CDC's main building, it appears to be fifteen stories tall, a dark and looming glass monolith. We vault over a hedge of evergreen shrubs and enter a service stairwell through the emergency exit. The alarms stay silent and the door closes behind us, a loud echo through the vertical shaft.

"You're on the main level," he says. "I have security monitor access for this floor and two sub-levels. The levels beyond that aren't outfitted with surveillance, which is crazy sketch. I see two security guards at the front desk, and a handful on the second sub-level."

We descend two floors, where the service stairwell ends. We're thirty feet underground and not yet finished burrowing. There's an unmarked heavy door hidden behind the stairs. Locked.

"She's below us. I'd rather not fight our way to the elevator," I say. "The

CDC's basement has to have stairs, because of Federal regulations. I bet they're behind this door."

The texture of Puck's cellphone connection has changed, growing thin and spotty. "Puck can't open that door. It's not locked electronically. I think you're on your own, starting now. We'll lose connection after you enter."

"Thanks, Puck," Samantha Gear says. "We'll breach, release the hostages, shoot Blue-Eyes in the head twenty-five times, and return back here. Should take ten minutes max."

"Puck is not religious," he says. "But Puck is going to be praying. A lot."

Samantha screws a short silencer onto her pistol, and I pull the Thunder Stick free from my vest. "Ready," I say. My heart pounds so hard it hurts my eyes.

"Ready."

I punch through the door, at the handle. It's reinforced metal alloy and the sound is uncomfortably loud, and my knuckles bruise. But the tissues of my body have hardened to the density of steel and leather, and I'm able to grasp the locking mechanism and wrench it free. We step inside and quickly pull the door closed again. We wait and hold our breath, but no alarms sound; we're saved by the rudimentary nature of the lock. The designers built it simply to ensure no outside source could electronically activate it. It's a heavy metal door, after all, like a bank vault. But they didn't anticipate mutants simply ripping it open.

There are no lights, but we don't need them. Our vision adjusts rapidly and we descend the rough concrete stairs. We're below the mechanical rooms, the air circulation systems, the plumbing, the gas tanks, the generators. We plunge approximately forty-five feet before finding a solitary exit door.

No words needed.

We find her. We kill her. We run.

The thick door is unlocked and opens with a hiss of air into an airlock. Beyond, the hallway is vacant. We crowd the airtight chamber, close the door behind us, and open the hatch into the brilliant hallway.

There are Variants nearby. I *Feel* their heat, *Hear* their heartbeat.

There's a security camera at the far end of the corridor, where the hallway breaks off into perpendicular directions, and another camera above our heads. Puck never saw these, so most likely they're on a closed system, unable to be accessed from the outside on short notice.

This is going to be a fight. No way around it. Best we can do is confuse our enemies. Samantha raises her pistol, aims around the doorway, and fires. The camera lens at the far end, one hundred feet away, cracks. I rip the camera above our heads off the wall, and we run down the corridor.

By busting the cameras, we've begun a countdown. Armed resistance will arrive soon.

I feel like an exposed insect skittering down the sterile hallway under ultraviolet lights.

There are doors marked with numbers. The first we encounter is 'Twenty-Eight.' Unlocked, but it's a simple supply closet, packed with equipment.

The next door, 'Twenty-Six,' requires us to pass through an airlock portal, but the chamber beyond is empty. Long and dark, and it reeks of piss and blood. Hastily-constructed restraint apparatuses, which look like crucifixes, are empty. It's obvious the room has been used recently, and for a nefarious purpose; Blue-Eyes kept mutant prisoners here.

We exit the room and nearly collide with two guards. One mutant, and one Secret Serviceman, coming to investigate the malfunctioning cameras.

It's a silent, savage, one-second struggle.

Samantha brings up her pistol, but the Variant is quick. He gets a hand on the barrel and desperately redirects it away from his throat. I crack him in the temple and he slumps; if the Variants have a weakness it's their fragile skulls, prone to concussion. All this happens before the Secret Serviceman, who is un-enhanced, can reach his pistol or shout. I snake an arm around his neck and haul him back inside the dark chamber.

I've closed his windpipe and he struggles in vain. Samantha relieves him of his sidearm and radio. I release.

"We're looking for Blue-Eyes," she says, and she places her pistol's nozzle against the man's groin. "And we're in a hurry."

His face pales and he swallows "*Who?*"

"Mary," I say. "Secretary of State. The girl you're most likely in love with."

He shakes his head, and begins to tremble. "You'll have to kill me. Never will I betray her."

"He's right," I say. "He's brainwashed. It'll just waste our time."

"Fine." She places the pistol under his jaw. Her pistol clicks, and I hear a wet, pulpy burst of air. Instant death. The man collapses into a heap.

"Samantha!" I hiss. "We could've tied him up!"

"Ohmygosh, Outlaw, you're still on this pacifist kick? We're at *war*."

"He didn't have to die. We're in a room full of restraining devices!"

"We don't have time for this!"

I return to the hallway, ignoring her grumbles behind me about one of us being a wimp. There are two more doors on this hallway. 'Twenty-Four' is locked with an electronic keypad but I force the door open. The bolt screams and rips free. Another airlock and another dark chamber, but this one's occupied. Five Guardians are strapped to the metal crucifixes, pinned by heavy chains at the ankles and wrists.

I see no immediate signs of mistreatment, other than skin rubbed raw by the chains. They see me, see my mask, and their eyes snap wide.

"Outlaw!"

I hold a finger to my lips. There is no collective release mechanism; each captive is bound by an individual system of chains and locks. I move to each one, strain at the links near the lock, and break them.

"Where is she?" I ask. "Blue-eyes."

I'm releasing a girl I don't recognize, but she's a Guardian, one of Katie's. She radiates the pent-up aggression and fear of a pit bull. "She's here," she girl whispers, close to a snarl. "Close."

"Are you hurt?"

She shakes her head. "But we're next. She's making connection with Queen Carmine, somehow. And executing us, one by one."

"You've seen it done?"

"Twice. Last night, it happened again. She killed the boy across from me. His name was Tom. Burned and shot him."

The boy next to her, still in chains, whispers, "The queen is getting stronger. We *Feel* it."

217

Samantha is at the airlock's hatch, keeping watch.

I ask, "You're immune to the witch's persuasion?"

"I think we're protected, because of the queen," the girl says. "But the witch is wearing us down."

"How many more of you does she have?"

"We're the last remaining hostages. I think."

I snap the final chain, releasing the fifth Guardian. All five stretch atrophied muscles and grin at one another. Freedom.

"We're here to kill her," I say, and the group shivers with excitement, like wild animals. I press a piece of paper into her hand. The paper contains directions to our U-Haul, and to our private jet on the other side of Atlanta. "Get out of here. Follow these directions. All goes well, we'll see you there. Otherwise, the jet will take you home."

At once, like flicking a switch, the group flinches. They exchange a worried glance and turn their gazes in what I assume is a western direction.

Samantha asks, "What's going on?"

"Queen Carmine," the girl breathes.

"What about her?"

"She's excited about something. But it's different, somehow. She's…"

"She's *what?*" I demand.

"She's alone. She's not near the others. It feels faint."

"She's alive?"

"Yes."

I glance at Samantha. This is killing me, and she knows it. I'm getting an ulcer, worrying about her.

"You five, run. Get free, don't stop, get to the jet at Fulton County airport," Samantha says. She jerks a thumb over her shoulder. "Stairs are that way."

"They'll sound the alarm," I note.

"That's okay. A fight will be cathartic," she says. "I want witch blood. Besides, they'll be a diversion."

The five thank us and run. It's about to get interesting.

Samantha and I enter room 'Twenty-Two.'

This chamber is larger and well-lit. There are workbenches along the walls, next to big canisters of oxygen. Rolling metal trays full of surgical equipment I don't recognize. Tubes and wires dangle from the ceiling. A refrigerator full of blood bags.

There are two men, most likely physicians, both wearing airtight bodysuits, both too surprised at our appearance to move.

But that's not what gets my attention.

There is a cage in the middle of the room. All four walls and the roof of the cage are constructed out of either impermeable glass or transparent plastic, providing the physicians full view of their subject. The edges are connected by metal seams. Inside is a man.

I know the man.

The prisoner and I went to the same high school, but I haven't seen him in over a year. We played football together, both of us quarterbacks. He was kidnapped by a madman named the Chemist, and forced to undergo the same surgery as Katie, injected with the Hyper Virus too late in life, giving him strength and power while also breaking his mind.

I have no idea how he got here.

"Andy?" I say. "Andy Babington?"

The prisoner looks up, his eyes bloodshot. His head is shaved. He wears a hospital gown, which hangs loose.

Samantha points to Andy's back, where something alien and awful and heavy has been surgically attached to the bones of his spine. "Is that... Is he strapped to a nuclear bomb?"

- 5 -

Carmine

I park my Land Cruiser at the Montgomery-Gibbs Executive Airport, eight miles north of my target: downtown San Diego.

In the distance, uncontrolled fires throw an angry glow into the night. This city isn't being cared for and tended the way New Los Angeles is, and there is an impalpable smog of burning commerce, pollution, spoiled food, and human odor in the air. Manifest anarchy. No wonder Russia plans to invade the Kingdom tomorrow; he's consumed San Diego to the point of ruin.

The executive airport is pillaged. Private jets have been drained of fuel and food, maybe now used for sleeping cabins. I'm not waiting to find out. Deep inside the airport there's a hanger for corporate helicopters off John J Montgomery Drive and I haul heavily on the sliding doors, which part slowly on creaking wheels. Thankfully, inside I discover unsullied helicopters.

In order to to avoid detection I work in darkness, a crepuscular thief. I select a sleek gray Sikorsky S-76 chopper with dials showing a full fuel tank, and connect the forward landing gear to a motorized trolley. Inch by inch, I'm able to jockey the executive helicopter out of the hanger and into the open air.

Other than San Diego's stench, I decide it's a beautiful evening. The sky full of stars.

I set my supplies into the passenger compartment and climb inside the cockpit. PuckDaddy gave me a checklist to perform and I follow it to the letter. Soon the instrument panel is completely lit, a thousand glowing gadgets, and the engines are humming.

Deep steady breaths.

I can do this.

New Los Angeles is worth it.

The Outlaw is worth it.

I call Dalton and he answers on the second ring. "Go ahead."

I say, "Your progress?"

"Half a mile out. You were right. Kayla just smiles at these jackasses and they move aside."

"She's similar to Blue-Eyes, but not as powerful. I'm lifting off in five minutes. Wait for my signal."

"Roger that. And Carmine. Be careful."

"You too." I hang up and text Puck.

Puck. You ready to do this?

I got a Sikorsky-76

>> one sec

>> helping outlaw and shooter

>> ready in 60 secs

True to his word, he calls me in one minute. "What's up, girl."

I ask, "What about Chase? Is he okay?"

"Chase is…fine."

"You hesitated," I say. Katie squirms uncomfortably between my ears. She's worried about Chase too. Her anxiety is my anxiety, one and the same.

"PuckDaddy does not hesitate! Chase is fine, sheesh. He's with Shooter, and they're at the CDC. You freaking white people."

"I'm not white. I'm Hispanic." Despite the stress, I can't help smiling.

"Whatever. Puck's just nervous. Are you really going through with this absurd plan?"

"Absolutely. Helicopter's warmed. Dalton and Kayla are in place."

"Promise Puck that you'll keep Kayla safe."

"I promise…I'll try," I say.

"You hesitated."

"Puck!"

"I can't help it! I love her!" he shouts.

"Yeah. Well. I know the feeling. You keep Chase alive, and I'll keep Kayla alive. Deal?"

"Deal," he grumbles and I hear clicking. "I'm loading the program. Connect your phone to the helicopter using your cord and the USB port."

I comply and he mumbles something about downloading specs and information. "Are you sure this will work?"

"Hell no PuckDaddy isn't sure. Only tried it once before, and that helicopter was empty."

I watch the panel and witness Puck's remote control over the instruments. The dials change with no input from me. He increases the throttle and the helicopter begins shaking and screaming.

"Carmine, are you religious?" he asks.

"I think so."

"Are you praying?"

Yes! Katie answers.

"Nonstop," I say.

"Good. Me too. Alright, here we go."

The Sikorsky's vibrations rise in intensity and the landing gear lifts off. My stomach drops and I set my jaw.

I can do this. We can do this.

"The autopilot program will keep you level and pointed in the right direction," Puck says. "I control the speed and altitude. We've only got a couple minutes before they shoot you down. Ready?"

"Ready," I lie. "Punch it."

The helicopter rockets upward rapidly enough to press me firmly into the pilot's chair. The nose pitches forward and the aircraft begins packing on speed, flying south.

Like riding on an out-of-control meteor.

Below is the darkened city, illuminated only by smoldering wreckage. The altimeter climbs over three hundred feet. Four hundred. Four-fifty. On the distant ground I spot brilliant bursts of gunfire. I'm too high and moving too fast for Russia's mercenaries to hit, but they're trying anyway. Probably the first aircraft they've seen in a month and they're trying to shoot it down, no questions asked. No reason other than hate.

I consulted with PuckDaddy and the Resistance; all intelligence indicates that Russia lives in the splendor of the Electra condominium skyscraper downtown, the tallest residential tower. It's easy to spot, a spire of glass and balconies, because there are dim lights burning at the pinnacle.

"Go to five hundred feet," I advise, and there's another surge of power. We're skimming the skyscrapers now and I'm trying not to look down. "Are you filming?"

"Puck is recording off four different cameras," he says. "Although I can't believe you want the world to watch you die."

"Not my death. Russia's."

As we near the Electra tower, the giant black flag becomes visible, an acre of fabric ruffled by the winds. His totemic emblem, planted to lay claim to the city.

I'm going to rip it down.

I exit the cockpit, squeezing backwards into the passenger cabin. I put him on speakerphone, slip my shoulders into the backpack, and pick up Hurt - the massive sword, needed once more. It's almost too long for the small cabin.

"Okay, Puck, decelerate. We're nearly there."

The Electra slides into position below us and I guide Puck until the Sikorsky is hovering twenty feet above the zenith of the roof, aggravating the air and heavy flag with its rotors.

"Better hurry, Carmine. Your time runs short. If you plan on going through with this," he says.

I wrap my hand through a safety loop, lean far out of the cabin, and drive Hurt into the helicopter's fuselage. I thrust from my shoulder, and the blade cuts deeply through the fiberglass and gashes the gas tank. There's a spurt of gasoline, and I withdraw the blade. The rush of air creates a vacuum and unleaded kerosene begins pumping freely from the aircraft.

This is insane, this is insane, this is insane.

"You're losing fuel pressure," Puck warns.

The gasoline is caught and whipped by the rotor blades. Gallons and gallons of the stuff, flung into the ether.

"Bingo! Incoming! You've got incoming! Time to go!" he shouts. I untangle from the safety loop, cinch the backpack tighter, and drop.

My fall isn't far but the downward wash of the rotors makes it tricky. I aimed for the uppermost service walkways but miss, instead landing on the penthouse balcony, four feet from disaster.

Ohmygosh, that was too close!

A heartbeat after I jump, a surface-to-air missile intercepts and shatters the Sikorsky. I'd been banking on itchy trigger-fingers, and the rocket-totting mercenaries don't disappoint.

Fuel ignites and the helicopter blooms into a fireball. The inferno travels the gasoline trails, creating an expanding umbrella of gaseous blazes, far beyond a normal eruption.

The sky is on fire, directly above the terrorist's headquarters.

Death tolls for thee, Russia.

And she's pissed.

The atmosphere relinquishes its hold on my helicopter; burning wreckage from the Sikorsky plummets and collides with the western side of Electra's roof. An ear-splitting, tremendous sound. The impact shakes the entire structure, windows shattering on all four faces.

The penthouse doors are unlocked and I slip inside. I hear the panicked screams of men and women in the bowels of Electra. The tower is still ringing like a bell, kitchen gadgets falling out of cabinets, books cascading from shelves.

There are women in the luxurious master suite, bound by their wrists and secured to the California king bed. They cry desperately for help. I hold my finger to my lips but the poor captives are beyond reason, unable to be quieted; I want them to understand they'll be released but not until after threats are eliminated, but it's a lost cause. I leave them behind, a heart-wrenching act.

Puck is buzzing my phone. Wanting to know if I'm alive. I don't have time to answer. I'm sneaking around corners, tiptoeing on the thick carpet and scuffed wooden floors. It's apparent that Russia has redesigned the top levels by inexpertly removing walls and floors. It's a madhouse of juxtaposition - opulence and raw deconstruction.

From deep inside the Electra, a voice booms. **"She is *here*. Little queen from Los Angeles! Come to fight Russia. Find *her*. Bring *her*."** Russia. Such a voice. Cold and lifeless, like a tomb, but imbued with deep authority. The syllables are issued from around every corner, up through the very floor.

All is darkness. I don't need the lights; his men do. I encounter the first squad in the grand entrance hall of the penthouse. Gunmen, white and hispanic, bearing shotguns, working blind, fumbling with flashlights. Hurt has been sharpened into a razor and this four-person squad dies with one mighty sweep of the great sword. I barely feel the resistance.

My body is an ocean of crashing adrenaline and blood. Violence sweeps aside all sanity and consequences.

There is no penthouse front door. The walls are gone, and there is a gaping maw near the elevator. Five levels of elite condominiums are exposed, a large atrium created by explosives. Like the center of the uppermost floors has been hollowed out by an gigantic fifty-foot drill bit. From my perch at the apogee I see - an active fireplace at the lowest level; electric lanterns interspersed top to bottom, nestled inside bare living rooms and kitchens; more captive women, chained and hysterical; scrambling gunmen; and a truly shocking panoply of explosives and ammunition on the bottom floor of this sick theater.

The northern side of Electra is gashed open; a large scar which runs down the uppermost three floors, freshly gouged by the falling Sikorsky.

Russia himself stands near the fireplace, sixty feet below. He is tall and strong, artificially swollen by a herculean amount of body armor. A blast suit which rises all the way to his chin. His face is like stone, his eyes black. **"There is queen. There is little girl."** He effortlessly raises the largest machine gun I've ever seen. A belt-fed .50 caliber monster.

Not even the Incredible Hulk would enjoy absorbing those rounds. I'm forced backwards as he opens fire and disintegrates the floor on which I stand.

It's like a ray of death, liquifying anything the stream touches.

"I know boyfriend, little queen! I helped fight Chemist. I owe boyfriend favor. You abandon Los Angeles, you and boyfriend live."

"It's too late for negotiations, Russia! I am your executioner. This is your final night."

He roars and destroys another portion of the Electra's ceiling with his almighty machine gun. "Little bitch! You know nothing! I have lived over century. I fight in Soviet civil war, general in Red Army. I win wars in Czechoslovakia, in Angola, in Hungary. You, little girl, die like wolf! Alone. Hung as ornament."

His voice rattles me, shaking my confidence and vision. I get a taste of the Guardians' fear when Chase *Shouts* at them. He's *so* powerful.

Focus, Carmine!

Focus, Carmine. He sent a suicide bomber to assassinate you and nothing's been the same since. He's going to attack New Los Angeles tomorrow. He will crush everything we've worked for.

More of his men are invading my floor, pumping through the stairwells. I retreat from the gaping center atrium, withdrawing into the catacombs of broken condos.

I stalk and eliminate them. They're simple mercenaries, overmatched and weak. They smell of alcohol and marijuana, and they move in slow motion. Hurt sings in my hand, warming with the butchery.

The gunmen don't have a chance to aim their gun. Those lucky enough to get a shot off don't fire accurately, and they are quickly executed. Anger gives me wings.

The last man falls and I scan the battlefield, *Probing* through halls and rooms with my senses. I find no one.

Without warning and without a second thought, I *Launch* into the gaping maw and plunge towards Russia. Between my ears, Katie Lopez holds her breath. I do too. His back is turned. I aim for the spine at the base of his neck, Hurt poised to fall like an executioner's axe.

At the last second, Russia hears my rush of air. He twists, which saves his life, and my blade bites deeply into his shoulder. A normal man would be cut in half, but his armor and freakish body composition stay the steel after only a few inches.

He *Roars*, a thunderous sound, and somehow swings far enough to crush me with a fist. I don't release my hold on the hilt, and Hurt shatters. Shards of metal erupt like confetti. I land against the fireplace, holding a jagged sword now only eighteen inches long. A longer two-foot chunk is still imbedded in his left shoulder.

I attack again, while he's wounded and stunned.

Even encumbered by the blast suit, he's still quicker than me, and infinitely stronger. Russia is Infected, a pure-born. He knocks my blade to the side and kicks me in the abdomen. My ribs break.

"**Little queen!**" he *Bellows*. "**Little queen will die!**"

I'm flung across the room, coming to rest near the boxes of rockets, the rounds of bullets stacked five feet high, crates of grenades. His treasure, an unending supply of pain.

"**You don't know. *Strong* survive. Victors get spoils. Mighty and powerful rule. But little queen falls. Should have run.**"

He picks up his machine gun.

I hurl the broken blade, tomahawk-style. He's forced to block it, leaving him vulnerable. I'm already mid-air. My knee connects with his face, breaking his nose. I latch onto his shoulders. The soft skin under his jaw peels away in thick slices, surrendering to my nails, but I can't dig deep enough. A savage, disgusting, but ineffective attack.

With one fistful of my hair, he yanks me off and I crash though an exquisite set of dining room chairs, probably once valued at five thousand dollars a piece.

He aims with the .50 cal.

Get up!

I can't. I'm going to die…

"Hey handsome!" Kayla calls, a melodious sound. She steps out from behind a broken door like a guardian angel. "Over here!"

Yes! Kayla, way to go!

Kayla's voice carries power, enough to stagger the Infected beast. "That's right, big guy, just hold steady!"

Dalton reveals himself, emerging from the crumbling stairwell. He's holding a rocket launcher on his shoulder. A deadly unguided RPG.

About time these two showed up. With firepower.

The four of us are in close proximity. A direct impact might be lethal to us all. But it's worth it.

Russia is shaking his head, dislodging Kayla's influence.

She keeps chattering.

Katie Lopez rages.

I try to rise. My abdomen protests.

Dalton aims and depresses the trigger.

Compressed gas erupts from the rear of the launcher, a fiery backblast.

- 6 -

Samantha Gear

Andy Babington is groaning. I remember that kid. The little twerp was upset when Chase became the starting quarterback at Hidden Spring High School.

Feels like eons ago. Back before the world went off axis.

Chase approaches the glass and presses his hands against the surface. "Andy," he says. "Can you hear me?"

Andy stares at him but doesn't respond.

A black case is surgically attached to his back, secured with bolts screwed into his…ribs, probably. The skin surrounding the six insertion points are inflamed. Unquestionably a bomb - a permanent and heavy backpack. There's a small digital panel on the right side, green lights blinking.

I've seen a lot of sick stuff. But this makes my stomach turn.

Chase points at the two men dressed in airtight suits and says, "You two. Are you loyal to the Secretary of State?"

One man remains silent, glowering.

The other man gasps and his face breaks with relief. "No! I was abducted from Georgetown University Hospital yesterday! They flew me in and demanded I consult on the surgery. This is inhumane! This is madness!"

His fellow surgeon, deep within the clutches of Blue-Eyes's supremacy, picks up a small scalpel, screams, and charges Chase. The Outlaw is a powerful man, towering and muscular, and he gives off the impression of being bigger than his physical dimensions. He casually knocks the surgeon aside. The little man crashes into a collection of metal carts and doesn't get up.

"You. Georgetown," he says. "What'd they'd do to Andy? Is that a bomb?"

There are multiple security cameras in this room. We'll have hostile company before long. I move to stand beside the airlock, pistol in one hand, grenade in the other.

Where are you, blue-eyed bitch.

The surgeon from Georgetown answers, "Y-yes. But I don't know much about the explosive. I caught the phrase Mk-54."

"Which is a small nuke," I confirm for Chase. "Like a suitcase bomb."

"How small?"

"Less than ten kilotons. Maybe five."

"Samantha. Talk English. What's that mean?"

I search my brain for information. "The bomb dropped on Hiroshima was approximately fifteen. So this has a third of the yield, but will still wipe out multiple city blocks. In a dense city, fifty thousand casualties. Maybe a lot more."

Chase glares at the surgeon. "Disarm it."

"I cannot."

"Remove it."

"Any tampering will detonate the payload!" The man is close to hysterics, ragged breaths fogging his face-shield. "The mechanism monitors the patient's biology. Specifically, his heartbeat and blood pressure. If he dies...it detonates. If he's removed from the sensors, it detonates."

"That's the most deviant thing I've ever heard," I growl. "Not even Andy's sorry ass deserves that fate."

The boy in the cage begins unlimbering and he slowly stands, his head nearly touching the glass ceiling. His muscles possess a sinewy, twitchy strength.

"There's more," the surgeon says. "I've reviewed the surveillance footage. The Secretary of State herself has spent hours with him, talking through the glass. Inculcating him with instructions and a mission."

"She's using her influence to brainwash Andy. What mission?"

"He'll be released and sent to hunt down Queen Carmine. The mutant leader in Los Angeles," the man states, unaware his words pierce directly into our hearts.

He's an assassin.

He's Katie's assassin.

Chase is going to lose his mind.

Andy and Chase are inches apart. The hero and the surgical freak. I see Andy's vitals on the digital display. His pulse is racing, over one-twenty. Chase's shoulders slump and his face tilts forward until his forehead rests on the glass cage. "And if Katie kills Andy, even in self-defense, the bomb will detonate and incinerate everyone within a half mile," Chase says.

"That's right. And once the patient is out of range of the CDC, the bomb will grant him the ability to detonate at will. So he only needs to get close," the man says.

"A suicide bomber. With a nuke. Brainwashed to track down and execute Katie. And everyone near her," Chase mutters. "Our world has gone to hell."

"Outlaw. We need to go."

"What about Andy?"

"I...I don't know. But we're not here for him. Let's accomplish our objective and then worry about Andy," I say.

Without removing his forehead from the glass, Chase nods.

I don't know if Andy has been listening or not, but he makes a fist, draws his arm back, and strikes the glass with his knuckles. The glass cage rings; the struck wall buckles slightly, and the structure itself shifts forward half an inch.

"Oh hell. Doc, can he get out of that?" I ask.

"I don't know! Remember, I just arrived."

I shove open the airlock's inner door and hold it open with my foot.

Andy punches the glass wall again with the force of a battering ram. There's a splintering sound, but the cage remains intact.

Chase asks, "So the bomb is armed? You're positive?"

The surgeon nods.

"But he can't detonate it himself yet?"

"Correct."

"But if he dies in this room...?" Chase asks.

"I think…I-I'm not sure, but I think the bomb will detonate. I was brought in to help keep him alive, but I don't think he needs assistance. He's exceptionally robust."

"So we just keep him alive. Easy," I say. Andy strikes the glass again. His face is turning red, and the cage's ringing has taken on a fractured sound. "Chase. Let's. Go. We're making him mad."

I step inside the airlock and shove open the broken outer door.

Blue-Eyes is waiting in the hallway. Surrounded by a security detail. Wearing a revealing cross-over drape top. She gasps in pleasant surprise, the most beautiful sound I've ever heard.

Her scent.

Her face.

The noise she produces.

She's an intoxicating bouquet of pleasure, one which goes straight to my brain. I'm not immune to her disease's manifest charms because I'm a women or because I'm heterosexual. I'm overwhelmed by the banquet of desires to serve and obey. Instantly ensnared.

We're saved from disaster only by my training, my military instincts. My left hand, of its own volition, flicks loose the grenade's safety pin and releases the spoon, starting the countdown. Her eyes, beautiful blue orbs which shine like the gulf off Florida's coast, swivel down to witness this act of rebellion.

Live grenade.

Tick tock.

"No!" she cries, a sound so mellifluous my heart could break.

I drop the grenade, which bounces off the airlock's doorjamb and rolls into the midst of her security detail. They scatter. The bravest among them, thinking he has time, bends to retrieve it.

But it's a three-second grenade.

Chase grabs my vest and hauls me backwards.

I watch the detonation in supercharged slow motion. The weapon expands to twice its original size before the metal bursts.

The brave man disintegrates.

The force blows the airlock's door off ruined hinges.

Screaming in the hallway.

The spell she cast over me is broken by the noise and the concussion.

Chase yanks a second grenade from my vest and throws it into the hallway, fastball style, ricocheting out of sight. Another explosion rocks the CDC's basement.

We're SO close!! I can't BELIEVE she caught me by surprise! I'm so mad I might shoot my own foot.

The once quiet sterile hallway is now a riotous red.

I'm up. Pistol in my hand. I empty the clip into the two security guards in my field of vision, a staccato of noise. Reloading takes half a second and I come up with a third grenade.

Behind me, Andy Babington crashes hard enough into the cage to splinter it, and the glass wall partially separates from the joining metal seams. He'll be free any second.

Chase goes *through* the lab's outer wall, bulldozing into the hallway. He's the bait, the tank intended to absorb damage so I can get a clean shot. Truly the Outlaw is a wonder to behold. He can dodge bullets or block them with his stick of death, and even though he's fighting a superior number of Variants he's too much for them.

I leap through the bore he created, glaring down my pistol's front sights. Blue-Eyes is ready. She raises her palm to me and says, "Desist, please, my love. Lay down your weapon and come with me."

I can't fire while she's talking. Her words impact me like physical blows. She nearly has me again, but she makes a mistake; she quits speaking. As soon as her mouth closes, I clench my eyes and pull the trigger. My hand is shaking as the gun kicks. The bone in her right shoulder, likely the acromion adjacent to the clavicle, shatters.

A pulpy mist. She screams.

I'm reeling and shooting, but her guards leap in front, absorbing the hollow-point bullets. More security is pounding down the hallway, some running barefoot along the walls.

Our tiny battlefield is compacting with warm bodies.

I release the third grenade's safety spoon and cock my arm. She's too far from an exit. This grenade should—

Andy Babington, released from his prison, hits me from behind. Like being crushed by a tow truck. The grenade pops free from my hand, wavers midair, two seconds from detonation.

The Outlaw sees it, grabs it, *Throws* it, probably over a hundred twenty miles per hour. The noise is deafening. Men fall. Ceiling tiles collapse, and shrapnel digs into Chase's right flank.

Enraged, I spin and get my pistol under Andy's jaw. He's not as fast as I am, and I'm not thinking lucidly. I'm going to remove most of his face. I yank the trigger.

"No!" The Outlaw grabs my weapon, his pinky wedging between the hammer and firing pin. The gun blast is aborted. "If he dies, we die."

My eyes widen. I'm pinned under an armed nuke.

Oh yeah…

Andy hits Chase, a colossal right cross which would kill other men, but the Outlaw simply spins with the punch and tackles the oncoming Variant guards.

Pinned beneath Andy, I hammer my forearm into his throat. Once. Twice. And then into his jaw, and the human bomb rolls off, coughing. I get to my feet. Still woozy from her voice. I get a glimpse; she's being helped at the far end of the hall.

I fire the remaining bullets in my clip and jack home another. Andy plows into me again, and pins me against the wall. He hammers my ribs and my shoulders and my skull with his iron fists, but I still aim at Blue-Eyes. Yanking the trigger almost faster than the mechanism can respond. Have to hand it to her security detail - they willingly intercept bullets. A shield of flesh. But most of them now bleed on the ground.

I'm grinding my teeth against the pain. Andy is freakishly strong.

That oozing shoulder wound won't put Blue-Eyes out of commission. I need another clean firing lane.

The Outlaw grabs Andy by the throat and pulls him off.

Two seconds before she turns the corner. Last chance.

I aim. Andy breaks loose, spins, and drives the Outlaw back into me. We're a writhing mess, like an octopus mashed against the hallway wall.

I see the pistol's theoretical terminus, an invisible target generated in my mind's eye by natural tendencies and practice, as though the weapon had a laser sight. Usually steady and pinpoint accurate, now it weaves wildly across the hall; the trusted connection between my brain and finger is malfunctioning, the coordination broken by Andy.

I fire all three rounds left in my magazine. Possibly the most important of my life.

The first bullet catches her in her left side. Likely puncturing a lung.

The second digs into her left buttock.

The third misses.

"Got her!" I scream. "Three hits total! She's wounded!"

Chase finally puts his shoulder behind a punch, connecting with Andy's jaw, and the crazed patient goes limp.

Alarms scream and lights flash. Took them long enough. A security door is dropping at the end of the hallway, where Blue-Eyes's retreat is being guarded by at least two dozen secret servicemen and Variants. We duck into the airlock to avoid incoming gunfire.

"Is she fatally wounded?" Chase asks.

"I don't know! I tagged her shoulder; her back, near her lung; and her ass."

He nods, wincing with each breath, and I finally notice his injuries. He's bleeding from…everywhere. The grenade, the Variants, the bullets, and Andy have taken their toll. "So maybe not fatal."

"Maybe not."

"Samantha. I didn't come all this way to let her escape."

"We can't fight through the hall. There's too many now, and half of them are mutants. Our element of surprise is gone. And so is she."

He takes a deep breath, which hurts him, and he nods into the hallway. I follow his gaze. Andy Babington is on all fours, struggling to rise.

"Him," Chase says.

"What about him?"

"Shoot him. In the head. And Blue-Eyes doesn't escape."

I don't respond. He's suggesting we detonate a nuclear bomb. On American soil, in a crowded city. A very un-Outlaw-like suggestion, but I immediately understand; the sacrifice would be worth it. We die, she dies, her Variants die, and so do thousands of civilians - but we might be saving the future of everyone else.

If I don't execute him now, I could spend every day hereafter wishing I had.

"Shoot him and Katie lives," he grunts. "Shoot him and the President is free from her."

I eject the pistol's exhausted magazine and jam a fresh one home. Chamber a round. Aim at Andy's temple. He's shaking his head slightly, as though he's trying to wake up. The casing on his back has been bent slightly, but the lights still blink green.

"You sure?" I ask, and my voice wavers.

"No. But Katie's worth it. Her Kingdom is worth it. Right?"

The sights on my gun won't hold steady. I increase the pressure on the trigger, thinking about how this whole thing could be over. My headaches. My anxiety. The war. Blink of an eye.

"Why don't *you* do it?" I ask.

"You know me." He gives me a lop-sided grin. A sad one. "I could never go through with it."

I glare at Andy. And I pull the trigger - part way.

Memories land like lightning strikes in my mind.

I remember spying on Chase, over two years ago. I watched him for a couple weeks before registering as a student at his school. I introduced myself to Chase on a football field, same time I met Andy Babington, and I liked him immediately. I witnessed him grow into his abilities. Later, somehow he discovered my perch on top of the City Hall tower and confronted me. He taught me to live again. Taught me the meaning of bravery. The first person to love me in ten years. On multiple occasions I was ordered by superiors to execute him but I couldn't, and I still can't.

"No way, Outlaw," I say, and I lower the pistol. "Without you, there's no Chase-and-Katie. There's no happy ending. And that's really the only reason I get up in the morning."

He nods, hands on his hips. His complexion has paled. "I'm fond of

Chase-and-Katie too. Okay…" He inhales. And does it again, like he can't gulp enough oxygen. His body is already hard at work, repairing itself, but that doesn't help with the pain. "Let's intercept her on the main floor."

The security door has fully closed, sealing us off from Blue-Eyes and her security team. We rip our way through the locked stairwell doors and egress upwards, towards the surface. Andy Babington staggers after us, his face a mask of hate.

We exit onto the main level and into a scene of madness. Both our phones beep with messages. Police cars are arriving en masse. There is shouting and gunfire. Helicopters overhead. And the Cheerleader.

Hannah Walker followed us! She's screaming. And she's aflame. Like a comet among the CDC's defenses, steadily demolishing the main floor. She's out of control, gone berserk. The temperature in the hall has risen to an easy eighty-five. Sprinklers should kick in soon.

"Your girlfriend's here," I note the obvious. "She's going to chase you until one of you dies, you know."

He nods grimly.

Puck messages again.

>> hey u 2

>> cant talk

>> but u should know

>> the cheerleader followed u

>> police have been called

>> and the army

>> and fire department

>> and every1 else

>> so u should probably run

"What a mess," Chase mumbles, from our hiding spot.

"Hannah? Hannah Walker?" Andy is standing beside us, slightly unsteady on his feet. He holds his head and peers down the CDC's primary hall towards the chaos. "I remember…Hannah."

"That's right," I say slowly, catching Chase's eye. "Andy, didn't you and Hannah used to date?"

He doesn't respond. I wonder how much brain power he has left, after all he's been through. He could be operating with the faculties of a two-year-old.

"Maybe," I suggest slowly, "you should go give Hannah a hug. But provide us a five-minute head start."

Chase mutters, "You got a twisted mind, Shooter."

Andy has begun a broken shuffle down the hallway. "…Hannah…"

I hiss at Chase, "Two birds, one stone. Maybe three! We don't know where Blue-Eyes is, but she's probably still on campus. She'd die in the blast. Right? I suggest you and I run. Quickly."

There's a wheezing, rattling sound when Chase breathes. "I keep expecting life to settle down. To grow less ridiculous," he says. In the reflection of his eyes, I see Andy walking slowly towards the growing blaze. "But now… I don't know. Andy is my former teammate. And Hannah was my girlfriend. And one is on fire, the other is strapped to a bomb, and I'm hoping they both die in a nuclear blast. How can it get weirder?"

"This isn't the best time for you to get sentimental."

"There's never a good time anymore."

I grab his vest and haul him towards the emergency exit. "Come on, Outlaw. We need to run."

"I wish we could do it all over again. Go back in time, and fix this," he says. "You know? There's gotta be something we could have done…"

I tug him again, and he follows me through the emergency exit. Time to go…

Except about a hundred police officers are waiting for us. Guns drawn. Shouting orders.

We freeze, and I wonder how long before Andy reaches the fire…

- 7 -

Kayla

That Russia dude is *huge*! And ugly!

"That's right, big guy, just hold steady!" I *Shout* at him, throwing all my personality into the words. He staggers, and his awful machine gun swerves crazily. I can't hold him long, not like his army of mercenaries. He's Infected, vastly more powerful than any of us, and he's going to kill Queen Carmine.

She's hurt. On the floor, trying to rise.

Dalton, I want to scream. Fire your stupid *rocket!*

He does, *finally*, but it's a disaster. This tower has sustained considerable damage, and the floor he's standing on buckles. The rocket ejects from his launcher, but misses! It passes within eighteen inches of Russia and connects with the burning fireplace beyond. The western face of the Electra tower bursts outwards, exposing the black sky and Pacific ocean.

The explosion rocks the tower and we're all thrown down. Like someone hit a giant reset button.

My ears ring. My vision is white at the edges. Limbs are numb. I try to speak but the heat scorches my throat; my words come out as rasps.

Queen Carmine was too close to the eruption. She's holding her ears, and rolling around in a pile of chairs.

Everything is on fire, except Russia. His blast-suit protected him from the worst. The broken sword lodged in his shoulder is gone. He slowly stands, a gargantuan man, and laughs. His voice box is damaged but still functioning, like disgusting rocks breaking against one another.

"Little babies! Come to play with grown man."

Dalton rises to his feet but the launcher is missing.

Queen Carmine is no longer moving. She lays limp. Poor thing, she's been through SO much.

I'm *super* close to freaking out!

Before Dalton or I can move, Russia pulls a *huge* knife from his belt and kneels next to Carmine. They are close enough to the fresh gaping hole in the tower that I worry he'll simply fling her into the sky, but he doesn't. He says, **"I like this one. This one is strong. Maybe I keep her."**

"No, you maybe don't!" I shout but it's a harsh squeal. No effect. I shamble towards him, and so does Dalton, but Russia holds up a finger.

"You come closer, and little queen dies."

Get up, Carmine. Get *up!*

But she doesn't.

Oh my gosh oh my gosh oh my gosh…

"I think maybe I cut queen's hair. And cut out queen's eyes. And I keep her. With other women. I like queen's strength. You two watch and go home. Tell the world. About Russia." He raises his knife. **"Let this be lesson. Don't resist powerful men. Might always makes right."**

Suddenly, Queen Carmine's eyes pop open. "You were born strong, Russia…" she snarls, and she punches him in the nose. Hard. It was already broken, and now she drives it inward with an audible crunch. He rears back and *Roars*, which I bet is the sound tyrannosaurus dinosaurs used to produce. His recoil gives her room to bend her knee and kick upwards, catching Russia in the chest. A kick powerful enough to rock him backwards into an unsteady standing position. "…but don't confuse that with the ability to rule."

"Carmine!" I scream, and it's sufficiently loud to affect Russia. A little. He's dazed and injured.

She kicks him again, in the groin.

Dalton is at a full sprint. He lowers his shoulder and hits Russia in the abdomen. Text-book tackle, except Dalton doesn't tackle the monster.

Instead he drives him. Toward the hole in the tower. Toward the black sky and Pacific ocean.

How do you kill an Infected? Drop them on their head from a tower!

Carmine sees it the same moment I do - Dalton intends to finish the job. He isn't planning on going home. Maybe he never was. He's going over the edge and he's taking the monster with him.

We scream.

The two men reach the brink of the abyss and teeter. The Infected warloard is off-balance, Dalton underneath him, and Russia can't get purchase. Can't stop the awful skid.

Russia rams his knife into Dalton's back. Again and again. But the queen's bodyguard won't let go. Failure is not an option.

With the last of his strength, Dalton gives a final thrust from his leg, and slowly they tip into the atmosphere and fall from view.

Russia roars for the duration of their fall.

Dalton, who might be the finest man I ever met, doesn't complain.

Carmine and I reach the side. With our enhanced eyesight, we pierce the dark gloom below. Two bodies, broken on the railroad tracks. Never to rise again.

After the vicious battle, the subsequent calm feels phantasmagorical. Technically the Queen Carmine's plan worked, and we understood beforehand it might cost all three of our lives. We won, and with fewer losses than anticipated, and yet… And yet.

And yet, Dalton.

He's been gone mere minutes but I miss him so MUCH already. I want him to growl when Carmine gets too close to the tower's edge. I want him to intentionally turn away and not stare when I stretch or smile. I want him to glare when I tease him.

I wish PuckDaddy was here. I could use a hug. From a boy.

Queen Carmine weeps, curled into a ball, for almost an hour. We cry on the one remaining undamaged couch. It's during this interval that I recognize the subtle transformation. The queen has changed. Like the quality of her aura is altering. She's still the queen. It's still her voice. Still her body. But somehow there's been a shift.

When she finally stands, her posture is perfect, but perhaps not as ramrod straight. Her eyes hold a gentleness I'm unaccustomed to, and she hugs me fiercely. That *never* happens, but I love it so much. She kisses the top of my head, and I'm embarrassed by how happy I am. "Sweet sweet Kayla," she says. "How glad I am that you're here with me."

The queen's intensity is still present, but it's of a brighter, purer texture. "Carmine? Are you…are you okay?"

"No. No I'm not. But I think the trauma has broken a few barriers in my mind." She smiles weakly. "I've found more of myself."

"You mean Katie Lopez?"

She stares into the distance, like searching the corners of her brain, listening for something. "Katie and Carmine are two sides of the same coin. And I'm both of them."

I nod, though I don't understand.

She asks, "Any news of Chase?"

I check my phone, but Puck hasn't texted. "Not yet, sweetie. What do we do now?"

She sets her jaw and glares at the bizarre atrium of exposed penthouses above us. "Now you let the world know Russia is dead. Then we release his chained victims. And tear down that flag."

I get to work immediately on my phone while she staggers and limps around Russia's super weird penthouse prison. The ceiling and floors of at least four or five levels have been removed, and I can hear women crying on all of them.

Releasing the hostages takes hours, because we're moving slowly, the chains are thick, and the liberated women are hysterical. Convincing them we don't have food and that Russia is really dead takes a while. They recognize and cling to Carmine, and she tells them to wait on the third level of the tower, and we'll all travel north together.

Dawn is purpling the eastern horizon by the time we reach the roof. Queen Carmine is exhausted, but I'm not. I go days without sleeping. Even hurt and tired, she's the most beautiful person I've ever met. Inside and out, and I love her so much I nearly glow. I would die for the queen, that's for sure.

I use my phone to film her taking down the immense black flag, and releasing it over the side. She strikes an exotic and heroic figure, the angry muscles in her arms pumping and flexing, strong hands ripping the material. The fabric catches the wind and drifts northwest, toward the ocean. A tattered American flag is balled up near the base of the pole Russia used to hang his black banner, and Carmine carefully attaches Old Glory to the rope, and hauls it into the air. Even though the President is trying to kill us, and we seceded from the United States almost a year ago, I get a lump in my throat watching it ascend the spire. Red, white and blue never looked so good.

She speaks into my phone, "America the Beautiful is no more. But the dream is not dead. This flag doesn't represent the President or his witch. This flag represents what it did originally. Hope. And freedom. The crime lord known as Russia has been vanquished, as will be all enemies of hope and peace."

I turn off the camera, transmit the video, and we sit on the edge of the tower, feet dangling five hundred feet in the air. We snack on fruit she brought in her backpack. Without food and without a firm leader, this city will descend into anarchy and violence. The mercenaries will wake up in the next few hours, realize Russia is dead and...well, it'll be ugly.

Queen Carmine is unnaturally still beside me. She's staring steadily toward the east and chewing on her lip. A tear leaks out of her eye and she takes a shaky breath. "I remember the first time I met Chase. He was new to the neighborhood and he came out to play. There were older kids nearby who had never been very nice to me, but Chase was. I loved him from day one, when he chose to bounce a ball across the street with me rather than play with the bigger kids."

I'm stunned. Her memory *has* returned. Maybe I should be recording this.

She continues, "They lived in the newly built subdivision. When his mom died, his father used the life insurance money to pay off their townhouse. His father, a good man named Richard, got depressed and hurt his back, and Chase raised himself. His grades dropped, he couldn't focus, couldn't concentrate. And when he finally found himself again, the disease struck…" She stops to wipe her eyes, but it doesn't help. She's a wreck. "Life has been very hard on Chase Jackson. And now…"

"And now?" I ask.

"And now," she repeats and draws another shaky breath. "And now he's gone."

"Gone?" I take her hand and squeeze. The sun will be up soon, less than an hour. We are running low on time. "Sweetheart, do you mean Dalton?"

"I'm not talking about Dalton."

"Then I'm confused."

"Chase." Her voice beaks. "His heart stopped. I *Feel* it."

- 8 -
The Outlaw

We're being pursued by most of America. Or at least that's what it seems like.

Samantha and I evaded the contingent of police officers on CDC's campus, but we're still stuck in Atlanta. We're hidden on the black, sprawling roof of North Dekalb Mall, safely removed from a nuclear blast. I hope. The Army has arrived. The Reserves are here. A thousand police cruisers search the streets, lights blaring, sirens wailing. Hunting for us.

For the moment, the rage inside our bodies has unclenched. We sit in the dreamlike aftermath of the shoot-out, an eye of the hurricane, quickly evaluating our options before plunging again into the maelstrom.

Is it wrong to pray for Blue-Eyes's wounds to be fatal? Probably, but I am. She's trying to murder the love of my life, and we came so close to stopping her. So. Close. I'm a little surprised the bomb hasn't detonated by now. Andy apparently survived his pursuit of the Cheerleader. As awful as it is, I'd been hoping it would blow.

Andy and Blue-Eyes, both hellbent on killing Katie.

"Any news?" I ask.

Samantha is texting PuckDaddy, searching for an escape route. "About Katie? Puck hasn't mentioned anything."

I grunt with displeasure, and it hurts my lungs. "He's not telling us something. Tonight has not gone well."

"We released the hostages," she says. "And shot Blue-Eyes three times.

Tonight wasn't a total failure." I don't respond. Katie's still in mortal danger. Which means total failure.

The western horizon is blue with police lights, turning the earth into a ghost zone, but the sun is minutes away from climbing in the east. The night passed in a blink.

"Okay," she says, glancing up from her phone. "Puck says there's another airport, five miles north of here. This one isn't abandoned, and in fact Blue-Eyes's personal jet is waiting there on the tarmac."

"Let's steal it." And go home. Home to Katie. I ache for her.

"My thoughts exactly."

There's a squad car near us, in the mall parking lot. The driver leans against the hood, listening to his radio squawk. We slip silently down the wall, catch him by surprise, and break his radio and cellphone.

"Sorry about that," I tell him. "Also, it'd be great if you gave us a couple minutes head start."

"Are you really the Outlaw?"

"For as long as I have to be," I say.

"You kill the Secretary of State?"

"Tried. Not sure if it worked or not."

He nods grimly and salutes us. "She's a terrorist, you ask me. Every day I think about packing my car and driving to California."

"We need good men like you."

"Can't. Got a kid on the way, you know? But anyway. I won't report my stolen vehicle for a couple minutes. Good luck to you both."

I'm about to duck into the driver's seat but Samantha says, "Hey, Outlaw. You're hurt. Besides, I've always wanted to drive one of these things."

I hate riding shotgun. "But I usually—"

"Tough. You're bleeding heavily. Move." And she slides behind the wheel.

The police officer is true to his word - we hear no reports of a stolen squad car over the in-dash radio until we've parked at an eclectic restaurant called The 57th Fighter Group, directly next to the airstrip. From our vantage standing on the roof, we spot a government jet waiting, engines warming, lights on, near a series of small private hangers.

Samantha says, "There's our ride."

I speak into my blue-tooth headset, "Puck, what happened to those prisoners we released? Did they make it to our other jet?"

"Not yet, homie. But that's a long hike. Puck bets they will show up soon, and I'll fly them home. Also, the mighty PuckDaddy has news; Queen Carmine is alive and Russia is dead."

"Wow," I say, and I grin so big it feels as though my face might split. "How'd that happen?"

"Carmine, Dalton, and Kayla intercepted him at his headquarters before he began his march north."

"And Katie is safe?"

"*Carmine* is safe, yes," he answers.

"See, Outlaw? Tonight wasn't a total bust," Samantha Gear says.

"Get that plane in the air," he tells us. "And get yourselves home. I'll put it on cruise control once you're airborne."

We vault the security fence and run to the jet. The sun has broken the horizon, and for a moment we're in plain view. Airport servicemen and security personnel mill around the nearby hanger, their backs to us momentarily. We storm aboard, and find it vacant but for the co-pilot. Samantha puts a gun to his temple and says, "I'd rather not. But I will. Get me?"

"Y-yes, ma'am."

"This jet ready to fly?"

"Ah, well," He gulps. "Before takeoff we'll run through the checklist—"

"But we're fueled?"

"Yes, ma'am, she's ready for takeoff," he stutters.

"Wanna go with us?" I ask. "We're headed to California."

"You're the Outlaw."

"Yep. Wanna go?"

He turns white. "I...I'd prefer to stay, sir. But I'm a big fan."

Samantha slides into the pilots chair and looks over the myriad of controls. "No sweat. Let's do this."

I jerk my thumb over my shoulder. "Time to get out, co-pilot."

He scrambles and trips down the stairs. I haul the hatch closed, and Samantha revs the motors. "Let's go," I call.

"We're gone!"

The jet lumbers forward and slowly pivots onto the slate-gray tarmac. She clamps a set of headphones over her ears, and she grins. I can't hear the incoming tower chatter but Samantha responds, "Copy that, Tower, but I'm only taking her for a test-drive. How's she handle, anyway?"

This plane is stocked with ice cold drinks and snacks, and I select an armful to bring with me to the front. I'm famished.

Samantha pivots the jet again, in a 180-degree turn, and now the long black airstrip stretches before us to a dot on the horizon. My heart accelerates, analogous to the engine's increasing RPMs. Marveling at her technical acumen, because after all she only recently learned to fly, I pop a strawberry into my mouth and savor the familiar flavor. Can't remember my last strawberry.

Airport servicemen and security are running toward our airstrip, waving their arms. Samantha releases the brakes. We pack on the speed and the world begins to blur.

"Yeah, well. Same to you, Tower," she barks into the radio. "Mind your manners and maybe I'll return the plane in one piece." She tears off the headset and grumbles, "People get so attached to their stuff."

She hauls back on the control wheel and we nose gently into the atmosphere. Airborne. Headed home.

Puck calls me on the radio as we arc northward.

"Listen carefully, you two. Puck advises you stay low to the deck. The Federal Government isn't going to let infamous war criminals escape easily. You've got incoming F-22 fighter jets scrambling out of Moody Air Force Base, and they'll be given the order to shoot you down. You copy that?"

Samantha nods and she banks east. "Roger that, Puck. I'm flying low and east. Hopefully we'll throw them off our trail by taking an indirect route. You disable whatever features our aircraft uses to communicate with the FAA."

Instead of flying home, we're headed directly opposite; aiming toward the sun, which is now fully above the horizon and climbing steadily. She says,

"Let's fly south above the Atlantic and cross Florida into the Gulf. Whaddaya say?"

"I say I trust you."

"Pass me the strawberries and cashews. And is that a cold ginger ale I see? Good heavens, hand it over."

Forty-five minutes later, we cruise low over the beach at Hilton Head and she alters our course south. As if on cue, PuckDaddy calls again. "You've been spotted!"

"Damn it," she growls.

"F-22s a couple miles off your starboard."

She dips the plane lower, now dangerously close to the ocean's surface. "Can't outrun them, can't out maneuver them," she mutters. "This was a short flight."

I say, "Time to abandon the ship."

"But they'll spot our parachutes."

"But possibly not our wing-suits. Get us some altitude and we'll jump. Land in Savannah."

"This sucks. I like this jet."

She flies silently a moment, considering her options. But there are none.

"Get us higher," I say. "I want room to glide."

"F-22s have a visual on you," Puck warns. "Lethal force has been sanctioned!"

This is all happening too quickly. Samantha points our nose at the sky and punches the throttle. I'm thrown backwards through the cabin. "Let's go!" I roar. "Get back here!"

Our little jet begins shaking.

I yank on the emergency hatch's release and kick the door outward. Our air rushes out and enormous noise pours in.

"Oh crap! They fired! Missiles incoming!"

Our aircraft is climbing at a forty-five degree angle. Samantha drops through the cabin's walkway, but crashes into a chair. She can't get her feet under her.

"Move, move! Go, go!!"

I grab her vest with one hand, and the emergency hatch with the other. With one giant pull, I bodily haul her up and through the opening. She's gone with a loud whomp of air.

"Outlaw!" I hear her cry through my bluetooth earpiece. "Hurry!'

The first missile collides with and detonates against our starboard wing. The metal is sheered off and I'm thrown backwards, deeper into the cabin.

I'm disoriented, stricken nearly insensate by the intense eruption, but I'm aware of a second missile punching through the jet's cockpit. All is pain and sound. It's like being caught inside a tumbling inferno. The fuselage breaks in half. Our forward momentum evaporates and the wreckage begins a free fall.

I can't move, no longer functional. My injuries are too great.

The jet's tail begins cartwheeling, and I'm flung limply into the sky. My awareness feels loose, as though barely stitched to my bones.

The planet spins. More jet fuel ignites. Can't breathe.

I want to haul on my parachute.

I want to engage the wing-suit.

But I do not possess the capacity.

In my ear. "Outlaw! Outlaw! NO!!"

"What?! What's going on??"

"He didn't make it out!! No parachute! I don't see him!"

"Find him!!"

"There's no parachute! No wing-suit! He's gone! I don't see him!!"

He's gone, the voice says.

He's gone.

He's gone.

Before I enter the Atlantic Ocean, a drop which would kill most people, I become dimly aware that my heart has stopped.

- 9 -

Carmine

A kind of saturnine numbness has settled across my mind. I operate on instinct and impulse, simply doing what I must without thinking. One foot in front of the other.

Chase is dead. I don't understand why I know this.

But I do. Some preternatural awareness. I *Felt* his heart stop.

Puck isn't responding to Kayla's texts, further confirmation.

However, at the moment, I cannot focus on that. I will weep for weeks later. But for now, there are scared women to usher out of San Diego, a city which will break open into madness soon. There is a functional San Diego Metropolitan Transit bus at the ransacked terminal. The interior is filthy and the tank is half full, but it should carry us far clear of city borders. I sideswipe a few derelict cars in my wild ride back to the tower, but for the twenty-three released hostages it may as well be a chariot made of gold. Their ticket out of hell.

They load, bringing no belongings. Kayla steps in and wrenches the doors closed, and the bus coughs and lurches forward. A half-hearted, exhausted cheer is raised.

Five minutes later, I bring the bus to a stop on Interstate 5, near Middletown. Kayla and I climb onto the bus's white roof. She says, "Should be any minute."

"Film it," I say. "I want the footage."

"Yes, Carmine."

Sixty seconds tick by, and the timer on a wad of C4 detonates inside Electra's upper levels. Much of Russia's gruesome pile of ordnance ignites. The rockets, the grenades, the C4…it creates a spectacular explosion which blows part of the tower's roof off. Bright coils of fire unfurl upwards. Weakened from the crashing helicopter, Dalton's rocket, and now Russia's stockpile of firepower, Electra's structure wavers, and slowly the top third of the tower succumbs to gravity. Like watching a popsicle melt in fast-forward.

Afterwards, she stops recording. "Now what?"

"Now you practice driving this bus."

"What?? Me? But you're so good! Why would I?"

I lay down on the bus's roof and lay a forearm across my eyes. Because I need space, Kayla. Because I want to be alone. Because I want to drive Dalton's Land Cruiser again and cry by myself. Because… Because…

Puck calls. Finally. But he doesn't ring Kayla's phone. He calls mine.

I already know what he's going to say. I answer, "Hello, PuckDaddy."

"Hey, Carmine." His voice is shaky. I put it on speaker for Kayla's benefit.

"How did he die?" I ask. He's quiet and the lack of response is deafening, and my voice is thick with hurt. "Don't ask how I know, Puck. I just do. Tell me. Please."

He stumbles through the explanation, half-crying. "He and Samantha. In a plane. Federal fighter jets…shot it down. She got out…he…didn't…"

Kayla gasps and covers her mouth. I nod, having been preparing myself for this for an hour. No body to bury. As I predicted when last I saw him. "Okay. Thank you, Puck. Did they kill Blue-Eyes?"

"Unconfirmed. Samantha shot her. Several times. But…we aren't sure."

"Where is Samantha?" I ask.

"I don't know. Her equipment malfunctioned when…she landed in the water. So. I'll hear from her soon."

I nod again and want to ask more, but my mouth won't form the words. As though talking is no longer worth it. As though the fires inside the furnace of my heart have gone cold, and the rest of my desultory facilities are losing power.

"There's more," he says in a groan.

"We're ready," Kayla answers for me. She smells like rain and wind on a winter day.

"Before he died, Chase found Andy Babington. He was a prisoner inside the CDC."

Katie Lopez remembers Andy. No, that's not right. *I* remember Andy. A grade older than me. Arrogant. Handsome. Self-appointed nemesis of Chase.

There's a long pause, and Kayla says, "We're still listening."

"Andy Babington has been brain-washed by Blue-Eyes," Puck says.

"To do what?"

"To find Carmine. And...to kill her."

I make no response. On top of all the other obstacles I face, this new terror makes no impact. Let him find me. I don't care.

"But, to make it worse," he says, "he has been surgically fused with a nuclear bomb. He'll be able to set the bomb off himself, or it will detonate when he dies."

Ah. That *is* a problem.

This time, it's Kayla who is struck speechless. Her mouth hangs open and she stares at me as though I'm already lost.

Which I am.

Puck says, "You still there?"

I take a deep breath and force out the words. "So...if he finds me in New Los Angeles, then he'll simply get close...and..."

"And detonate it."

"...and kill everyone I love."

"Basically, that's exactly right."

"Where is he now?"

"No idea. Possibly...possibly already on his way to California," he says. "I wouldn't put it past the President to fly him out there."

"I need a moment to process this, Puck."

"Yeah, me too."

The moment turns into five minutes of silence. Then ten. The women in the bus are antsy and scared, but Kayla and I are powerless to help them until we make up our minds. I don't know what to do. There are no good solutions remaining in the world, and I can't be pragmatic enough to pick the least terrible.

The sun is finally clear of the horizon and it'll be warm soon. "I can't go back," I say.

"What?!" Kayla cries. "No! That's crazy! Where else will you have more protection than in New Los Angeles??"

"There is no protection from a nuclear blast, Kayla. He could kill half our population."

"No," she repeats, fresh tears rolling down her perfect cheeks. "No, no, no. You can't leave."

"I have to."

"Stay together, stay alive," she evokes my Kingdom axiom.

"If I stay…we won't."

"But…how…where will you go?"

"I don't know, Kayla. I'm figuring this out the same time you are."

"No."

I indicate the remains of Electra tower. "I think perhaps it's best if Queen Carmine accidentally died in that explosion."

Fortunately one of the liberated women knows how to drive big machines. I stand beside the Land Cruiser and wave as the bus rolls away from the airport. Kayla cries fiercely, pressed against the inside glass of the doors. Poor thing, she's been through a lot.

"You've got to be strong, Kayla," I told her. "You and Mason and the General and the Governess, you have to keep the Kingdom intact. Let the Guardians bond with Tank. Or maybe with Saul. It's your best shot. Walter won't give up. That guy with the wolves, he'll be back. You've got to be ready."

"But—" she said.

"This is not the end," I told her. "This is just a safety precaution until we deal with the nuke."

But she didn't believe me.

I'm not sure I believed me.

I'm not sure of anything.

Kayla has already released the footage of Electra's destruction, with a statement that Queen Carmine died in the blast. It's a ruse which won't last forever, not with a busload of women who've seen me alive, but it should buy me time. Buy New Los Angeles time. But maybe not. Who knows. Not I.

Soon the bus is out of sight. And I'm alone.

And, for the moment, I don't care.

I pat the hood of my vehicle. Dalton's final present to me was packing this thing full of supplies, enough for weeks. He didn't know it at the time, but I'll use it all.

Thanks, Dalton.

Please say Hi to Becky for me.

And…to Chase…please give him my love…

…

Nope. Not ready to say goodbye to Chase yet.

Can't even pretend I'm ready.

Not yet.

I get into the driver's seat, and start the engine. It roars to life and settles into a deep purr, a healthy sound, an eager machine ready to go anywhere and everywhere.

But…which direction?

I have options. Stay nearby. Head to the East Coast. Settle in Texas. Join the Resistance. Live on a boat.

My life has changed so much in the last hour and a half. So I simply sit. And cry. And pray. And think.

But I can't make sense of it. Everything coming too fast.

Can't stay here. Mercenaries will wake soon.

I briefly consider suicide. Simpler. Easier. But that's not truly an option. I haven't finished writing this story yet.

If my story ends here, hate wins. Evil wins.

Chase would die for nothing.

No.

Even though I'm broken, I can't stomach that idea.

I'm still hoping for a happy ending.

Or at least the happiest I can manage.

Which reminds me. There's one final thing I need to check.

Within an hour, the newscasters on satellite radio are tentatively speculating on the video originating from San Diego and the attached statement, that the queen's dead.

Could it be true? Could she have died in a freak explosion?

Of further interest are the statements issued by the Federal Government. The Secretary of State was wounded in a terrorist attack, but is receiving the best medical attention possible. The culprit, the infamous extremist known at the Outlaw, was discovered in a private jet over the Atlantic Ocean and killed.

I turn the radio off.

And I turn my cellphone off. Puck's been texting me, but I don't read it. I want to disconnect from Puck, to dislodge myself from the grid. At least for a while.

I park in Oceanside, on the Wisconsin Avenue bridge, and walk to the shore. A half mile north, a beautiful sight greets my eyes.

A gleaming Disney cruise ship, the Disney Wonder, rides at anchor a mile off shore. Black and red and white and chuffing a faint trail of smoke, it rides like a bobber, easy on the swell. The enormous cruise ship's tenders are traveling to and from the Oceanside Pier, plucking the Inheritors and their mothers out from harm's way and ferrying them to the safety of the Wonder, where no crazed mercenary can reach them.

Apparently the Navy couldn't put down their mutinies fast enough, and so General Brown adapted by commandeering a nearby liner. Or at least that's the way it appears to my eyes. Well done, General. The kids are safe. Safe to destroy the planet eighteen years from now. May God forgive us.

Saul, the Zealot, will know what to do with them. Or least, he'll have a better idea than I would have.

I take a deep satisfied breath, filling my lungs with ocean air, and return to my vehicle. It's time I vanished. I drop the Land Cruiser into drive and turn east. Toward the Interstate. Toward the unknown future.

The End

Epilogue One
(out of four total)

Tank Ware stands on the Balboa Bridge and glares northwest, up Interstate Five. In the direction of Santa Clarita. In the direction of Walter's army of freaks, and the anticipated attack which never came. He and the queen's Variants, and the giants, and Mason and his Falcons, stood guard the entire night, prepared for a battle to the death. Now that morning has come, rays of light falling on the western strata of the valley, he grunts in frustration. His body is a temple of unused adrenaline, enough to make him queasy. Weighing over three hundred pounds, most of it rock hard muscle tissue, he is forced to consume calories constantly to maintain energy, which is difficult while his stomach roils.

Where are they, he wonders. When didn't the cowards attack? Why was last night different?

When finally the titan releases his hold on the bridge's guardrail, and admits to himself the fight will not materialize, only then does Walter make an appearance. A black truck crests the far rise, and brakes. Tank's eyesight isn't as good as the queen's or as the Outlaw's, but he can see better than most - it's Walter who emerges from the truck, carrying a white flag.

Mason McHale, the dangerous little man bristling with knives, spits over the side of the bridge. "That sonuvabitch wants to talk."

"Too bad," Tank grunts. "Should've showed his face hours ago. I'm tired."

"I wish the Shooter was here. She could pick him off clean at this distance," Mason says. "One shot, pow."

Tank doesn't respond. He's personally been shot by Samantha Gear, more than once, and he has mixed emotions about his current alliance with her.

The Zealot steps forward, his face hidden inside his cowl, and he says, "I will parlay with this man."

No one on earth makes Tank Ware as uneasy as the Zealot does. Well, except perhaps the Cheerleader; his face will never recover from his fiery encounter with her. Tank respects but does not fear the Outlaw, nor Walter. But the Zealot? The man radiates calm strength and Tank swears he's felt the strange man inside his mind, poking around.

"No," Tank says. "It could be a trap."

"He cannot hurt me," the Zealot quietly replies. His name is Saul but Zealot suits him better, Tank believes. "And any gambit is worth taking, to end this senseless violence."

The Zealot requests use of a jeep from one of the military captains. A large contingent of soldiers and Variants are watching this transpire, and Tank falls under the conviction that he's being viewed as a coward. That the Zealot is usurping some of his authority by willingly parlaying with Walter. "Fine," he says, and he gets into the driver's seat, forcing the Zealot into the passenger role. "Fine. You can come with me, old man."

"Very generous." The Zealot places his large satchel into the rear, a satchel which Tank has noted holds a bible, a journal, and medical supplies. Like the guy's a nurse.

He's not a nurse, though. He's a pure-born Infected, like Tank himself, and he's old. With age comes power, and Tank cannot fathom why the Zealot wastes his on healing lesser mortals.

"Stay here," Tank tells the military captain, unnecessarily. "I'll see what Walter wants."

The jeep creates a noisy rattle and the two Infected men race beyond the Kingdom's defenses and motor up the gentle incline, where Walter waits. The trip lasts three minutes and Tank parks at a distance of twenty feet.

Walter leans backwards on his truck, elbows resting on the hood. He's chewing on a splinter of wood and grinning. "Look'it this. They sent a brother to deal with me. Finally."

"Hello, Walter," the Zealot says, and Walter jolts upright as though he's been shocked. He's wearing designer sunglasses but even so it's obvious he's inspecting Saul curiously.

Something about the Zealot's voice.

"The hell?" Walter says. "Should I recognize yo' wrinkled ass?"

"No. But you should recognize what's inside."

"Which is?"

"I am cursed. Like you. Like my friend Tank. Three of the very few Infected stand on this hill, and I believe we should come away with a new peace. Don't you?"

"I heard of you," Walter says.

"As I have of you."

"One of the old guys."

Tank rumbles, "What do you want, Walter? The white flag mean you surrender?"

"No. Means I willing to accept yours. On account of my deep generosity."

Saul asks, "Why would we surrender?"

"Because yo' queen just got her ass cooked. Or maybe you didn't hear." Walter grins again, his mouth full of metal, and he drums the claws of his fingers onto the truck's hood.

Tank feels as though he's been dumped into ice water. For a moment, shock replaces anger. "What do you mean? Katie? Didn't hear what?"

Walter laughs, an unpleasant rasp. "Oh! Oh this is good. You two fools don't know."

"Don't know *what*!"

"Lil queen got herself blown up inside a tower. Check the news, don't believe me. She gone. Even yo fine lookin' girl Kayla say so."

Saul doesn't move.

Tank doesn't breathe.

"So!" He laughs again. "How 'bout that surrender now?"

"You better hope that rumor ain't true, Walter," Tank growls, a dangerous tone in his voice. "Because she's the only reason I haven't burnt you to the ground yet. If she's gone…"

"If she's gone *what*? If she's gone *what*??" Walter rises off the truck and spreads his arms wide. He is muscle and sinew and power. "Look'it, I'm right here, you fat, overgrown lapdog. You an errand boy, a simple messenger."

"Gentlemen—" Zealot says calmingly, but it's too late.

All of the suppressed rage, the enormity of hate and arrogance, it's too much for Tank to control one second longer. He's on Walter faster than a lightning bolt, far quicker than his bulk should be able to move. So fast even Walter, the instigator, is unprepared. Tank gets both hands on Walter's skull and squeezes. Like trying to break open an overly ripe coconut.

Walter's skull fractures. His brain compresses and his eyes bulge. He has just enough time to rake the razors attached to his fingertips across Tank's throat. Despite skin as thick as cow leather, the razors slice cleanly through Tank's esophagus and jugular.

The Zealot arrives in time to receive a mist of blood in his face. He forces the injured men apart. Walter staggers into the truck, bleeding from his ears. Tank wobbles after him and then drops, hidden from view of the Kingdom's army by the crest of the hill.

Walter stares stupidly at his surroundings, as though operating from inside a deep concussion, and considers attacking the Zealot, so desperate and fierce is his confusion. The old man points north and says, "Go."

Walter obeys.

His truck swerves wildly back the way it came, its driver on the verge of blacking out, until running off the road and coming to rest in a drainage ditch beside the guardrail.

Tank will die. Saul sees that immediately, as he sits beside the enormous man. If Tank's body held seven liters of blood, approximately two have already pumped onto Interstate 5, a rich stain trickling south.

He will die, Saul thinks to himself. Unless.

From his satchel, Saul retrieves medical equipment. The wound is too grievous and too wet to sew closed, but Tank is Infected. If he lives long enough, the injury will heal itself. Saul drags Tank into a position so the blood won't fill his lungs, and he presses the thick vein together. It's a disgusting mess, but Saul works calmly. In less than a minute, the tissues have knit together a thin gossamer sheath, which connect the broken tubes.

The curse keeps him alive, Saul thinks. It's a miracle.

He could call for help. He could radio for additional medics. But this moment feels ordained. As though it was meant to happen.

"You may yet live," he tells Tank, whose face has lost all color. "But. To be safe, I would make peace with your Creator." Soon, most of the blood loss has been staunched.

Tank cannot respond. The injury is too traumatic, and he's lost four liters of blood. Over half. Far too much to survive.

Saul attaches himself to an empty blood bag, which immediately begins filling with his own life. He watches it a moment and nods in satisfaction. He attaches the outgoing line to Tank, and soon Saul's blood is freely entering Tank's body.

The richest, most powerful blood on the planet, freely given to a man who doesn't deserve it. How perfect, the Zealot thinks. Because Tank will require every drop.

He begins dribbling a fresh bottle of gatorade into Tank's mouth, and continues until he's too weak. Until his fingers grow numb. Until the world fades…

Tank's awareness returns thirty minutes later. Weakly he vomits to the side. He will live, but is unable to rise, too sick and weak. With each movement of his head, tender muscles break at his neck.

The Zealot, lying prone next to him, has been waiting to issue his final words. Tank's eyes widen at the sight. The old man looks like a withered skeleton, enervated by blood loss, depleted of life. Every drop of it.

Saul whispers, "Tank, my brother, you no longer belong to evil. But to good. It is your soul that I have bought. With my blood." The man, about to die, smiles to himself as he quotes from his favorite book. "And I give it to God."

And with this, Saul, the Zealot, pleased with his manner of death, surrenders his spirit back into his Creator's embrace.

Tank watches the world from a distance, through blurry lenses. Can't concentrate, can't focus.

It is your soul I have bought? The final words ring in his mind. They don't make sense.

Nothing does.

Not even the collection of wild animals which are creeping down the valley walls, cautiously entering the interstate, coming to inspect him, the giant on the road. The giant whose body, teeming with blood over a hundred years in the making, calls to them.

Epilogue Two
(out of four total)

A woman sits at an open-air bar on the Savannah beachfront, staring with bleary eyes at the television newscast. Every few seconds she drops her gaze to inspect the sand. The surf. The sky. She finds nothing.

Queen Carmine is dead, the anchor repeats again. But the woman knows that isn't true.

The Outlaw is dead, the anchor repeats. Again. And the woman knows that he is. She's been waiting here for a week, hoping Chase Jackson will surface.

But he won't.

And it's time she moved on.

But not to the Resistance. She's tired of warfare. For the time being.

She finishes her whiskey, which doesn't affect her body to any great extent, and stands. The clothes she's wearing belonged to the rider of a Harley Davidson until recently. They don't fit her well. But the Harley does.

Her drinking companion watches her rise. He's been plying the tools of seduction for over an hour, hoping for a glimmer of response. So far, he's been frustrated in his efforts.

"Leaving? Just now?" he asks the striking woman. "The sun's about to set."

"Leaving," she answers.

"Going to see someone?"

"I am. A good man in Utah, named Richard Jackson. He and I both need to raise a glass to the fallen hero, and then have a good cry."

She walks out of the bar, stares a final time at the Atlantic Ocean, and gets on her new motorcycle.

Epilogue Three
(out of four total)

The Disney Wonder reaches the Island of Hawai'i, the southernmost and largest of the isles. Off shore of Hala Point, she releases her anchors and comes to rest, surrounded by a deep dazzling blue.

A small boat sets off from the rocky surf to meet her, and is received at the Wonder's forward hatch. A bald man steps aboard and is escorted to the bow to meet the Wonder's most recent owner. There, perched over the water and caressed by a gentle Pacific breeze, the bald man lights a cigarette and shakes the hand of a man known only as the Priest.

The bald man's name is Carter. He is the second oldest living Infected and he chuckles darkly. "A stroke of genius, Priest, getting the kids aboard this boat. You'll be rewarded."

"I have no doubt, sir."

"You heard the news? Both the Outlaw and Queen Carmine are dead?"

"I heard. Though…I'd sleep better if I saw their broken bodies."

"Me too, kid. I've got resources looking into it." Carter secretes blue smoke from his nostrils with each syllable. "What a cargo you've brought." He eyes the length of the massive ship, a rapacious glint to his eye. "What a bountiful future we have before us."

Epilogue Four

Chase Jackson's body is found after three days adrift, a mile off Jekyll Island and seventy miles south of Savannah, by the captain and owner of a thirty-six-foot catamaran, a man named Ervin Simms. Chase's body is hauled onto the stern's swim platform and raised from the water.

Despite multiple sun blisters, a waterlogged face, and the absence of the infamous red mask, Ervin Simms recognizes the Outlaw instantly. After all, Ervin is a long-time admirer of the Outlaw, and he is living at sea in quiet protest against the traitorous President and his wretched Secretary of State. He's seen the news, knows the Outlaw's plane was shot down about fifty miles north.

But does he live? Ervin places his ear to the Outlaw's chest and presses his finger's into the Outlaw's neck. And listens.

And listens.

Finally. And barely. He detects a sluggish and cagey heartbeat. The Outlaw lives.

Chase is brought out of the sun, slung inside a hammock, and revived with sips of water and juice, until he's able to stomach slices of banana twenty-four hours later. He is delirious, vacillating between fever and extreme chills. His caloric debt is so vast it'll be weeks before strength returns. If it ever does.

On his fourth night aboard, a measure of sanity takes delicate hold between Chase's ears. For the first time in a week, he isn't stark raving mad. He clamps his chattering teeth together, and opens his eyes.

He cannot process the vigorous assault on his sensorium yet, so he drifts back to sleep. He naps another two hours, and now the sun has fallen and his eyes hurt less. But still, it's better if he just listens. His ears don't hurt him like his eyes do.

So he listens. And listens…

To a man singing to himself somewhere above deck.

To the lap of waves on the pontoons.

To the radio.

To the dominant story on the newscast.

Finally, after the statement has been repeated for the fourth time, its meaning settles firmly into Chase's mind. The queen is dead, the news anchor says again. Queen Carmine is dead. Her funeral was held yesterday in downtown Los Angeles.

She is dead.

She is dead.

Chase Jackson, swinging inside his hammock within the dark starboard cabin, is too weak to do anything but groan.

Stay tuned for the thrilling conclusion (maybe! probably!) of the Chase/Katie saga! Due late 2017.

Dear reader,

I hope you enjoyed City of Broken Angels! Despite the many heart breaks. The next book in the Carmine series should be the last, a conclusion to the Chase and Katie saga. They've been through a lot. However, the story MIGHT require an additional book. There is still much to be done, possibly too much for one novel. We'll see.

I'm often messaged by readers, and one common theme is this - "You're too mean to Chase. And to Katie."

And the readers are probably right.

But I respond with this quote from Jim Gordon about Batman, near the end of the movie *Dark Night*: "He's the hero Gotham deserves, but not the one we need right now. So we'll hunt him. Because he can take it."

Much is asked of Chase and Katie. Because they can take it.

Many many thanks to the readers who have stuck with me through both Outlaw and Carmine series. You are the best!

As always, Amazon reviews are golden - they keep me in business.

If you'd like to read Book One of the Outlaw series, I'll send you a copy for free. Click here —> **http://eepurl.com/b95Bgj**